What was it

Kelly was a fascinating combination of rancher, mother and desirable woman. Letting her go may have been the worst mistake of Josh's life.

"What's going on in that head of yours?" Kelly whispered.

"The past and the present."

"The boys?"

"Partly."

Her eyelids flickered and she moved backward, almost imperceptibly. "I shouldn't have asked," she said. "This isn't the time."

Josh glanced at his sleeping sons. However much he wanted them to know he was their father, he didn't want it to happen by accident. "Mostly I'm hoping the rodeo will be as successful as everyone thinks it'll be. It helps the town, which means it helps Casey and Marc. As for the rest? Being a celebrity isn't what it's cracked up to be."

"You used to enjoy the attention."

"Maybe I've grown up since then."

He wished he could tell if she believed him.

Dear Reader,

Once upon a time, I thought I'd never write a story that had anything to do with rodeos, then I moved to a town that has an annual rodeo. The excitement in the community, the events leading up to the rodeo and the competition itself were too rich with possibilities to ignore. Very quickly, Kelly Beaumont and Josh McKeon came knocking at my mental door, demanding that I tell their story. In *Twins for the Rodeo Star* (the first book in my new Hearts of Big Sky series), Josh is Canadian and, unbeknownst to him, is the father of Kelly's sons. Both Kelly and Josh are strong individuals and they need a lot of growing, learning and compromising to work things out between them.

Rodeos are amazing to watch, but contestants risk injury, particularly in bronco and bull riding. Classic Movie Alert: *Pure Country*, with George Strait. I haven't seen this film in years, but I still remember the sweet, romantic ending.

I enjoy hearing from readers and can be contacted on my Facebook page at Facebook.com/julianna.morris.author. If you prefer writing a letter, please use: c/o Harlequin Books, 22 Adelaide Street West, 40th Floor, Toronto, Ontario, Canada M5H 4E3.

Best wishes,

Julianna

HEARTWARMING

Twins for the Rodeo Star

—

Julianna Morris

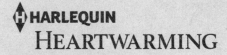

HARLEQUIN
HEARTWARMING

HARLEQUIN®
HEARTWARMING™

ISBN-13: 978-1-335-88980-5

Twins for the Rodeo Star

This edition published by arrangement with Harlequin Books S.A.

For questions and comments about the quality of this book, please contact us at CustomerService@Harlequin.com.

Harlequin Enterprises ULC
22 Adelaide St. West, 40th Floor
Toronto, Ontario M5H 4E3, Canada
www.Harlequin.com

Printed in U.S.A.

Recycling programs for this product may not exist in your area.

Julianna Morris still remembers being read to by her mother in a rocking chair, wrapped in a patchwork quilt. She learned to read by herself at an early age and remains a voracious book consumer on everything from history and biographies to most fiction genres.

Julianna has been a park ranger, program analyst and systems analyst in information technology. She loves animals, travel, gardening, hiking, taking photographs, making patchwork quilts and doing a few dozen other things. Her biggest complaint is not having enough hours in the day.

Books by Julianna Morris

Harlequin Superromance

Bachelor Protector
Christmas with Carlie
Undercover in Glimmer Creek

Visit the Author Profile page at Harlequin.com for more titles.

To Burt and Emily, who first introduced me to cows. Lots of them.

CHAPTER ONE

KELLY BEAUMONT REINED in her horse and looked down the small Montana valley where her mother's Irish family had settled in the 1800s. Once the Flannigans had dreamed of owning the kind of vast cattle empire they'd heard about in Texas, but it hadn't happened.

Kindred Ranch was enough, though, and she loved it…the way her father never had. Of course, he hadn't been born here, he'd married into the Flannigan clan, but his lack of devotion was mostly because his first love was competing in rodeos. Everything else came a distant second.

Her mouth tightened and she urged Lightfoot into a trot. Usually she tried not to get annoyed with Harry Beaumont, he was what he was, but he'd arranged for one of his rodeo buddies to stay at the ranch for a few days.

Kelly didn't like it.

Her twin sons were already thrilled by their grandfather's stories about the professional rodeo circuit, and the last thing she needed was another beat-up bronco rider telling them tall tales of his glory days. It wasn't that she had anything against rodeos—they were exciting and she admired the courage and skill of the contestants—but it wasn't the life or career she wanted for her boys.

She rode into the ranch center and saw a late-model truck parked near the main barn, bearing an Alberta, Canada, license plate. At least this pal of Harry's wasn't entirely broke, and she'd have time to check him out before the twins got home from their after-school soccer practice. She could also ask that he keep his stories to himself.

A tall man moved in the shadow of the barn door and Lightfoot half reared, snorting with anger. The stallion didn't take well to strangers.

"Whoa, boy," urged a vaguely familiar voice. Kelly was busy keeping the Appaloosa under control and didn't look up, but she spotted the newcomer's hand reaching for Lightfoot's head.

"Don't touch him," she ordered.

"Just trying to help. I breed and raise horses now."

"You didn't raise this one." She leaned

over and scolded Lightfoot in his ear. "Stop that, you big lug. You are *not* a watchdog. You're a horse."

The stallion let out another snort, but stood quietly as she got off and walked him into the barn. It wasn't until Kelly had tied him to a post that she turned around and the breath was knocked out of her lungs.

Josh McKeon.

The most handsome and talented rodeo competitor she'd ever seen, the subject of her youthful romantic dreams...and though he didn't know it, the father of her six-year-old sons.

"Hello, Josh. What are you doing at Kindred Ranch?" Kelly asked, proud there wasn't the faintest quaver in her voice.

"A long time ago you invited me here."

She narrowed her eyes. "The invitation was revoked when I found you kissing another woman."

"Still upset about that?"

"Not in the least. It was a lucky escape and taught me a lesson I'll never forget." Kelly removed Lightfoot's saddle and put it on a rack in the tack room. She'd been up since before dawn, working in the barns, then riding and repairing fences. She didn't have the energy to go over old territory with an ex-boyfriend. Still, she knew Josh well enough to realize that if she immediately ordered him off the ranch, he'd wonder why she was in such a hurry.

"What lesson?" he asked.

"That Canadian cowboys can't be faithful any better than cowboys from somewhere else."

His jaw jutted, the way it used to look before he got on one of the broncos he was such an expert at riding. "It was simply an enthusiastic kiss from a fan, but you were looking for a reason to break up with me when you came back from the hospital. I wish I could have stayed while your mother was being treated, but it was the final round. I won a nice amount of money that day."

"And I'm sure the blonde helped you spend it," Kelly returned smoothly. "You married her not long afterward, didn't you? But you're wrong that I was upset about you competing instead of being with me at the hospital. I was upset that *Harry* didn't stay while Mom was having emergency surgery. He'd been eliminated, but he still left to watch the finals. I'll never forget the look in her eyes when she woke up asking for him, only to hear he wasn't there."

"I'm sorry."

Kelly shrugged, determined not to reveal how much it had hurt. Sweet, gentle Kathleen Beaumont still believed that someday she'd become a priority in her husband's life, but Harry was addicted to the adrenaline rush of competition. While he rarely won any longer, he kept trying, and sooner or later his obsession would likely kill him. The fees and travel costs had been sucking Kindred Ranch dry until Kelly had put an end to it after taking over management of the ranch.

Yet, in a way, Josh was right.

That day had reminded Kelly of the life she'd have if she stayed with a man who was so similar to her father. It had seemed romantic and exciting to fall in love with a rising professional rodeo star. But in reality it meant being dragged from one venue to another, no real home for months on end… and eventually watching him lose far more than he won, while he got thrown, kicked, stomped on, gored or even killed. And with a guy as attractive as Josh, there would have been no end of women competing for his attention.

Kelly had grown up in that life, but at least she'd had Kindred Ranch and her grandparents as a stable foundation during the school year. She'd only travel with her parents during part of each summer, particularly when they were closer to Montana.

"So, why *are* you here?" she asked, plying a currycomb over Lightfoot in firm, even strokes. Unlike some horses, he enjoyed all aspects of grooming. She would do a quick job now to make him comfortable, and return to finish...after Josh was gone. In the meantime, it allowed her to focus on something besides her unwelcome visitor.

"Your dad and I still see each other at rodeos and professional bull-riding events," Josh explained. "He asked me to come for a visit, saying his health is bad and it's time to begin making amends for the past. He never did anything that needed amends, but he was a big help to me when I started and I want to find out what's bothering him."

Kelly gritted her teeth.

Josh McKeon was the "old rodeo pal" her father had invited? She rested her forehead against Lightfoot's neck for an instant. His warmth and scent filled her senses and she wondered how she could love one kind of horse so much and want nothing to do with the ones that were bred to buck men to the ground in a few seconds.

"Harry's health isn't bad," she said finally. "He was diagnosed with slightly elevated cholesterol and mild angina a few weeks ago. That's all."

"I don't know much about health privacy laws in the United States, but it's possible you don't know everything the doctor told him."

Kelly took out a hoof pick and leaned into Lightfoot's left shoulder. He obligingly shifted his weight off the leg so she could lift his forefoot to clean it.

"In case you haven't noticed, Harry is a hypochondriac. He'll ride a bull with three cracked ribs and a separated shoulder, but one sneeze and he's convinced it's bubonic plague. Mom overreacts, so I'm the one who takes him to all of his medical appointments. Mostly Dr. Wycoff wants him to stop eating fried foods and fatty meats, which is exactly the advice he's been getting for the past twelve years—advice Harry hasn't followed, at least when he's on the road."

She glanced toward the barn door, gauging the time of day by the length of the shadows. By her calculations, she had less than an hour to convince Josh to leave for Canada. Otherwise, when the boys returned home he'd come face-to-face with fatherhood; it was something she'd rather avoid. While she felt guilty for not telling him about the twins, his knowing would have complicated life for all of them.

Josh probably wouldn't have believed her, regardless.

And he'd repeatedly said he didn't want children until he could buy his own ranch. From everything she'd heard, he had won big over the years, yet he was still competing. Her father would periodically mention the winners at various events, and inevitably, Josh McKeon's name would come up. He'd gotten top honors at the Pro Canada Series final multiple times over the past seven years, along with being the All-Around Cowboy champion on the National Rodeo Circuit. Curiously, she and Harry had never discussed Josh being the twins' father and whether he should be told.

Was that the "amends" Harry hoped to make? She seriously hoped not.

It wasn't Harry Beaumont's secret to tell.

JOSH WATCHED KELLY working with the Appaloosa, automatically noting the animal's strong,
clean lines. The stallion was a beauty, mostly
black, with a nice pattern of blurred white
spots on his rump. He was large for a woman
of Kelly's petite size, but Josh knew she had a
special love for the breed. They were popular
with rodeo contestants, as well.

He'd first met Kelly when she was a gangly
fifteen-year-old kid, all knees and elbows.
Over the next four years she'd blossomed into
a beauty, but it wasn't until she turned nineteen that he'd really noticed. She'd come up
from Montana to watch her father compete
at Leduc, and one look from her intense blue
eyes had taken his breath away.

Her flat chest had become sweetly rounded,
her hips shapely, and her chestnut hair, like
a flame in the sun, had drawn his attention,
wherever she was sitting in the stands. The
relationship had progressed from flirting and
a few dates the first summer, to love the next.
At least he'd thought it was love.

"So, how are you doing on your ranch
plans?" Kelly asked, picking up a body brush
and running it over Lightfoot's coat.

The stallion nickered, plainly loving the
contact.

"Actually, I bought a spread south of Edmonton three years ago. It's called McKeon's Choice. We raise cattle and have a small horse breeding program."

"But you still compete." It was a flat statement, rather than a question.

"Sure. Mostly in the Pro Rodeo Canada series. Some in the United States as well, especially the larger venues. The money is good and I like saving against a rainy day."

"I'm sure the thrill of winning has nothing to do with it."

Josh frowned at Kelly's cynical tone. "I enjoy competing. There's nothing wrong with that."

"Except sooner or later you'll start losing more often and the money won't be so good. You'll decide it's just a bad year and the next one will be better. After a while it will cost a whole lot more to compete than you're actually winning, but it won't matter. You'll keep going."

"That's my concern, isn't it?" Josh asked, though he knew plenty of men and women like that, Kelly's father included. Harry was a nice guy, and while he'd never become a top champion, he'd been one of the better-known names. Now he encouraged young competitors and accepted losing with grace.

"You're right—it's entirely your concern. But since I've assured you about Harry, why don't you head back to Alberta?" Kelly suggested. "I'm sure McKeon's Choice would benefit from your presence. Not to mention the daily training you need for your next rodeo."

"Kelly, that's no way to treat a guest," Harry Beaumont scolded as he walked into the barn.

A strained look passed between father and daughter.

"I don't have time for guests, Harry. Maybe the two of you could head for Canada together. You talked about going to Grande Prairie for the Pro Wrangler event."

"That's all right. I may give it a pass this year."

"You never give it a pass. Besides, you haven't gone up to the Bucking B for months. Doesn't your foreman want to see you once in a while?"

"Forgot to mention—I sold the Bucking B to Rory and his son this winter. It was too much to handle, what with me being away so much, and they've always wanted it."

Another unfathomable look passed between Harry and Kelly. She was far more closed and wary than she'd been at twenty, though it was inevitable that she'd changed. She wasn't a kid any longer and had responsibilities. Harry didn't say much about the family, but he'd mentioned that she ran Kindred Ranch for her grand-parents. Josh hadn't asked why Harry wasn't in charge—much as he liked the older man, he wouldn't have put him in charge, either.

"Then where are you going to do your bull and bronco training?" Kelly asked crisply. Obviously she didn't expect it to be on Kin-dred Ranch.

"Bill Fenton has offered to let me practice with his training barrel. You've met Bill. He has that big spread near Medicine Hat. We stayed there a few times."

"I remember. By the way, Josh is under the impression you have serious health issues."

"The doc said my heart was bad. You heard him."

"Dr. Wycoff said you have very mild an-gina and some cholesterol issues, that's all. You're supposed to eat smarter, take low-dose aspirin every day and carry those little pills in case you get pain in your chest."

"Yeah, for my bum ticker," Harry insisted. "And I got that rash on my arm again, the one that looks like poison ivy. Except I haven't been near the stuff."

Plainly it was a discussion they'd had more than once and Josh didn't want to get in the middle. Until Kelly had mentioned it, he hadn't thought of Harry as being overly concerned about his health, but it was true. Harry Beaumont had endured some of the worst injuries a rodeo competitor could face, yet he worried about everything from hangnails to the state of his stomach.

"Fine. Make an appointment with Dr. Wycoff." Kelly's face was tight as she ran a soft cloth over the stallion's coat. "But this time give me more warning about when you're supposed to see him."

Josh shifted uncomfortably. She was more beautiful than ever, but he was in the wrong place, at the wrong time. "Maybe I should head back home."

"Great idea," Kelly announced at the same moment Harry let out an emphatic "no."

KELLY COULDN'T BELIEVE her father was forcing the issue.

"Harry, can I have a private word?" she hissed.

"Now?"

No, next Wednesday, she wanted to scream, but sarcasm was lost on Harry. Instead she nodded curtly. "Yes, now."

Once they were outside the barn, she glared at him.

"What do you think you're doing?" she demanded, struggling to keep her voice down.

"Josh has gotten more settled. He'd be a good father to the boys. His marriage didn't last more than a year. Now he's talking about finding someone and starting a family."

"So you decided to hand him one that was ready-made?" Kelly wondered if she'd ever stop being astonished at Harry's thoughtlessness. "Or maybe you don't think I should have any choice in the matter."

"I just want you to be happy."

"I *am* happy. Telling Josh is my decision to make, but as usual, you did what you wanted."

Harry blanched. "I just thought it would be easier for you to have someone to share the responsibility. My parents are long gone and your mama's folks are in their seventies. It could be hard on them to finish raising the boys if needed. What will Casey and Marc do if something happens to the rest of us? At the very least, I thought Josh should know."

Kelly shook her head, still furious. "What happens if he files for custody?"

"He wouldn't."

"You don't know that. We're from two different countries and Josh just told me he bought a ranch near Edmonton. That's around four hundred miles away. A little far for weekend visits, don't you think? Or did you think at all? Even if Josh and I agreed to a custody arrangement, I'd never be comfortable letting him take the boys to another country for visits. It would be too risky."

Abruptly her father looked twenty years older. "It's just that my age is catching up with me and your mother has never been strong. I worry about the boys and their future. And I worry about you. Don't you want to get married and share your life with someone? You were in love with Josh, once."

Kelly resisted yelling at him. As a kid she'd idolized Harry, but growing up had taught her that somebody had to be the adult, and it wasn't going to be her father. As for sharing her life with someone? Did Harry honestly think he'd shared his life with his family? They'd mostly been spectators, following him around while he did his best to dig himself an early grave.

The whole thing had made her resistant to marriage. A few weeks ago, she'd even turned down Grant Latham's proposal. Grant was a veterinarian in the nearby town of Shelton; he was a decent, settled, hardworking man, yet she hadn't been able to accept. There just wasn't any spark with him. Sharing her life with someone was a nice thought in theory, but not with the wrong someone.

Spark or not, Josh McKeon was wrong in capital letters.

Even if he was more responsible than Harry, he was still a rodeo competitor. Not to mention a heartbreaker. She couldn't deny being hurt when she found him in a passionate kiss with another woman, but ultimately, her common sense had made the decision to break up. He'd simply made the split easier by proving he couldn't be trusted. And look how easily he'd transferred his affections. By the time she'd realized she was pregnant, he was married to someone else.

"It was a kid's crush, nothing more, Harry. I can't be sorry, I adore my sons, but it wasn't love."

Her father made a helpless gesture. "All right, I'll get Josh to leave. But even if he stayed, he wouldn't necessarily assume Casey and Marc are his kids."

Kelly hoped that would be the case. She'd gotten pregnant right before her mother had collapsed with a perforated ulcer. On top of that, the boys had arrived two weeks late, which would confuse the issue if Josh calculated the dates.

As for Casey and Marc sharing his dark hair and eyes? Two-thirds of Shelton's population had the same coloring.

JOSH HAD BEEN unsuccessfully trying to coax Kelly's Appaloosa into accepting attention from him when Harry walked back into the barn with a discouraged expression on his face.

"Sorry, pal," Harry murmured. "I thought my daughter had forgiven you for the past, but I was wrong."

"I told her nothing was going on with the woman she saw kissing me. I'd never met Doreen Bigelow before that day."

"Yeah, but you married her a month later. That doesn't sit well with someone like Kelly. She's real proud."

It was ironic. Josh's rebound marriage to Doreen Bigelow had been the worst disaster of his life. In the time they were together she'd cheated, connived and spent money as if it grew on trees. He'd filed for divorce in less than six months.

"Fine. Do you want to drive back to Edmonton with me?" Josh asked. "We should be able to get to Lethbridge and I have friends there who'll put us up for the night. Or else we can sleep in my camper. Kelly is right about the event at Grande Prairie. You always go."

Harry looked tempted. "I'd love to, but I promised my wife that I'd stop being away so much. She was still coming with me during the summer, but her folks are older and she'd rather stay home to help out."

"With the ranch?"

"Heavens, no. We have a couple of cowhands and Kelly has a talent for running the place. She loves the land and animals. Ranching is in her blood. Don't think I've ever seen anyone with her eye for breeding horses."

Josh spared a glance for the Appaloosa. If Lightfoot was any example, Kelly was brilliant with horses. He would love breeding some of his mares with the stallion, but it was unlikely she'd agree, no matter what fee he was willing to pay. Maybe if she offered artificial insemination over the internet he could buy Lightfoot's sperm through a third party.

They walked out of the barn and Josh saw Kelly forking hay into a feeding trough in the corral. Seeing her again had awakened memories he'd tried to forget—of her fastening bandannas around his neck for good luck and knowing she'd be there for a victory kiss when he won. Of laughter and first love. Yet whether she'd acknowledged it or not, in the weeks leading to their breakup, he'd sensed her withdrawing from him. Her excitement before his events had been replaced by distraction and hints of anxiety.

He'd urged her to train seriously for ladies' barrel riding, because that way they'd both have a stake in rodeos where the event was offered. She'd learned the sport at her grandparents' ranch and was a natural. The few times he'd seen her practicing had been amazing; she could have become a champion.

Instead she'd found a reason to end the relationship. To his knowledge, she'd never attended another rodeo in Canada, though her father had continued coming to them.

A devil in Josh made him walk to the corral. "Looks like I'm leaving after all. Sorry we couldn't kiss and make up."

Kelly jabbed the tines of her pitchfork into the ground. "I'm sure you have ex-girlfriends all over the US and Canada. If you're desperate, some of them might be willing to kiss and make up."

"I don't have that many ex-girlfriends. Contrary to what you seem to believe, I don't get involved with every woman I meet."

"I'll take your word for it. Have a safe drive."

Josh tipped his hat. "Take care, Kelly."

She nodded and he noticed she was watching as he got into his truck and backed around the end of the barn. It was probably to make sure he left, though it would be nice to think she had a lingering fondness for him.

While the gravel road out to the small country highway was well maintained, he drove slowly to avoid throwing up too much dust. An incoming truck approached, so he pulled over at a wide spot to let it pass.

He recognized Kathleen Beaumont behind the wheel. She waved and the youngsters next to her waved, as well.

Cute kids, Josh mused after they'd passed.

He continued and turned north at the highway. Thirty minutes later he drove to the side of the road and flexed his hands on the wheel.

Cute kids.

But whose kids?

Over the years Harry had said nothing about Kelly getting married or divorced or having children. While the boys might belong to one of the Kindred Ranch cowhands, Josh didn't recall seeing any other residences aside from the large, rambling main house and what was obviously a small bunkhouse, no longer in use, judging by the weeds at the base of the door. Their cowhands must live elsewhere.

Nah.

It was ridiculous to question the situation, even if Kelly had seemed anxious for him to leave. Their relationship had crossed the line just once during their second summer together, but he'd used protection. It wasn't that he hadn't wanted a family, but starting one when he was still living out of his truck and going to rodeos all over the continent hadn't seemed the best idea. Some years he'd driven fifty thousand miles or more, getting to different venues.

Kelly had agreed.

Well, he thought she'd agreed. Looking back, he wasn't sure if she'd just decided not to debate the point. In the ranching tradition they both came from, kids were part of the life. Not that his father had ever achieved the dream of owning a ranch, instead growing prematurely old working someone else's cattle. Now he bossed McKeon's Choice. Having somebody he trusted implicitly to run the place gave Josh the freedom to compete whenever he wanted.

In his mind Josh envisioned the two faces he'd seen. Undoubtedly they were boys, alike as two peas in a pod, wearing small cowboy hats tipped back on their heads. Likely the same age, which would make them twins. But how old? Five? Six?

A chill crept through him.

Six was hazardously close to being an issue. Six could mean they'd been conceived up in Canada, in a cramped camper over an ancient pickup truck.

Jaw set, Josh checked for traffic in both

directions and did a U-turn, heading back toward Kindred Ranch. Most likely it didn't mean a thing, but he'd never have any peace of mind if he didn't find out the truth.

CHAPTER TWO

"I'LL DO IT, MOM," called Casey, running from the house after changing out of his soccer uniform. His brother was close at his heels and Kelly breathed a sigh of relief that Josh was gone.

The boys loved to help, just the way she'd loved to help at their age. They were still too young to do much, but they participated with the orphaned calf feedings and did other chores as far as their small arms and legs would allow. Lark, one of the family dogs, followed them from one task to another, an ever-present guardian.

Kelly's heart melted as she looked at her sons, filling a wheelbarrow with fresh straw for the horse stalls. In her mind she could see the years rushing ahead, Casey and Marc growing into strong, fine young men who cared about Kindred Ranch as much as she did. They were well on their way. Both of the boys were crazy about horses and animals and were always asking questions and wanting to participate, eager to learn about ranching.

Of course, they also asked endless questions about rodeos, enthralled with their grandfather's stories. She kept explaining that life as a professional rodeo competitor rarely included making enough money to pay for more than getting to the next event and having their bodies beaten to a pulp in the process. But they didn't care. They were still too young to recognize their grandfather was a dreamer who didn't deal well with reality.

Casey and Marc each lifted a handle of the wheelbarrow and pushed it as a team to Lightfoot's enclosure. The stallion quietly moved to one corner, letting them work. He might dislike strangers, but he was as gentle as a newborn kitten with the twins.

With another sigh, Kelly continued cleaning the last horse stall. Even if Kindred Ranch wasn't a major spread, there was plenty of upkeep. Her dad did what he could when he was home and felt well enough, but most of the work was left to her and the cowhands.

The sound of a truck driving into the ranch center made her frown. They didn't get many visitors in the afternoon; their fellow ranchers were just as busy as they were at that time of day.

She stepped outside the barn and went rigid.

It was Josh.

First, casting a quick glance at the boys spreading straw in Lightfoot's stall, she hurried toward the truck. "Forget something?" she asked, struggling to sound casual as he got out.

"Not exactly. But it's later than I thought and the sky looks as if a thunderstorm is brewing."

A thunderstorm? Kelly knew he'd driven through hail, floods and tornado warnings to reach rodeo competitions, so she was skeptical that he'd balk at a few clouds.

"Hi, mister." Marc had come out of the barn and was looking curiously at their visitor. "Are you Grandpa's rodeo friend?"

"Yes, sir. I'm from Canada. The name is Josh McKeon."

Marc's eyes widened with excitement. "Grandpa is from Canada, too." Marc was less reserved with new people than his brother, a trait he'd inherited from Harry, who could talk the ear off a grizzly bear.

Kelly tried to ignore the dread in her stomach. "Marc, get Casey and go inside."

"Aw, Mom, can't I stay?"

"Now, Marc."

Dragging his feet, he went into the barn and emerged a couple of minutes later with his brother. Obviously he'd explained that Josh was "Grandpa's rodeo friend" because they both wore the same starstruck expression. Casey looked longingly at Josh, but didn't protest being banished to the house.

"Lark, go," she said to the Australian shepherd, who was keeping a watchful eye on Josh. The dog trailed after the boys.

"I don't think the weather is that bad," Kelly said, taking a long look at the horizon, where a few thunderheads could be seen. "Surely you could get as far as—"

"Hello there," interrupted her grandmother's voice from the front porch.

Now Kelly was in even deeper trouble. Grams was fierce about the rules of hospitality.

Grams hurried down the steps and smiled. "Welcome. I'm Susannah Flannigan. My great-grandsons told me someone had arrived. Are you one of Kelly's friends?"

"Josh McKeon, ma'am." He lifted his hat, a proper cowboy. "I'm—"

"Mr. McKeon is Harry's rodeo pal," Kelly interrupted quickly. She didn't think Grams had ever met Josh. Her grandparents weren't huge rodeo fans and had never attended one of the big events, in either Canada or the United States.

"That's right," Josh said easily. "When Harry invited me to visit, he mentioned your local rodeo fundraiser, the one in a few weeks. I've decided to compete in it."

"Goodness, I should have realized you were my son-in-law's guest, but I expected some-body older. Now, we have spare bedrooms in the house, but if you'd prefer something more private, I can give a bit of cleaning to the bunkhouse. We aren't using it these days, but I don't think it's too bad."

"The bunkhouse will be fine, Mrs. Flan-nigan. And just leave the cleaning to me. I'm an old hand at it. Actually, I live out of the camper on my truck a good part of the year and can just sleep in there."

Susannah chuckled. "For several weeks? Nonsense. You'll be much more comfortable in the bunkhouse. I'll get fresh linens and cleaning supplies. I hope you like chili. My husband is cooking tonight and it's one of the few things he makes."

"Chili sounds great."

Silence fell when Susannah went inside. Kelly dusted her hands. She couldn't let Grams handle the cleaning, and while it galled her to do anything for Josh, she would have a chance to ask that he refrain from telling grand rodeo adventure stories to the boys.

"There's a bathroom in the bunkhouse," she said briskly. "Everything got a good scrub when we winterized the building, so it shouldn't be more than dusty."

"Where do your ranch hands live?"

"Down the road. A neighbor's husband passed away last summer and her kids aren't happy about her staying on the property alone. So Mike and Thaddeus board in the Galloping G bunkhouse and work both ranches."

"That means less help for you, then."

Kelly shrugged. "They don't have a lot to do there. The Galloping G is larger than Kindred Ranch, but Dorothy's husband didn't do much with it for years. Mostly there's a small herd of cattle and several horses that Mr. Gillespie loved. We keep horses and cattle there, too. I help by riding fences on both properties and checking on her herd. We also mow and bale quite a bit of hay over there. It works."

Josh looked surprised. "Don't her kids want to take over?"

"There are two daughters who live in Helena and a son in Minneapolis, but they aren't interested in ranching. Dorothy is hoping I can buy the Galloping G someday and let her continue living there."

"I see."

KNOWING HARRY WAS a financial disaster, Josh doubted Kindred Ranch would ever have the funds to buy another spread.

The real issue was whether Casey and Marc were his sons. He'd returned, intending to demand that Kelly tell him the truth, only to decide that discretion was a better idea. Otherwise he could make the situation worse.

Kelly's uneasiness could simply be that she'd gotten involved with someone else soon after they'd broken up. He didn't like the idea, but considering how quickly he'd married Doreen, he didn't have a leg to stand on. For all he knew, she'd had a boyfriend back in Shelton the whole time they were dating. After all, she'd gone back and forth between

Kindred Ranch and the rodeos where her father competed.

Susannah came out of the house with an armload of linens and Kathleen followed with a bucket and mop. The two women possessed an ageless beauty; it was easy to see where Kelly got her looks.

"Hello, Josh," Kathleen said, smiling gently. "How nice to see you again."

"My pleasure, ma'am."

He tried to determine if there was any deception in her face. If she believed he was the twins' father, he couldn't see it in her expression. But then, Kathleen was a sweet lady whose health had been fraying during that long-ago summer. Maybe she genuinely didn't know who had fathered her grandsons.

Josh focused again on Susannah Flannigan. Her eyes were as bright and alert as a meadowlark. In that, Kelly obviously took after her grandmother, rather than her mother.

"We'll have none of the *ma'am* and *Mrs.* nonsense," Susannah announced firmly. "We're Susannah and Kathleen to you. And my husband is Liam."

"Yes, ma'am. I mean, Susannah," he corrected himself, reaching to take the stack of bedsheets and blankets she carried. His father had strictly taught him to show respect to his elders, particularly women, so it would have been easier to stick with "ma'am" or "Mrs. Flannigan."

"Thanks, Mom. I'll take care of it," Kelly said, collecting the cleaning supplies from Kathleen. "When is dinner?"

"Not for at least an hour. I'm making corn bread to go with the chili."

"That should give us enough time to get everything in order. Let us know when you're ready." Kelly gestured to the porch, where a heavy iron triangle hung from a hook. It had probably been used for over a hundred years, calling ranch workers to thousands of meals.

"All right, dear."

Josh followed Kelly to the bunkhouse. She unlatched the door—obviously it wasn't kept locked—and went inside. He inhaled the scent of ancient timber, permeated with wood smoke. A potbellied stove even stood in the corner.

"Does that thing still work?" he asked, temporarily distracted from questions of fatherhood.

"Few things can go amiss with a properly maintained woodstove," Kelly said in a dry tone. "But if you're asking whether the stove pipe is hooked up, then yes, though it hasn't been used for a while." She set the bucket and mop next to a table and rolled up her sleeves.

"There's no need for you to stay. I can handle the cleaning." Josh wasn't sure he wanted Kelly there; having a quiet moment to think was appealing. "You were in the barn when I got back, so you must have work left to do."

Kelly shook her head. "Nothing that can't wait awhile. Grams is all about hospitality. She and Mom would have had the bunkhouse ready in case it was your preference, but Harry didn't tell us someone was coming until this morning and they had commitments in town. Something to do with rodeo week. There are a number of activities surrounding the event."

That sounded like Harry. He was a fine friend, but he probably wasn't so great with family. Josh understood how Kelly felt, but she was blaming her father's failings on rodeos and his compulsion to compete. She didn't see that if Harry hadn't become obsessed with professional rodeo, he would have found something else to compel him. He was that kind of man.

"I'll turn on the water and electricity," Kelly said, heading for the door again.

Josh looked around. The floors had begun as hand-hewn planks, but they'd been worn smooth by decades of contact with heavy boots and polishing. Assorted lamps and braided rag rugs added a cheerful note. Winterization must have been done after their autumn storms, because dust was at a minimum. Overall the building was well maintained and could sleep four, though the original number had likely been eight to ten. Sleeping space would have been sacrificed to add the bathroom, along with the small kitchenette.

Kelly returned, switched on the wall furnace and opened the faucets. They burped and hissed as water replaced the air in the pipes. "It shouldn't take long for the water to heat if you want a shower," she said, filling a bucket. "I'll start in the bathroom."

He turned on the lamps, then removed the plastic covering from one of the beds and made it up. Sheets and blankets would be a pleasant change from his sleeping bag. The camper was comfortable, but he didn't bother with the niceties.

"Why keep the potbellied wood burner when there's a wall furnace?" he called.

"In case the electricity goes out, which it

usually does in a storm. Since we're a distance out of town, it takes longer to get back on the grid again. We have a generator, but mostly to run things like lights and refrigeration. There's always a huge stock of firewood for when it's needed."

It was the logical explanation. Josh would have guessed the reason if he hadn't been distracted by more disturbing thoughts.

Kelly reappeared and poured something from a bottle onto a dust mop. The smell of lemons rose in the air and she swiftly ran the mop around the room while he made a stab at removing a light layer of dust from the higher surfaces. The bunkhouse was already cleaner than his ranch house in Canada, so he wasn't sure why they were bothering.

After vacuuming the braided rugs, she took patchwork quilts from a chest and spread them over each of the beds. Since he didn't think it was for his benefit, he assumed it was a standard custom when the bunkhouse was in use to make it homier.

"This is nice. Thanks," he said awkwardly. "I'm afraid the bunkhouse on my ranch is much more utilitarian."

Kelly cocked her head. "How many ranch hands do you employ?"

"Pop keeps tabs on that. We hire extra in spring and summer. I believe we have nine at the moment, but he mentioned planning to advertise for a real cook instead of rotating the duty around. The bunkhouse has space for twenty. We also have a cookhouse with an attached mess hall."

"What if he hires a woman to cook, or are you opposed to equal opportunity?"

Josh was flummoxed by the idea. Why would a woman want to prepare three squares a day for a bunch of rough-talking cowboys? It would require massive adjustments on everyone's part.

"Not opposed," he muttered. "I suppose she could sleep at the main house. My dad will make the decision, but he'll need someone with a wide range of skills."

Kelly lifted an eyebrow. "Oh?"

He'd seen the same look on her face when they'd been dating; it usually meant he was going to get nailed on a point of logic. "It's just that we'd need someone who can be called on for other tasks, like splitting wood, rebuilding a fence or riding out in bad weather to help look for lost animals. That kind of thing."

"You mean everything I do at Kindred Ranch."

Right.

Nobody looking at Kelly would think she could tame a horse or split a log, but what was the saying...work smarter, not harder? What she lacked in brute strength, she unquestionably made up for in smarts.

"I'm sure Pop will hire the best-qualified person available," he said.

"Uh-huh." Kelly sounded skeptical. She tucked the cleaning supplies into a small utility cabinet and turned around. "Look, I'd be grateful if you don't talk about bull riding or other events in front of my sons, or encourage Harry to tell stories. The boys already have romanticized ideas about chasing rodeos."

"It's a good life," Josh asserted, though it was unlikely Kelly would change her mind.

Her eyes chilled and she looked more determined than he'd ever seen her. "It might be a good life if you're in love with performing, but family gets the short end of the stick."

Josh's pride instantly went on edge. "I'm an athlete, Kelly, not a performer. Everyone has a purpose at rodeos and bull-riding events, including the clowns. As a matter of fact, rodeo protection athletes are critically important, whether or not they're dressed in costumes."

"Oh, please, it's *all* a performance," she scoffed. "Don't tell me that you don't love hearing the fans clap and scream and cheer. Rodeos wouldn't exist if there weren't spectators and a showman factor."

"That's true of any sporting event."

"I also hope my sons won't become professional hockey or football players," Kelly returned promptly.

He glared. It seemed as if all his choices were being put on trial and found lacking. "So you aren't going to give them a choice. It's ranching or nothing."

"Wrong. They have a choice. I just don't want them being unduly influenced when they're too young to understand how dangerous competing can be. It's exciting to hear about winning while sitting at the dinner table or as a bedtime story, but they also don't get there are only a few big winners and that a huge number of rodeo performers live hand to mouth at best."

"Ranching can be dangerous, too."

She nodded. "Sure, but ranchers don't take risks, just for the sake of putting themselves in danger. That's exactly what bronco and bull riding is about. Especially bull riding. You're pitting yourself against a thousand pounds of bad-tempered animal who doesn't know the game is over once he throws you to the ground or you jump away. There's no purpose beyond the thrill of challenging yourself, entertaining the crowd and winning."

Josh didn't agree that was the whole picture, but he didn't want to argue the question further.

"Fine. Believe what you want. I'll do my best not to talk about rodeos," he said, "but I can't control your father."

"Nobody can control Harry. Look, I'm going back to work now. I'll be in the barn if you need anything."

She left before he could offer to help— an offer he was certain she would have refused. No one would have guessed they'd once shared something special, or that they'd talked about getting married someday.

KELLY SWIFTLY TOOK care of one task after another, her mind only half on the routine chores. Having Josh resurface in her life had been the last thing she'd expected.

And appearing in the boys' lives.

The mental reminder wasn't needed, though it reaffirmed her conviction that she didn't want Josh in contact with her sons.

Josh was just as rodeo crazy as Harry. Why couldn't he realize it was better to retire as a champion than to be overtaken by younger competitors? They were probably already nipping at his heels. Soon they'd start getting the top prizes and turn him into a has-been, trying to hold on after his time. She still remembered the moment she'd recognized the expression in Harry's eyes when he'd looked at a cocky young bull rider and known he was outmatched. *At thirty-two.* The same age Josh was now.

Bull and bronco riding, in particular, were a young man's game. There was the National Senior Pro Rodeo Association that held its own rodeos and finals event, but her father wouldn't join. He simply refused to acknowledge that in the rodeo world, the march of time had already marched over him.

Lightfoot remained on edge when she went into his stall to finish his grooming. Horses were sensitive and he always knew when she was upset. She'd been there when he was born and had worked with him every day since.

"Hey, boy," she murmured as she fed him a carrot, then took out a soft cloth to run over his body. The ritual helped calm them both. "Settle down. Everything will be okay."

The stallion nickered and nuzzled her neck. They were the best of friends and he likely sensed her doubt. She *didn't* know if everything would be all right. The idea of Josh finding out about the boys and filing for custody, or even just asking for visitation rights, had often kept her awake at night. Now the possibility had become very real.

"Hey, boss. Let me finish up in here."

She looked over at Thaddeus. He was the eldest of their ranch hands and had gone through high school with her mother. Kelly suspected he'd once been in love with a young Kathleen Flannigan, but he didn't seem to resent Harry, so maybe she was wrong. On the other hand, he had stayed at Kindred Ranch, even though there were larger spreads where he could have had the chance to become a foreman. Was it to remain close to a woman he cared about?

"Thanks, Thad. Where's Mike?"

"Looking in on the mares in the foaling barn. Mrs. Gillespie is expecting us for dinner, but he'll be back later."

Kelly and the ranch hands had been taking turns sleeping in the foaling barn to keep an eye on the pregnant mares.

"You know perfectly well that it's my turn," she said firmly. "Tell Mike to get a good night's sleep."

"But you have a guest."

"Josh McKeon is *Harry's* guest, not mine, and he's going to be here for a while. Besides, Fiona Chance is close to having her foal. She might deliver tonight, which means I'll be up with her, regardless."

Thaddeus bobbed his head, accepting her decision. He must have seemed dull to her mother in contrast to Harry Beaumont, who was far more colorful and charming. But Kelly appreciated Thaddeus's solemn, responsible nature. She couldn't rely on her father to wake up regularly and check the mares, no matter how good his intentions might be, while the two ranch hands were utterly trustworthy.

The iron triangle on the porch clanged and she gave Thaddeus a smile. "Thanks. I'll see you tomorrow."

Josh emerged from the bunkhouse as she stepped out of the barn. He'd changed into a newer pair of jeans and a dark blue shirt.

Generally folks didn't dress up for dinner on ranches, but it was customary to come to the table clean and neat. She hurried inside to wash and change her own clothes, racing back to the dining room in time to hear Harry introducing Josh to her grandfather.

"Nice to meet you, Josh," said Granddad. "Hope you don't object to mild chili. Half of us like it spicy. The other half doesn't. In particular, my great-grandsons. They don't appreciate food that bites them back."

JOSH CHUCKLED OBLIGINGLY at the older man's joke. "I enjoy it both mild and hot, sir."

"It's Liam. Any which way, we have cayenne powder and pepper sauce, so you can spice it up to your preference."

"Hi, Josh," called a young voice.

Josh thought it was the boy he'd spoken to earlier. "Hi. It's Marc, right? And your twin brother is Casey."

The kid's smile broadened. "Cool. Nobody can tell us apart, except at home. Are you coming, Casey?" he called toward the kitchen.

"Duh." His brother came out clutching a large bowl filled with squares of corn bread, followed by his grandmother and great-grandmother.

"Hello, Casey," Josh said.

"Are you really a rodeo champion?" asked the boy.

Josh cast a swift glance at Kelly. He couldn't read her expression and shrugged mentally. If he couldn't control her father, he also couldn't control her sons. "I compete often enough. What grade are you in school?"

"We're in the first grade," Marc broke in. "But they don't let us be in the same class because we're twins. It isn't fair. Me 'n' Casey do everything together."

Considering the annoyed look Marc received from his brother, Josh suspected Casey wasn't overly concerned about being in a separate class. Was that the only way he got a word in edgewise without fighting for it?

"What's your favorite subject, Casey?"

"History," he replied quickly. "Today we learned Montana became a state in 1889. But I already knew that part."

"I don't know US history as well as Canadian history," Josh admitted. "That's where I was born."

"My teacher says you have queens and kings instead of presidents in Canada," Marc said. "Do you bow to Queen Elizabeth?" He put one arm across his stomach and the other across his back and gave him an exaggerated bow.

Josh tried not to smile. "I've never met the queen, but I would probably bow to her as a courtesy."

"That's what Grandpa Harry says," Casey rushed to say. "But Canada has a different prime minister than they have in England. Right?"

"Boys, sit down and let our guest catch his breath," Susannah ordered. "Liam, will you dish up the chili?"

"Of course, dear."

Generous bowls were handed around the table along with the corn bread.

"You can lighten up with this if you'd like," Susannah said, passing a tray piled high with chopped onions, diced tomatoes and bell peppers, along with grated cheese. "Normally we eat healthier, but Liam volunteered to help today in the kitchen. It doesn't happen very often, so I take advantage whenever possible."

Liam chuckled. "Don't believe her, Josh.

My dishpan hands speak for themselves. My wife just doesn't like me competing with her when it comes to chili—she enters a cook-off every year during rodeo week."

Josh didn't believe either one of them. They seemed to be a close and loving couple, two equally strong-willed individuals who'd managed to live together for decades without killing each other. It was quite an accomplishment.

"I'm sure you work things out. Anyway, a homemade meal is a treat." He ate a spoonful of the tender meat crowding his bowl, flavored with the smoky essence of chipotle peppers. The sweet corn bread and hearty flavor of the chili blended well together. "I don't get anything close to this on the road. And the chow at my ranch is even worse."

"Hey, I love rodeo food," Harry protested.

"Josh mentioned his father runs his ranch when he's gone," Kelly volunteered, changing the subject. "They're planning to hire a cook instead of rotating the duty around the cowhands. Do we know anyone who might be interested in applying for the job?"

Liam looked thoughtful. "Could be. I can ask in town."

"They're open to hiring a woman," she

said sweetly, "so I wondered about Nellie Pruitt. She's bossy, but that's from cooking at the high school for twenty years. Anyone who can ride herd on all those teenagers wouldn't have trouble with a bunch of cowhands. She might welcome a change now that her husband is gone."

Josh groaned silently.

Whatever game Kelly was playing, he didn't think it was intended to end well for him.

CHAPTER THREE

LATER THAT NIGHT, Josh lay on his back in the bunkhouse, listening to the familiar sounds of a ranch. Cows lowing in the distance. The occasional neigh of horses. The call of a coyote. Crickets. A breeze rustling the trees outside.

The evening had been pleasant, but he hadn't been able to escape his underlying questions. While Casey and Marc were great kids—smart and inquisitive, with distinct personalities—he couldn't see himself in their faces or mannerisms. Yet that didn't necessarily mean anything. Kelly resembled her maternal grandparents much more than Harry or her mother.

As for Kelly? Her edginess hadn't necessarily meant anything, either.

Harry had been strangely subdued, but Josh had seen nothing unusual in the rest of the family. Apple crisp with ice cream had followed the meal and then they'd played a round of dominoes while the boys did their schoolwork. The cozy scene was topped by the two dogs curled up in front of the fireplace, one with a heavily bandaged leg and a cone around his neck. Very homey, unlike the thoroughly male world he'd grown up in. His childhood might have been different if his mother had lived, but she'd died when he was four, leaving just him and his dad.

Wanting to be a courteous guest, Josh had excused himself early and returned to the bunkhouse. But he was restless, which ordinarily wasn't a problem he faced. Being on the road so much, heading from one rodeo venue to another, he'd learned to sleep anywhere, anytime.

"Blast," he muttered to himself, sitting up and checking the time on his phone. It was almost 1:00 a.m.

He got dressed, thinking a walk would help.

Outside he saw the main barn was dark, but the lights were burning in a large barn on the outer perimeter of the ranch center. Instinctively he headed for it and went inside.

"Hello?" he called. Several horses stamped their feet and a few poked their heads over the stall doors to look at him.

"Is that you, Grant?" called Kelly's voice.

"It's Josh." In a large box stall he found Kelly standing by a pregnant mare. Her tail had been neatly wrapped for foaling, but it didn't look as if her water had broken. He rolled up his sleeves. "Who's Grant?"

"Our veterinarian. I called him a little while ago. It's Fiona Chance's first pregnancy and the foal isn't in the right position."

"Is she wary of strangers?"

Kelly slid a hand down the mare's flank. "She's usually mellow, but has gotten more high-strung the past couple of weeks. Approach her slowly and see how she reacts."

Josh stepped next to the horse and stroked her neck with a low, wordless murmur. The mare's tension radiated into his fingertips. "She's gorgeous," he said at length.

"Thanks. She's carrying one of Lightfoot's foals."

It made sense. Lightfoot was one of the finest Appaloosa stallions he'd set eyes on, even topping his favorite mount, Quicksilver.

"What can I do to help?" he asked.

Josh almost expected Kelly to order him away. Instead she pointed to the supplies she'd stacked nearby. "There's a sink in the rear of the barn. Scrub up, put on a pair of sterile gloves and be ready to lend a hand in case Grant is delayed. I've already given Fiona Chance a good wash."

He did as Kelly asked, waiting until he'd donned the gloves before making a comment. "I'm amazed you're willing to accept my help, considering how reluctant you were to have me stay at the ranch."

"When it comes to my horses, I'll take any qualified help. Granddad would be here, but he had knee replacement surgery a few weeks ago and I don't want to ask him unless absolutely necessary. As for Harry, he's too excitable. That's the last thing a foaling mare needs."

"What about your cowhands?"

"They're working with a colicky gelding over on the Galloping G. I told them not to come because I was calling Grant. He's the best vet in the county. We've helped birth more than one foal together."

Josh frowned. The warmth in Kelly's tone when talking about the veterinarian didn't have anything to do with him.

But he still didn't like it.

GRANT LATHAM PARKED near the Kindred Ranch foaling barn and got out, thinking he must have set a speed record getting there. Kelly didn't phone after hours unless she was really worried. He strode into the barn and noticed she wasn't alone; a man he didn't recognize was in the large, loose box where Fiona Chance was moving restlessly. The mare looked distressed, but not in immediate danger.

Yet. He had faith in Kelly's instincts.

"Grant, thanks for coming so fast," Kelly said. "Sorry about the late hour."

"Not to worry. We both know that horses, like human babies, rarely give birth at convenient moments. If I'd wanted to stay home at night, I would have become a podiatrist."

Kelly laughed, which was what he'd intended. She was a good mother and took equally fine care of the animals on the ranch. Strength and compassion were just two of the things he admired about her. He still wished she would marry him, but when he'd proposed, she'd left little room to hope she would change her mind.

It wasn't that he was lonely, as Kelly had teasingly suggested. True, in a place like Shelton, the singles scene was limited, but he'd known that when buying his veterinary practice six years earlier. In any case, there were enough unmarried women in his age range, eager to socialize, to keep loneliness at bay.

Just then the mare's water broke and Grant focused on the task at hand. He did an exam and was glad Kelly had called him.

It was going to be a long night.

DAWN WAS BREAKING when Fiona Chance finally gave birth to a colt that was mostly black like his sire, but with a broader sprinkling of blurry white spots on his rump.

Kelly was delighted.

Kindred Ranch had always raised cattle and she'd gotten the ranch certified as organic, but even before her grandfather had put her in charge, she'd worked to diversify the operation with horse breeding. It made sense. Horse sales were less likely to be affected by chronically rising and falling beef prices. She'd even resolved some of that concern, however, since now her cows were largely sold as breeding stock to other organic producers. Kindred Ranch cattle were in high demand.

She yawned, though the adrenaline was still running too high for her to feel the full impact of a sleepless night.

Apparently Josh understood that having too many people present following delivery could upset the mare, because he retreated without being asked. But it wasn't without a last, admiring look at the new arrival. She couldn't blame him. Whatever faults he might have, he loved horses, and the new colt looked promising, even as a newborn.

Kelly was proud of Fiona Chance. Though it was the mare's first foal and she'd had a rough time with the birth, she was quickly enchanted with her new baby.

"I never get tired of it," Grant murmured an hour later, grinning ear to ear. They'd moved the new family to a clean stall and Kelly hoped it would be warm enough later in the morning for them to go into a secluded paddock.

"Me, either."

"Do you have a name for the little guy?" Grant asked.

"Black Galaxy."

"Nice. That fellow who helped, is he a new ranch hand? He seems to know his business."

Kelly's breath caught. "Sorry, I should have made proper introductions. Mr. McKeon is a Canadian friend of my father's. He plans to compete at the Shelton Rodeo Daze and is staying in the old bunkhouse."

Grant's eyes turned knowing. "One of Harry's rodeo friends? You won't enjoy having someone like that at Kindred Ranch."

"You don't have to tell me. He'll need to train with Harry's horses, because he isn't doing it with mine. And you know we don't allow bull or bronco training at the ranch any longer."

Some time ago, Kelly had confided in Grant how she felt about her father's obsession with rodeos and how it could affect Casey and Marc. She regretted her openness with Grant, though not because she didn't trust him. He'd assumed it was based on a growing warmth between them, when she'd simply been blowing off steam.

She really didn't have anyone else to talk to about certain things. Rodeos were a sensitive subject in the family, one best left alone. The elder Flannigans loved their son-in-law, but they'd also seen what his obsession had done to their daughter. As for Kathleen? She didn't want to discuss it, *period*. If she spoke about rodeos with her husband, it was mostly behind closed doors, where no one else could hear.

Well, recently Harry had declared to the

family that he wasn't going to be gone as much, but Kelly didn't believe it.

Grant straightened. "I've checked and everything looks good. Fiona Chance's colostrum seems all right and she's letting down enough for the foal. Do you want me to take a look at Gizmo's leg before I leave?"

Gizmo was the stray dog Kelly had found in Helena two years earlier. He was pure mutt—part German shepherd, part golden retriever and part who knew what—and he possessed the instincts of a champion cattle dog. But he'd cut his leg recently and was still healing. He was confined to the house while he recovered.

"Thanks, Grant, but I think he's fine. We're keeping him quiet, like you said to do, and he's still wearing the cone. He doesn't fight it as much as I expected."

"You should be able to stop using the cone now, unless he fusses at his bandages. I'll come back later and check on Fiona Chance and the baby, but I don't have any concerns."

"Great. Will you be able to go home and get some rest?"

"Hey, I slept Sunday night. I should be fine for the rest of the week."

She was smiling as he left. Normally she

would have walked him to his truck, but she wanted to keep watch on Fiona Chance and the new baby for a while longer.

A few minutes later Kelly heard a faint sound behind her and turned to see Josh.

"It's okay," she whispered. "They're both asleep."

JOSH STEPPED NEXT to Kelly and looked into the stall.

The colt's black coat had dried and he lay nestled in the straw, a picture of tired contentment. Fiona Chance's fine lines were even more apparent now that she was no longer carrying the large foal, and his admiration grew.

He was developing a horse breeding program at McKeon's Choice, but if these two were anything to go by, Kelly had him beat, six ways to Sunday.

Maybe it would improve if you were home more often, chided his ego.

Josh pushed the thought away; it was too reminiscent of Kelly's indictment of his rodeo schedule. He was still at the top of his game in competition. The money was great and he was receiving offers to appear in ads and commercials for various products and services. So far he'd just appeared gratis in a few public service spots, but he was weighing his options.

As for McKeon's Choice Ranch?

His father made sound decisions for the spread, based on the long years he'd worked for other ranchers. But his strengths were in cattle, not horses. Josh disliked stepping on Benjamin's toes, so while he made suggestions, he didn't push too hard. Someday he'd have to find the way to strike a balance, such as leaving management of the cattle side of McKeon's Choice to his dad and handling the horse breeding aspect of the ranch himself.

He glanced toward the front of the barn. The doors were closed to keep the warmth inside, but he could hear the muffled sounds of the ranch stirring to life. The foaling barn looked new. It was also the most distant building from the ranch center, which was a smart location because it afforded more quiet for a new mother and baby in the critical first hours after birth.

"When did you build this place?" he breathed.

"A couple of years ago," she replied, in an equally soft voice. "I wore a short skirt and flirted with the bank manager so he'd give me a loan."

Josh choked back a laugh; Kelly was too forthright to flirt her way into a bank loan. "Tell me another whopper."

"His son and I were engaged in the second grade, but Clay broke my heart by wooing two other girls at the same time. Mr. Carson agreed I was owed reparation."

"What's the real reason?"

"Kindred Ranch is excellent collateral and I promised to pay the money back. People know each other in Shelton. They know whether you're good at what you do and how hard you work and if your family is reliable. The Flannigans have been here for over a hundred and forty years. So he trusted me."

That Josh believed, though he had limited experience at belonging to a tight-knit community. His father had been restless, moving around, always trying to get better-paying jobs with more responsibility. Even as a child Josh had wondered if staying put and working into a foreman's position would have been best. Yet all that traveling had provided opportunities to meet various rodeo legends. They'd taken an interest and worked with Josh from a young age, so it had benefited him, in one way.

"Clay and I *were* engaged, with a glass diamond ring and everything," Kelly continued. "He also broke my heart. Sort of. It doesn't take much to break your heart at that age. I suppose it teaches perspective for the future."

Josh didn't ask if *he'd* broken her heart. Once he would have sworn she was in love with him, but she'd quickly pushed him out of her life. So it was possible she could have found someone else right away. Grant Latham, for example. He seemed fond of Kelly and might be the twins' father. The veterinarian was tall, even taller than Josh himself, with dark hair and eyes. He was also local, with a career that kept him in one place. She'd appreciate that.

But if so, why hadn't they gotten married?

Over the hours Fiona Chance had been in labor, Josh had seen an easy comfort between Kelly and the vet. Obviously their friendship went back a while. They'd practically read each other's minds while caring for the distressed mare, though that wasn't unusual—anybody experienced at helping birth a foal could anticipate what needed to be done.

Josh cleared his throat. Speculation was useless without facts. "What does Clay the Heartbreaker do now?"

"He lives in Kalispell and owns an outdoor adventure-type company, taking tourists into the backcountry around Glacier National Park. They also host white-river rafting trips and that sort of thing."

"Ah."

Fiona Chance woke and nuzzled her baby. Josh rested his arms on the stall door and watched the colt lurch to his feet and begin nursing, its tail swishing. The silence between him and Kelly was almost companionable, but he wasn't fooled. She'd shown too much antagonism the previous day to think she was at ease with his presence now.

Finally she straightened and gestured to the barn door. They walked out together and she gave him a stiff smile.

"Thanks for the help with Fiona Chance."

"You would have managed without it."

"Grant is a great veterinarian. He could have chosen a more lucrative city practice, but he prefers doctoring cows and horses, with cats and dogs and other pets on the side. It isn't easy getting medical personnel to settle down in such an isolated area." An odd expression flickered in Kelly's face. "Luckily, Dr. Wycoff's daughter is doing a residency in family medicine and plans to join her father's practice when she finishes, so we should be okay for a while."

Josh understood the concern, though his ranch wasn't as remote as Shelton. Out of necessity, ranchers became proficient at dealing with a variety of animal and human problems. Kelly probably could have assisted Fiona Chance in delivering her colt without the vet, but considering the value of the mare and foal, she'd been wise to call for assistance.

"Go eat breakfast," she said briskly. "Then you should get some sleep."

"What about you?"

"I have a full day's work ahead. I'm going to change my clothes, check on the boys and get busy."

He couldn't sleep while she was working. "I'll help."

"Nonsense. You're a guest. I'm sure Harry is still in bed, but he said that you're free to use his horses. They're in the small gray barn." She pointed across the compound. "You'll find plenty of tack in there if you want to go for a ride. Later you can talk to him about a tour of the ranch."

"If I work with you, I won't need a tour."

"I prefer working alone," Kelly returned in a tone that didn't brook disagreement. "But if you want something to do, you can let Harry's horses into the corral."

She hurried to the house without another word and Josh fought renewed irritation. He'd met hundreds of ranchers and cowhands over the years and admired their strong, independent natures, but Kelly was taking it to an unnecessary extreme. He was experienced with cattle and horses. Why was she too stubborn to accept his help?

Josh went into the ranch house after a shower and shave. Inside Kelly was eating with the boys, still answering excited questions about Fiona Chance's new foal. She promised they could see the colt before leaving for school. There was no evidence in her demeanor that she'd been up all night; she even double-checked their schoolwork after the meal and took them out to the foaling barn. The morning activities echoed a sense of normality. This was their regular pattern, not a performance put on for a stranger.

Josh instantly felt guilty.

The truth was, he was looking for grounds that Kelly might not be the best mother, in case he felt compelled to file a legal action for custody or to obtain visitation rights. It was just one of the reasons he was accepting the Flannigans' hospitality under a false guise.

Assuming, of course, that he was the boys' father, something he still wasn't sure about.

BETSY HARTNER CHATTED with her customers at the small café, keeping their coffee mugs full and collecting her tips when they left. It was mostly men who frequented the Hot Diggity Dog Café in the early morning hours, and they appreciated someone with a quick smile, who made sure the coffee was hot and the cups were kept full.

Two weeks earlier, her aged van had broken down on the outskirts of Shelton. The repair shop had estimated she needed at least seven hundred dollars to fix the thing—which probably meant a thousand or more—so she'd gone looking for a job to earn the money, rather than draw it from her savings. Work could be scarce in small towns, but she'd learned in her travels that waitressing was usually a good bet. When she had saved enough for the repairs, she'd move on to her next adventure.

The door opened and Betsy saw the newcomer was Grant Latham, the local "vitinery," as the old-timers called him. He was good-looking, but according to gossip in the café, he was batty over a lady rancher who lived southwest of town.

"Hi, Grant," she said, automatically pouring him a mug of coffee as he slid into one of the booths. "Have an early call?"

He shrugged and gulped the contents of the steaming mug.

Betsy filled it again. "The breakfast special?" she asked.

Grant nodded and she marked it on his ticket. She'd already learned he wasn't the talkative sort, at least in the morning, so she simply topped his coffee again and went to give the order to Leonard in the kitchen. Leonard was a culinary whiz who could turn an ordinary egg into a masterpiece. Today he was whipping up omelets, filled with bacon, mushrooms, onions and pools of melted cheese. A mountain of toast and home-fry potatoes accompanied the omelet. He made his own bread and the fragrance while it baked routinely drew diners into the café. Betsy hoped to learn more about his baking genius before she left Shelton.

Leonard sent a practiced glance around the dining area. "I see Dr. Latham is here again. That's five times in the last week. He must like you," he said in a low tone.

Betsy rolled her eyes. "He likes your cooking. I doubt he's noticed that someone new is pouring his coffee."

"Fine. Just don't quit to get married. That's what all my waitresses do," Leonard grumbled.

"No need to worry about me and marriage," she said, deciding not to remind him that she didn't expect to stay for long, regardless. She never took a job without being upfront about her plans. "Besides, I hear Dr. Latham is interested in a rancher."

"Yeah, Kelly Beaumont. She's part of the Flannigan clan. The Flannigan women can cook real good, so they don't eat here. Except Harry Beaumont. He's married to Kathleen Flannigan. Harry sneaks by for food the doc doesn't want him having."

Betsy grinned. Leonard knew all the doings of his small town, despite the long hours required to run a restaurant. But she'd also heard he had a long-standing rivalry with

Susannah Flannigan over the annual chili cook-off, held the week of the rodeo, so he likely took special note of their comings and goings.

She was lucky her old van had broken down where it had. The Shelton Rodeo Daze sounded fun and would be a new experience, at least. Perhaps the magazine she freelanced for would be interested in one or more articles, not that it mattered if they weren't.

Her goal was to see as much of the world as possible. No way was she going to be like her father, who'd dreamed of visiting places like the Grand Canyon, Mount Fujiyama and the Roman Colosseum, only to die in an industrial accident at thirty-six. In the end, Dad had never gone much of anywhere, too busy with his responsibilities as a single father to ever have the chance. She just wished he could have done some exploring before she came along.

Betsy did a quick run around the tables, filling coffee mugs and getting extra salsa and ketchup for the customers who poured the stuff on everything. Grant Latham seemed discouraged as his gaze became riveted on the street outside. Though she tried to squelch her curiosity, she couldn't resist looking and saw a pickup truck approaching. As it passed, she glimpsed a redheaded woman behind the wheel.

Hmm.

Could that be Kelly Beaumont?

Leonard was putting the final touches to Dr. Latham's breakfast, so Betsy put six slices of bread in the toaster and was buttering the toast when he put the order on the high counter.

"Here you go," she said, sliding the platter in front of Grant, along with the plate of toast. "Anything else?"

"No, I'm fine."

A hint of feminine ego wanted him to focus on her instead of the food, but she resisted doing anything about it. She didn't date much. Socializing could get complicated when she wasn't planning to stick around.

AFTER BREAKFAST, JOSH returned to the bunkhouse, thinking about Kelly's intense focus while Fiona Chance birthed her colt. She'd changed over the years. Where was the girl with the bright smile and merry laugh? Once Kelly had been sweetly romantic, delighted to receive a bunch of wildflowers, and happy to just hold hands and gaze at the stars on

a blanket. Maybe that part of her was alive
and well, but so far he'd seen mostly a serious rancher with suspicion in her eyes.

He stretched and headed for the small gray
barn, which sounded as if it was dedicated
to Harry's needs.

Outside he saw heavy posts lying on their
sides, with concrete clinging to one end;
they'd obviously been pulled from the ground.
A large barrel stood nearby, along with heavy
springs attached on four sides. He had a bull-
riding training barrel at McKeon's Choice—it
did a nice job of simulating the sensation of a
wild bull or bronc ride. Harry must have done
bull and bronco training on Kindred Ranch at
some point, but someone had put an end to it.

Kelly?

Josh pushed the thought away. Inside he
found the barn was divided into two sec-
tions, with stalls on one end and exercise
equipment on the other. Inquisitive horses
thrust their heads over the gates and looked
at him, aware that he was a stranger. Josh
went to each, getting acquainted. At length
he opened the stall doors and led them out in
turn. He didn't think Kelly or Harry would
have offered them as mounts or suggested he
release them into the corral if they had be-

havioral issues, not without a warning, but he didn't take anything for granted.

At the corral he automatically checked the water supply and forked hay into the feeding trough. The air was crisp, but the sun was rising in a cloudless sky and he suspected it would get warm as the day progressed. Still, the weather changed quickly this time of year—pleasant days could be followed by snowy nights.

The crunch of footsteps made him turn around and he saw Harry approaching.

"Morning," Josh called.

"Hey, Josh. What do you think of my horses?"

"They look good." It was honest. They weren't in Lightfoot's class, but they were amiable and appeared sound. "Which is your favorite?"

"That one," Harry said, pointing to a sorrel quarter horse on the far side of the corral. "Come here, Woody," he called.

Woody left the tuft of spring grass he'd found and trotted over to Harry at the fence. He was a compact, muscular animal with powerful hindquarters, well suited to his master's wiry body.

"He's a fine horse. You know, I've been

thinking Lightfoot is big for a woman Kelly's size," Josh murmured, only to kick himself for bringing her up.

"She can handle him. My daughter can handle any animal." Harry's declaration was proud, yet he also seemed wistful.

"It's just that I would have expected her to choose a stock horse for working the ranch."

Harry gave him an odd look. "Appaloosas are Kelly's favorite, but she also breeds American quarter horses. Woody is the first foal where she matched dam and sire. I wasn't sure about it since the sire was old and broken down. She picked up Blue Thunder at an auction for practically nothing. Then it turned out he was registered and had been a fine stock horse in his day. Blue is too old for breeding now and lives over at the Gillespie spread. It isn't practical, but Kelly won't get rid of the old ones. Says they worked hard and deserve a peaceful last road."

Josh agreed. It wasn't practical—ranchers needed a healthy dose of practicality— but giving a home to retired horses fit the softhearted girl he'd once known. And since Kelly was doing well with Kindred Ranch, she couldn't be letting sentimentality get *too* much in the way.

"I noticed you used to have specific training equipment for bull riding," he commented, wanting to direct the conversation away from Kelly.

Harry looked uncomfortable. "We took the barrel and posts out a couple of years ago. Have you looked at my other equipment?" Plainly he didn't want to discuss the training barrel any further.

Josh shook his head. "Not yet."

"You're welcome to use it whenever you like, along with the horses. Woody included."

"I couldn't take your favorite mount."

"Sure you can," Harry urged. "He could use a good ride. I got seized up with arthritis over the winter, so I haven't taken them out as much as they need. The Kindred Ranch cowhands work them some of the time, but more would be best."

"Sorry about the arthritis."

Harry made a face. "The cost of getting old."

Josh wondered. Harry was around fifty, which wasn't old in the modern world. Yet more than most men or women his age, he'd gotten banged up over the years.

As with any sport, some athletes seemed more prone to injury than others, and Harry was one of them. There *was* a price to pay for the accumulated damage, so maybe it was understandable that Kelly worried about Casey and Marc competing.

He didn't know. She was making him think about things he'd never wanted to consider.

CHAPTER FOUR

KELLY TRIED TO clear her mind as she rode out to survey the north herd later that morning. She practiced the old ways of ranching, surveying the herds as often as possible to protect them from predators and other issues. When she'd checked the day before, there had been at least three cows that still hadn't dropped their calves, and she wanted to be sure they were doing all right. Normally she wasn't the anxious type, but nothing was normal at the moment.

Two of the cows had calved overnight and she observed them from a distance to spot any issues. Range cattle weren't domestic pets. They edged on being wild and you didn't interfere with them more than necessary.

Edged on being wild?

A smile pulled at her lips. This particular herd was the family's heritage cows. They were directly descended from the first breeding stock brought to Montana by the Flannigans, and they were a bunch of mean, tough survivors. And because of their long lineage, the calves were in high demand. Right now, anything labeled "heritage" was hot in the consumer market.

The animals moved restlessly and she glanced around to see a rider approaching. Her mouth tightened. It was Josh. She doubted his arrival was happenstance—Kindred Ranch wasn't so small that you could easily stumble across another rider unless you were looking for them. Particularly in the north section. For the most direct route from the ranch center, you had to follow the water flowing from a small spring, up to the ridge. The narrow opening in the rocky outcroppings was hidden by black cottonwoods. Otherwise, it was four times the distance.

Her great-grandparents had purchased the north arm of the ranch as an act of faith that both of their twin sons would return safely from the Vietnam War and need the land to support two families. Granddad made it home. His brother hadn't.

She deliberately looked back at the herd as Josh rode up, determined not to ask if he'd followed her or if someone had given him directions. During his visit she'd have to keep mum about her plans for the day. As a rule, she told the family where she expected to be, but it wasn't necessary—if anything urgent arose, she carried a satellite phone and a GPS tracker. Her ranch hands followed the same procedure.

"Howdy," Josh said.

"Howdy?" she repeated, turning her head. "You saw too many classic TV Westerns as a kid. We don't say that very often around here."

"I didn't watch television when I was growing up."

"Right. You were learning how to rope cattle, ride bulls and become a star." Kelly instantly regretted the cynical note in her voice, but she couldn't unsay the words.

Predictably, Josh's mouth tightened. "Being a star isn't the only reason I compete. Is this about Doreen again? How many times do I have to explain that I never met her before that day? A few women enjoy kissing the winner, but that isn't why I compete."

Kelly gave him a cool look. "Doreen hadn't crossed my mind. You, however, seem to think about her quite often."

"Only because I'm here at Kindred Ranch and she's the reason you left me."

Her fingers tightened on Lightfoot's reins; he snorted and tossed his head until she relaxed her grip. "Grow up, Josh. Doreen is old news. I didn't appreciate what happened, but that was a long time ago, and it wouldn't have been enough to make me leave. I simply didn't want to end up in my mother's shoes, breaking my heart over someone who cares more about a bucking horse or bull than the woman he loves."

"Don't compare me to Harry. We aren't the same."

"You're more successful than he ever was, but other than that…" She let her voice trail.

Josh scowled. "Do we have to keep discussing this?"

"You're the one who raised the subject."

"Because you goaded me with that crack about learning to be a star."

"Maybe it bothers you because it hits too close to home." Kelly took a breath, reminding herself that Josh's choices had been his to make. "Look, I'm sorry. I'm really glad you're successful. It's what you wanted. But you can't deny that you're one of the fortunate few. You've won big and never had a serious injury. There aren't many professional rodeo cowboys with your elite standing."

"I've done all right."

Kelly resisted rolling her eyes. *All right* was an understatement. He'd earned enough to buy his own ranch, and that wasn't chicken feed.

She leaned forward. "So, what do you want, Josh?"

A strange, dark emotion crowded his face. "Harry mentioned where you were headed this morning and gave me directions. He didn't think he'd be up to riding today and suggested I go out on my own."

Thoughts churning, Kelly stared at the craggy outcroppings beyond Josh without really seeing them. Her father was an old man before his time. Granddad was healthier than Harry, even taking his knee surgery into consideration. It was sad, because Harry had been a respected athlete in his day. Crowds loved him because no matter what—poor performance or not, injured or unharmed— he smiled and waved his hat. And he was always happy for the winner. One of the things she admired about her father was his sense of fair play and sportsmanship.

"I offered to have some of his fitness

equipment moved into the house for the winter to help him stay limber more easily," she murmured at length. "He refused, saying he'd go to the barn. But he never would, even when I offered to work out with him."

Josh tipped his hat back on his head. "Maybe he was worried about his heart condition."

"That only came up a few weeks ago, and honestly, it isn't as serious as Harry wants to believe. Anyhow, the doctor gave him guidelines for exercise, which are more strenuous than his usual training regimen. Even the cholesterol count is low enough to be addressed by diet, though that will require cooperation on his part."

JOSH REACHED DOWN to stroke Woody's neck. It had been generous of Harry to insist he take the sorrel. Woody was quiet and gentlemanly, in contrast to Lightfoot's fiery personality. But despite their opposite natures, the two horses appeared to be friends, communicating back and forth with small neighs.

"I saw the bull-riding training barrel had been pulled out," Josh said, straightening in the saddle. "Even if you aren't a fan of the sport, what's the harm in letting Harry train?"

Kelly's blue eyes narrowed. "Harm? Marc snuck onto that barrel when he was four. He knew he wasn't supposed to and did it anyhow. He stood and jumped to make it move up and down, only to go flying. Luckily we have a volunteer medical flight unit in Shelton because he had a subdural hematoma and a broken arm. He was flown to Helena for treatment. Harry hired a backhoe to pull the posts out while we were there. I didn't ask for that. He just did it."

Josh frowned. If Kelly had intended to underscore the challenges of parenting, she'd done a great job. A training barrel wasn't a toy. No wonder Harry had gotten rid of it as soon as possible.

He cleared his throat. "Does Marc have any lasting issues from his injuries?"

"The arm was a clean break and healed well. The hematoma was the scariest part. He's fine, but they had to operate to relieve the pressure. He was so little in that hospital bed." Kelly's voice cracked on the word *little*, but her expression was set. In her face he could see echoes of the generations of resilient Flannigan women who'd helped build a Montana cattle ranch.

"I'm glad he's all right."

Kelly focused on the herd and he followed her gaze. The cattle were still shaggy with their winter coats, but they looked exceptionally fit.

"Do you winter livestock on this part of the ranch?" he asked.

"It's too inaccessible to get feed over here in bad weather. We drive this herd to the other side of the ridge each fall, to an enclosed pasture. Though that one—" Kelly gestured to a bull that looked as tough and ornery as any Josh had ever ridden "—doesn't appreciate our efforts. Last winter he broke the fence down and disappeared, right before a bad storm. We found him over here, five days later. This is his territory and it's where he wants to be."

Josh glanced across the small, tree-rimmed valley; it appeared as wild and untouched as the land must have looked when Kelly's ancestors settled the area. "He was lucky to survive. A hungry pack of wolves wouldn't hesitate."

"He's collected a few scars over the years, though not from wolves. They've been reintroduced into Montana and are spreading, but the packs are mostly in the southern and western parts of the state."

Josh recalled the periodic reports of domestic animals being lost to wolves in Alberta. His father was convinced wolf packs had taken several cows two summers ago, although it seemed just as likely that grizzly bears had gotten them. Dad carried two loaded rifles wherever he went on McKeon's Choice, determined to keep it from happening again.

"How would Shelton ranchers feel about reintroducing wolves around here?" Josh asked.

A thoughtful expression crossed Kelly's face. "Some of us support the idea. Others aren't convinced."

"I'm one of them."

She smiled faintly. "Since you don't live in Montana, you don't have a horse in this race, so to speak. There's strong evidence that the land and waterways are healthier with wolves as part of the mix, but since no one has approached the community with a proposal, anything else is just speculation."

"Then why does anyone bother discussing the question?"

Kelly's eyes widened at his argumenta-
tive tone. "Are you trying to start a fight?
Another fight, that is."

Josh realized he'd mentioned wolf management just to get a rise out of Kelly, the way
she'd gotten one out of him. With ranchers,
lupine predators could be a touchy subject…
akin to throwing a lit match into gasoline.
When she hadn't reacted to his provocation,
he'd resorted to something else. No doubt
about it—the situation with Kelly was doing
strange things to his brain.

"The subject is raised periodically at the
Shelton Ranching Association meetings,"
Kelly continued when he didn't respond.
"Mostly because a cousin on Grams's side
of the family inherited a ranch near Yellow-
stone National Park, where they do have
wolves. Gideon hasn't lost any livestock to
them, though his neighbor hasn't been as fortunate."

Josh shook himself. "Do you think wildlife managers are hoping wolves will mi-
grate into the Shelton area, either up from
the south or down from Canada?"

KELLY DIDN'T KNOW why Josh was behaving
oddly. While he might have a strong opin-

ion about wolves, it seemed unlikely that he was concerned about them finding a home around Shelton.

"I have no idea," she said. "I don't have any wildlife managers in my circle of acquaintances. Did you ride out here to debate philosophical issues?"

"Of course not. I'm simply interested in the ranch. You told me about it when we were dating. As long as I'm here, I may as well see the place."

Okay, maybe she was too suspicious. She *had* talked about Kindred Ranch when they were seeing each other—after all, they both came from ranching backgrounds. Josh had also told her about wanting to buy his own spread someday.

"And I explained that I prefer working alone," she said.

"Yeah, why *is* that?"

Kelly gave him an exasperated look. "There's nothing unusual about it. I don't think people become cowboys or stay in ranching if they're social butterflies. A good many of us enjoy our solitude, present company excepted," she said, waving her hand at Josh.

"I'm not a social butterfly, if that's what you're suggesting." He sounded offended.

"Perhaps, but you're energized by crowds. Even when I traveled with Mom and Harry in the summertime, I didn't go to all the events. You called me Bookworm when we first met. Remember?"

The nickname would have bothered Kelly, except Josh hadn't teased her where anyone else could hear. She would have hated being called Bookworm by her father's rodeo pals. It hadn't been so bad with Josh, though, and it was when she'd first gotten a crush on him. He'd been handsome and self-assured, unlike the gawky boys she knew at home. For years she'd dreamed about growing up enough for him to notice her in a new way.

A reminiscent smile played on his face. "I remember. You'd find a stack of hay bales to lean against and read one of your books. Serious stuff about animal husbandry and ranch management. I never asked—did they belong to your grandparents?"

"Some. But others were from the Shelton library or borrowed from neighboring ranchers." Kelly patted Lightfoot's shoulder as he stomped his left foreleg, unhappy with Josh's presence.

She didn't want to discuss the way she'd prepared to take over Kindred Ranch one day. At a very early age it had been very apparent that her father wasn't interested in his wife's family legacy. Kelly had tried to understand. After all, Harry had his own spread, though he'd rarely spent time there. She'd visited the Bucking B just a handful of times herself.

And now he'd sold it.

Why?

Even as the question formed in her mind, the answer was obvious; he'd sold his ranch to have the money to continue going to rodeos and bull-riding events. The Bucking B had been in Harry's family since the early 1900s, but he'd given it up for the thrill of competition he had little hope of winning any longer.

"You didn't borrow textbooks from your local veterinarian?" Josh asked. "I know that couldn't have been Grant Latham. He's too young for you to have known him as a kid."

Kelly let out a brief laugh. "It was Dr. Pierson when I was young, and his textbooks were old. *Really* old. Veterinary medicine has moved on since he went to school, as he'd be the first to tell you. He was delighted when Grant bought his practice, although he still helps with some of the small-animal work and does volunteer shifts during the rodeo. Looking at him, you'd never guess he's in his late seventies. Fifties, maybe, but no older."

"Right."

An awkward silence fell. No doubt it would be one of many awkward moments until Josh left Shelton. She rested her forearm on the saddle pommel as she watched the herd. The old bull was nicknamed Hellfire and she'd miss him when he was gone, despite the challenges he presented. He was wild and free and protected the heritage herd with a fierce determination.

"I don't get it," Josh murmured a few minutes later. "We talked all the time when we were dating. Why is it so hard now?"

Kelly spared him a glance. "I told you a little about Kindred Ranch, but we mostly spoke about rodeos, or your wins and goals for the future."

A dull red crept up his throat. "I didn't talk about myself the whole time."

"That isn't what I said."

Yet in a way, it was true. She'd been awed that Josh was interested in her. He'd been handsome and talented and she had been content to listen as he geared himself up for his next competition, or the adrenaline wore off from the last one. She'd also loved his assumption they would be together in the future he envisioned, though he'd never actually asked her to marry him or to be a part of it.

Riding for a fall, as her great-grandmother would have said.

"What are you thinking?" Josh prodded.

She straightened and said, "About my great-grandmother. Nanna Mary was a wise woman who told you the plain truth, whether or not you wanted to hear it. She grew up in New York City. Then at the end of World War II she came out to Shelton as a schoolteacher."

Josh whistled. "Life on a ranch couldn't have been easy for a city woman."

"She told great stories about it. The funny ones were my favorites. But however comical she made it sound, I think she took the whole thing in her stride. So many men died in the war, she hadn't expected to get married. Falling in love with the most eligible bachelor in Shelton was a gift."

"Is marriage something you think about?" Josh asked. "With Grant Latham, maybe?"

The question jolted Kelly. Coming from

Josh, it felt inordinately personal. "That's my business," she returned shortly.

"Yeah, but I'd think with Casey and Marc to consider, you'd want them to have a father."

Kelly glared. "Are you suggesting Harry and my grandfather are inadequate male role models? Our ranch hands are also good men, so my boys are fine. As for Grant, our relationship is off-limits to you."

"I didn't intend to poke a sore spot."

"You didn't." Her chin rose. "But why don't you go register for the rodeo today? I'm sure you'll have time if you leave now. Just drive into town and stop at the sheriff's office on the main road. That's where they're taking applications. You could do it online, but I think the personal touch is best."

"Isn't registration available on the day of each event?"

"You can register up to an hour before competing, but doing it early helps the planning committee know how many contestants to expect. We've never needed to put a limit on the number."

"Fine." Josh gave her a hard look, then turned Woody toward the narrow opening in the ridge.

Tension exploded in Kelly's stomach. She had doubts that Josh would end up competing. The annual rodeo raised money for Shelton's emergency medical services and it was a small, local event. They had a fair number of contestants, but the registration fees were moderate, so there weren't large purses to divide among the winners. Why would Josh wait around when there were juicier competitions to tempt someone with his talent? Any number of other rodeos would take place between now and the Shelton Rodeo Daze.

"Josh," she called, riding after him.

"Yes?"

"I shouldn't have pushed. Maybe you should wait to register, the way you planned. That way no one will be expecting you."

A muscle in his jaw ticked. "I have every intention of competing, Kelly. I'm going to do exactly as you suggested and register today. *In person*."

She let out a breath as he rode away, hoping everything would be all right. The rodeo was still a few weeks away. What if he registered, got the town excited about the possibility of a big-name competitor, and then he didn't show up?

ON THURSDAY BETSY was in the last half hour
of her shift at the café when Grant Latham
walked in, looking tired and faintly smelling like the business end of a cow. It was an
odor she was getting used to, particularly
when the wind blew in certain directions off
nearby ranches.

"Hi, Grant. What can I get for you?" she
asked.

They'd had a long conversation when he'd
come in for a late breakfast a couple of days
earlier, but she didn't think it meant anything. Still, it was interesting to know more
about him. In return, he plainly didn't think
much of her mobile lifestyle.

"Coffee, and something that's fast, followed by your biggest, fattest cheeseburger,"
he said. "I've been out on cases since two
this morning. The Harringtons invited me to
have breakfast with them, but I got another
emergency call before I could eat. I have two
meals to catch up on."

"You got it." Betsy hurried to the kitchen
and gave her boss an order for the special
house burger, then filled a bowl with bean-
and-ham soup. Back at the table, Grant ate it
so fast she was worried he'd choke.

"That was great," he said a couple of minutes later.

"Really? I didn't think it spent enough time in your mouth for you to taste anything."

He chuckled and gulped his coffee.

She refilled his cup. "All this java is going to burn a hole through your stomach. At the very least, you should add cream and sugar as a buffer."

"Nah. My stomach is made of iron."

"Then maybe you should stock those energy drinks in your truck. The ones that are loaded with caffeine and stuff."

"Is that what you use on the road with all your traveling?"

Betsy put the coffeepot on the table and rested her hip against the high back of the next booth. There wasn't anyone else in the café and she'd finished her end-of-shift tasks, so she had a minute to talk. "I keep dried fruit and nuts on hand for munching. They're good for energy."

"Trail mix? Sounds very hippie-ish. I suppose it goes with being footloose and fancy-free."

"Ha." She slid down to sit opposite him, wiggling her toes. "There's nothing wrong with any of that, but I do it out of practicality. As for being fancy-free? Perhaps, but I earn my way."

"I guess that's possible when you live out of a van most of the time."

Betsy scrunched her nose. Most people didn't understand her life, but it worked for her. Since college she'd seen a good part of North America. Once she had enough money put aside, she'd park her van in a storage area and backpack through Europe, Asia and Africa. After that she'd check out Japan, the South Seas, South America and all the other places she'd marked on her world map. The North Pole and Antarctica were goals, as well. Was there any way she could talk herself onto a team studying or filming emperor penguins? It would be an incredible experience.

Grant wiped his mouth with a napkin. "How do you live that way, taking only what you can carry? My mom was in the navy and she's a no-nonsense type, but even *she* has sentimental stuff that she moved from posting to posting. My dad is worse."

"The other day you mentioned that he's navy, too."

"Yeah. Actually, they're both retired now.

They got a divorce when I was five. The military is hard on marriages. I was passed back and forth between them until I left for university—San Diego, Spain, the Philippines, Guam, Australia, to name just a few. After a while, all the travel and those navy bases and navy housing just blurred together for me."

Betsy sighed. She didn't have any memories of her mother. Her dad had said little about his ex-wife over the years, probably because Lena Hartner had left her husband and baby in search of greener pastures and he hadn't wanted his daughter to feel abandoned. She squared her shoulders. She'd had a wonderful father and refused to feel sorry for herself.

"But at least you were able to see amazing countries," she asserted.

Grant snorted. "Give me Shelton any day. This place is home. You can put down roots here."

"Except I don't want roots. I even hate goodbyes. As a rule, I simply pack up and leave when the time is right. It makes things easier on everybody."

Leonard hit the bell to say the order was ready, so Betsy got up and returned with

Grant's plate. The special house burger was practically obscene, with cheese and grilled onions oozing from the top of a thick, hand-formed patty and a colossal stack of fries on the side.

Grant's eyes gleamed. "That's just what I need."

"The Hot Diggity Dog Café aims to please," she said lightly. "I'm going off duty now, so let Didi know if there's anything else you want. She just came in."

Grant waved in acknowledgment, his mouth already full with a handful of fries.

Betsy gave his ticket to Didi and hurried out. She liked Grant, but while it was pleasant to get tingles in the company of an attractive man, they obviously had little common ground. It would be wise to remember that.

How could he say places like Spain and Australia blurred together for him? Well, he'd said the navy bases blurred together, but she couldn't imagine being blasé about any of the spots she'd visited. She loved all of them, whether it was a small town like Tucumcari, New Mexico, or a city such as Victoria, British Columbia.

Betsy walked toward the house where she was renting a room, her route taking her past the Shelton Veterinary Clinic, which Grant owned. The building was tidy and in good condition, but there wasn't anything visually appealing about it. The place needed a splash of color to make it less utilitarian. A grassy area would also be nice for his canine patients, but even the large front flower beds were just covered with faded bark chips.

Betsy pushed the thought aside and kept walking.

"Hello, dear. Are you ready for a cuppa?" called her landlady from the porch that ran across the front of her house. "I made lemon scones, and might find a biscuit or two."

"Sounds great. May I help?"

"Not at all. Just sit and rest yourself."

Betsy grinned. It was Mrs. Mapleton's determined belief that tea was the answer to everything. Maya Mapleton had lived in Montana since she was fourteen, the daughter of a United States serviceman and a British secretary. A widow for over ten years, she was good-hearted and had welcomed Betsy like a daughter. As for "finding" a biscuit or two, she'd probably baked a batch that morning.

Betsy sat on one of the wicker chairs, first lifting Spurs from the cushion and resettling the gray-and-white tuxedo cat on her lap. Miss Priss and Bootsy were curled up across the screened porch; they gave her a glance, purred their approval and went back to sleep.

"There, now." Mrs. Mapleton set a tray on the table. The biscuits—actually delicate shortbread cookies— were piled on a china plate and the scones were nestled in a basket next to a porcelain serving jar of raspberry preserves.

"It looks delicious," Betsy said. "But you shouldn't go to so much trouble."

Her landlady blushed. She was a dear lady who struggled with shyness and an innate reserve. "Tosh. I enjoy our chats."

"In that case, tell me again about the time you saw the queen before your family moved to America."

Betsy listened, feeling as if she was taking a flying trip to England. Afternoon tea had quickly become a ritual, and before she left Shelton, she was going to make sure that her landlady had plenty of tea-time company. With that thought in mind, she gestured to a woman on the opposite side of the street, who was digging in a flower bed.

"Why don't we invite your neighbor over?"

she asked. "I can get another cup from the kitchen."

Mrs. Mapleton looked uncertain and Betsy wondered if she'd overstepped, something her enthusiasm could lead her to do. But if her father's early death had taught her anything, it was the importance of never wasting time.

"Do you think Irene would mind?" Mrs. Mapleton asked tentatively.

"What's to mind? If she's too busy, she'll say so."

"Oh. All right. G-go ahead. I'll get the cup and make a fresh pot of tea."

Betsy put Spurs on the floor and went outside. She drew a deep breath of the cool, clean air; she loved all the seasons of the year, but spring in Montana was especially nice. It didn't hurt that half of her winter had been spent in high, snowy elevations in Canada. Gorgeous, but frigid.

"Hi, I'm Betsy Hartner," she called.

The other woman looked up and brushed a strand of short, graying brown hair from her forehead. "How nice to meet you. I'm Irene Norville. You're Maya's boarder, aren't you?"

"That's right. Do you have time to join us for a cup of tea?"

Irene immediately removed her gardening gloves. "That sounds wonderful. I'm ready to surrender. Every fall I ask my husband to mulch these beds, and he never gets around to it. Then I don't get it done, either. Honestly, I think the weeds keep growing, no matter how cold it gets."

Betsy laughed. "I've never gardened, but it must be fun."

"You're welcome to have all the fun you want in ours. You can't do it any harm. Compared to Maya, we're quite inadequate as gardeners. On the other hand..." Irene looked hopeful. "Maybe I could recruit you to do prep work on the upcoming rodeo. My husband is one of the committee members and they're always looking for volunteers. It's for a good cause."

"Sure, whatever you need. I work the early shift at the Hot Diggity Dog Café, but other than that, I'm free. I'd lend you my van, too, but it's barely working at the moment."

Her quick agreement seemed to surprise Irene. "I'll let Dalton know you're available. And don't think twice about the van. You're kind to consider it, but we're well supplied with transportation. Half of Shelton owns a truck."

An imprudent curiosity caught Betsy as they crossed the street together. "Is Dr. Latham helping with the rodeo? The veterinarian, I mean, from the clinic a few blocks over."

"I know Dr. Latham. He takes care of our dogs. Grant is working shifts during the event, along with other county vets. They inspect the animals and all that, but I don't know if he's involved in the prep work."

"Right. I imagine he's too busy with his practice."

Irene's searching glance threatened to send heat creeping into Betsy's face. Darn it, she didn't blush—after all, there wasn't any point to getting embarrassed. Besides, her travels had taken her through enough small towns to understand that most people just had a friendly interest in who might be involved with whom. Rarely was there anything malicious about it.

"I met your husband the other day, out walking the dogs," Betsy said quickly. "Genghis and Khan, right? They're adorable."

"That's right."

They went up the walkway and Mrs. Mapleton shyly greeted her new guest. She'd brought out a fresh tray, along with sugar and cream. The two women began talking about gar-

dening and which rose varieties grew best in
Montana. Apparently they knew each other
by name and said "hello" when they crossed
paths, but didn't visit that much.

Betsy smiled with satisfaction.

The first step in getting her landlady more
company at tea time was accomplished. Now
she just had to stop getting stray thoughts
about a certain tall, sexy, lovelorn veterinarian, and everything would be perfect.

CHAPTER FIVE

JOSH BRAKED HIS truck to a screeching halt and stared at the colorful poster attached to a telephone pole.

See Rodeo Champion Josh McKeon compete at the Shelton Rodeo Daze...

Sheesh. He'd only gotten registered last week.

He drove on and saw a long series of posters, some with his photograph, some not, and all with his name prominently featured. Considering Kelly's attitude toward rodeos, it could make matters worse in an already tricky situation.

He still had more questions than answers, with the biggest question yet to be asked—were Casey and Marc his sons?

Kelly kept trying to avoid him, sometimes successfully and sometimes not. His efforts to learn more about her relationship with Grant Latham had failed miserably. He didn't know why it bothered him so much, except she hadn't shown a shred of interest in his own love life. It was annoying. They'd once shared something special, and just because it had ended badly, it didn't mean he no longer cared about her.

Now he needed to decide what to do next.

Keep probing?

Ask Harry?

Confront her?

He was leaning toward the last idea. Confronting Kelly might be the only chance he'd have of finding out what he needed to know. She was too careful to blurt anything out inadvertently.

Tense with frustration, Josh parked in front of the Shelton Saddle and Boot shop. Before going inside, he pulled his cowboy hat low over his forehead, hoping to escape notice. It didn't help. The moment he stepped inside, he heard an excited "Hey, that's Josh McKeon."

A kid, maybe eighteen or nineteen, rushed over to ask for an autograph. Josh obliged.

"Thanks, Mr. McKeon. My father owns the Barky K. It's well south of town, but we're still in Shelton County," he said emphatically. "I'll be in all of the adult events at the rodeo and my sister will do girls' barrel racing, pole bending and breakaway roping in the junior rodeo."

"The best of luck," Josh said. He'd never forget the rodeo legends who'd encouraged him.

"That's real nice of you, sir."

"Owen, leave Mr. McKeon be," scolded the clerk, a no-nonsense woman with short iron gray hair and an incongruous slash of iridescent pink lipstick on her mouth. "What can we do for you, Mr. McKeon? The name is Avery and I own this joint. This young fellow is my nephew, Owen Corcoran."

"Pleased to meet you both. I need saddle soap and other tack care equipment."

"Right over there." She gestured to the left side of the shop. "I can contact my supplier if I don't carry the brands you prefer."

"I'm sure you'll have what I want."

He filled a cart with everything from saddle oil to polishing cloths, along with buckets and a plentiful supply of grooming tools. Some of the brands were different from what he ordinarily used, but you didn't make points in a small town by acting as if they carried the wrong products.

"We're pleased to have you registered for the rodeo," Avery said as she rang up his purchases. "I hear you had horses sent down from Canada for it. Wesley at the gas station got a look at them when your employee stopped to ask directions to Kindred Ranch. He says they're real fine."

Josh had known the news would travel quickly in such a small area. After registering, he'd called and asked his father to send a cowhand down with Quicksilver, along with his favorite stock horse and three saddles. He would have preferred fetching the horses himself, but he hadn't wanted to leave Kindred Ranch, even for a few days. They'd arrived the previous evening.

Dave Dubret, who'd driven the horse trailer down, had spent the night in the bunkhouse and left after an early breakfast with the family. Josh couldn't help noticing that Dave had received a much more cordial welcome from Kelly than he had himself.

In plain words, she'd dazzled Dave.

For an hour after they'd hit the sack in the bunkhouse, he hadn't been able to stop talking about Kelly's horse savvy, along with her eyes "like blue larkspur in the sun," her shapely figure and rich hair.

"It isn't red, exactly," Dave had said, gazing at the ceiling, his hands tucked behind his head. "Or brown. There's gold, too, like a halo when the late sun hits it. I like how she keeps it long. A lot of ranch gals cut their hair short for convenience. What do you think?"

I think you should shut up, Josh had wanted to shout. He wasn't Dave's pal or confidant, and he sure didn't want to share his thoughts about Kelly with one of his employees or anyone else.

"You should get some sleep," Josh had told him finally. "It's a long drive back to McKeon's Choice."

Unable to rest himself, he'd stared at the ceiling for most of the night, his mind filled with memories. He couldn't blame Dave for being bowled over by Kelly. She'd gotten even more beautiful with time, like a picture that had come into full focus. If they'd just met, he would have done his best to get her attention, if only for the sheer pleasure of looking into her remarkable eyes.

Josh pushed the tantalizing image away and focused on Avery.

"Thanks, ma'am. I'm proud of my horses. Harry told me I could use his stock horses to train and compete, but I didn't want to impose." Eager to change the subject, he leaned forward. "I'm curious—why did your nephew make a point of saying his family's ranch is in Shelton County?"

Avery gave him a quick smile. "I'm surprised the Flannigans haven't told you about it. The Patrick Flannigan Memorial Buckle is awarded to the top Shelton County contestants in both the junior and regular rodeos. Owen has won it twice at the high school level and is a favorite for winning this year in the regular rodeo."

"That's great." Josh knew that many rodeos reserved prizes for local residents to ensure that some winners came from the area.

He carried his purchases to the truck and checked the time. It was a short day for the twins at school; they were getting out of class at noon. He'd offered to pick them up so no one would have to make a special trip into town, but Kelly had refused, saying she needed to have her dog checked by Grant and would fetch them herself. Kathleen had looked unhappy in turn; apparently it was her special time with the boys.

Josh had then offered to handle the veterinary visit, too, only to be refused once again.

"I also have other errands to run," she'd claimed. "And Gizmo doesn't like you. It would be too stressful for him."

She might be right.

Gizmo was entirely Kelly's dog. He tolerated the rest of the family and the cowhands, but his adoration was reserved for her alone. According to Harry, she'd rescued him in Helena when Marc was hospitalized after his misadventure with the training barrel. At the time Gizmo was an abused, half-grown stray pup, covered with fleas and ticks. His devotion to Kelly had been instantaneous, but it had taken months before he would let anyone else get near him without baring his teeth.

Grown now into a magnificent adult, Gizmo was intensely protective of his mistress. Between Gizmo and Lightfoot, a man would be lucky to get near her.

Shelton wasn't a huge community, so Josh drove over to see where the twins' school was located, then continued down the street before school officials or a deputy sheriff could wonder why he was loitering.

He would have appreciated spending time alone with the boys, not that he had any experience entertaining kids. With Marc, experience didn't seem to matter; he was spontaneous and craved being the center of attention. Casey was another matter. He worked things out in his head, and while his brother's determination to always grab the spotlight could annoy him, most of the time he didn't seem to care about having it himself.

Josh rubbed his chin.

At a guess, he'd say Casey took more after his mother than anyone else in the family. Kelly was strong and quietly confident. She kept her own counsel. Did that come from being a single mother and needing to manage the ranch?

No, he decided.

She'd always had a private streak. Kelly had suggested they'd only talked about *his* dreams and hopes when they were dating. Perhaps. But it was also because she didn't open up easily.

As he approached the veterinary clinic, Josh saw one of the Kindred Ranch trucks parked in the small lot. He hesitated before pulling in next to it; might as well find out how uptight Kelly was about those posters advertising the rodeo. A few minutes later she came out with Gizmo on a leash, accompanied by Grant Latham. The dog's tail swayed when Latham reached down and rubbed behind his ears. At least Gizmo accepted Grant. Was that a reflection of how Kelly felt about the veterinarian?

Kelly's mouth flattened when Josh walked over. It was just a guess, but she probably *was* miffed at seeing his name on every telephone and light pole in the community.

"I thought you would have returned to the ranch by now," she said.

"I was just passing on my way back."

"Uh-huh."

Okay, if she wasn't going to mention the gaudy posters on every available surface, then neither was he. "Did Gizmo get a clean bill of health?"

She exchanged a glance with Latham. "He's recovering well. Fairly light days for a while, that's all. Fortunately he didn't have muscle or tendon damage, or else he'd need rehab."

Josh looked down at the energetic dog. "You might have trouble explaining 'light' to him."

"I'll manage. Come, boy. We need to make a few stops, then pick up Casey and Marc."

Gizmo jumped into the cab before she could help him up, fairly dancing with excitement. He was free of both stitches and bandages and must know it meant he wouldn't be left at the ranch center while Kelly rode away without him.

Grant Latham cleared his throat after her truck had disappeared down the block. "I didn't realize you were prominent in the rodeo world until I saw all those posters. Of course, I don't follow rodeos or professional bull riding. The Shelton event is more than enough for me."

"I wouldn't call myself *prominent*. I've had some success."

"Modesty doesn't suit you."

Josh settled his hat more firmly on his head. "I win more than I lose. Does that suit me better?"

Latham just shrugged. "Kelly tells me you have first-rate horses. I look forward to seeing them. At the rodeo, I hope, not for veterinary care."

"Right. See you there."

GRANT WATCHED JOSH MCKEON drive in the opposite direction that Kelly had gone. In an odd way he liked Josh, though his presence had to be a thorn in Kelly's side, given his status as a rodeo champion.

You can't fight her battles, warned an inner voice.

It was true, and would have been true, whether or not she'd agreed to marry him. From the moment they'd met, Kelly had impressed him as stubbornly independent, already handling most of the management responsibilities for Kindred Ranch, despite being just twenty-one and the mother of newborn twins.

Grant sighed and went back inside to speak with his office manager. "Jill, Gizmo was my last appointment for the day, so I'm heading out to the Peters Ranch. Fritz is worried about his prize bull—something about a funny look in Rumble's eyes."

Jill laughed. "Honestly, Fritz worries more about that bull than the rest of us worry about our families. Just a reminder—unless something comes up, you offered to help at the rodeo grounds this afternoon. But if you want, I'll let the chairman know you can't make it. I'm sure they'd understand, seeing as you've been out the past three nights on emergency calls."

"Nope, I'm fine. I'll catch up on sleep once foaling and calving season is over."

Jill made a face. "You say that every year."

"And that's what happens every year."

She pursed her lips. "You could get a veterinary resident to take some of the load off. And they could handle the lab tech duties when Chuck retires. That way it wouldn't be as expensive."

"We'll see."

Chuck Adams had started work as Dr. Pierson's lab technician and lately he'd been making noises about retirement. Grant hated to think about it. Finding a new tech in a town like Shelton wouldn't be easy, which meant he'd probably have to run the tests himself for a while. Bringing in a veterinary resident was an option, but they weren't permanent, which meant he'd have to work with someone new on a regular basis. He wasn't big into change.

Grant drove to the Peters Ranch and found Fritz in the barn with Rumble, a misnomer when it came to the amiable Angus, who was gentle as a kitten. Grant carefully examined his patient, though his every instinct told him the animal was sound.

"I can't find anything wrong," he said finally. "Can you be more specific about his symptoms?"

"Oh..." Fritz waved his hands vaguely. "Just a look in his eyes. It's gone now."

Grant suppressed a combined yawn and

grin. Ranchers tended to be pragmatic when it came to livestock, but Rumble was more pet than livestock, and Fritz had a gift for blowing something small into something huge. Despite that, a veterinarian couldn't risk assuming that a client had imagined a problem that didn't exist. He'd had people rush their cat or dog into the clinic, showing every apparent sign of good health, only to discover something serious was going on.

"Okay, Fritz, keep checking on him and contact me if anything changes. I'll also run basic blood tests."

"Thanks, Doc. That'd relieve my mind."

With some animals, drawing blood could be a challenge, but not with Rumble. He stood quietly, and when it was done, he rubbed his huge head against Grant's leg and licked his wrist.

"Good fella," Grant said, petting him like a thousand-pound puppy.

He made a couple of other quick calls and then left Rumble's blood sample at the office for Chuck to do the tests. He was getting close to the start of his volunteer shift at the rodeo grounds, but he had just enough time to stop and get water to share with everyone.

He parked at the Shelton Market and hurried inside.

BETSY'S JAW DROPPED when Grant Latham brushed past her at the market without returning her smile or casual "hello."

She dropped her shopping basket on the stack of empties and followed him out to the small parking area.

"*Excuse* me," she said as he opened the passenger door of his truck and deposited a case of water.

He turned around. "Yes?"

"For your information, it's common courtesy to acknowledge other people, especially in a place like Shelton, where most everyone seems to know everyone else. Instead, you acted as if I'm invisible."

Grant frowned, a nonplussed expression in his brown eyes. "Sorry, Becky. I'm sleep deprived right now and on autopilot."

"The name is *Betsy*," she snapped. "You've seen it on my name tag often enough at the Hot Diggity Dog. I'm sorry you're tired, but that's no excuse for being rude. Or maybe you think you're better than me, just because you're a veterinarian and I'm a waitress? I suppose service employees are a faceless mass to you—people who smooth your life, but don't count in the grand scheme of things.

For your information, I'm proud of any job I've done. I work hard and give value for pay."

"Look, that isn't—"

"Forget it." Betsy turned on her heel and marched back into the market. She was silly to get her feelings hurt. So they'd had a few interesting conversations at the café—hardly a friendship, much less a grand romance.

She collected her shopping basket again and went to get a selection of miniature cream puffs from the store's small bakery. Mrs. Mapleton had invited Irene Norville and another neighbor for tea that afternoon and Betsy wanted to contribute her part to the event.

By the time she'd walked the few blocks home, she was regretting her outburst with Grant. Okay, he wasn't Prince Charming. What man was? And she'd definitely over-reacted. But everyone was so warm and friendly in Shelton, it had been a shock when he ignored her greeting.

Maybe he *hadn't* seen or heard her.

He'd been carrying a case of bottled water on his shoulder and his working hours were insane this time of year, according to the re-tired ranchers who hung out at the café each morning. The old guys were wonderful characters, along with being gentlemen in their own gruff way.

Right.

She knew how it felt to be tired. She'd worked full-time *and* taken a full course load at college. Most of the time she'd just put her head down and plowed forward, daydreaming about getting a good night's sleep. And it was easy to get the names Betsy and Becky mixed up. One of her professors had never gotten it right.

Maybe she owed Grant an apology.

WHEN KELLY AND the boys arrived back at the ranch, she got an argument from them about doing their homework right away.

"But, Moooommmm, we have hours and hours," Marc protested. "Can't we go riding with you?"

She was tempted. It was the ever-present challenge of being a working parent—wanting to be with your kids, while other responsibilities pulled you in a different direction. She was lucky. Her sons loved animals and were eager to be active in ranch life, which meant they could be with her part of the time. Once summer arrived and they were no longer in school, it would be even easier.

"Not now." Kelly hesitated. "After you do all your assignments."

"Yippee!" shouted Marc. He dashed toward the house.

"Thanks, Mom." Casey gave her a hug and rushed after his brother.

Grams stepped onto the porch. "I'll make sure they get their assignments done. Goodness, times have changed. I don't recall being given homework at their age."

"That was before the 'new math' arrived in Shelton. Now all the subjects have to keep up."

Grams shook her head. "I still don't understand what was wrong with the old math. It was good enough when I was a girl. After all, I don't need to count on my fingers."

Kelly grinned and patted Gizmo, who was eager to be active after being kept quiet while convalescing. He followed her to the main barn, where she found Josh stripped to the waist, forking straw into freshly cleaned stalls.

A tremor of awareness startled Kelly.

Her life was full. She rarely had a moment to think about much except the boys and the rest of the family, along with running the ranch. If anything, she'd figured romance would have to stay in the past. Yet the sight of Josh, tanned and well muscled, was taking her breath away.

"You… You shouldn't be doing that," she protested.

"I need to work, Kelly. Consider it the conditioning I require for competing."

Kelly grabbed a pitchfork and began spreading straw in the remaining stalls, hoping to stop the quivering sensation in her body. It was too reminiscent of how Josh had made her feel when they were dating.

She cleared her throat. "Harry has a bench press, weight machine and other equipment in his barn. I'm told there's a scientific approach to working all your muscle groups with those gadgets."

Josh swiped an arm over the sweat on his face. "Sure, but my philosophy is that real work enhances agility. I also stand on a fifteen-pound medicine ball every day. Often for a couple of hours or more. It's great for balance."

A picture flashed through Kelly's mind of the boys trying to improve their balance by walking fence rails or atop more risky locations. "You haven't mentioned that bit about balance to Casey and Marc, have you?"

"No, and I haven't mentioned the medicine

ball to anyone, either. It's private. I feel ridiculous on the thing, but when something works, it works." Josh didn't add a request that she keep the information to herself, which she took as an oblique compliment. He had faith she wouldn't say anything.

They worked in silence for a while. Though the moment seemed almost comfortable, Kelly wasn't fooled. Josh had been asking a lot of questions over the past few days… questions about the twins. Either he suspected they were his, or his ego was bruised by the idea that she'd gotten involved with someone immediately after their breakup.

"I've been wondering about Gizmo's injury," he said, breaking her concentration.

Kelly blinked, startled that his comment was so far from what she'd been thinking. "What about it?"

"From what I've seen, the cut is jagged."

"There was more than one, actually, and it would have been worse if he didn't have such thick fur. We were checking stock on the Gillespie spread when he howled and flew out of some brush in a gully." She shivered, remembering how alarming the wounds had been, miles from help. "I put compression bandages on his leg and rushed him as fast as possible to the Galloping G ranch house. Grant met me there. I'm not big on technology, but thank heaven for satellite phones."

"Have you gone back to find what did the damage? I've been wondering if it could be from old barbed wire. Gizmo seems too smart to tangle with a standing fence, but what if some wire is down, hidden in undergrowth? It would be best to deal with it before another animal is injured."

Kelly forked another load of straw into Lightfoot's stall. "I've wanted to return and check, but haven't had time. It's possible that a fence used to run through the gully. Mr. Gillespie ran both Hereford and Angus cattle for a while and needed to keep them separated. The boys and I are going for a ride later and we can look."

A smile spread across Josh's face. "I'll ride with you. I gave Quicksilver a workout earlier, but Chocolate Lad needs to stretch his legs, too, after that long drive from Edmonton."

She ground her teeth. "Then you should take him out now."

"It would be best to go with you and the boys. Chocolate Lad will be antsy, but he's too much of a gentleman to get rowdy around kids."

"Woo-hoo! We're going to go riding with Josh," yelled Marc from the barn door.

Kelly turned around, relieved she and Josh hadn't been discussing anything more personal. "Did Grams say you were done with your schoolwork and could come out here?"

"Uh-huh. We didn't have that much."

"All right. I'll check your papers before we leave." The twins were good students, but with the prospect of being able to go riding on a school day, they could have gotten careless.

Casey showed her his assignments first. They were the neatest, as usual. His brother's work was fairly accurate, but sloppy, revealing Marc's impatience with sitting quietly for more than ten minutes.

Just like Josh.

The unbidden thought twisted Kelly's tummy.

Lately she was seeing Josh in the boys, more and more. But at least the relationship didn't appear obvious to her grandparents and mother or they would have said something. Well, Grams or Granddad might speak up; she wasn't so sure about Kathleen.

As for the people around Shelton?

Kelly wasn't overly concerned they'd connect Josh with the twins; they were too thrilled that he was competing in the rodeo to think about anything else. Besides, enough time had passed that speculation about the boys' father must have died down, so it seemed unlikely that anyone would say something out of turn to Casey and Marc.

"Okay, guys, everything looks fine. Get your riding clothes on. We're heading to the Galloping G."

They rushed upstairs to their bedroom. Riding was a favorite activity at any time, but going with a rodeo star like Josh was the ultimate excitement. Lark sensed their enthusiasm and followed them with small yips.

At the main barn Kelly found the boys' horses already saddled and tied to the corral rail. She gave points to Josh for being observant enough to know which horses the boys rode and which tack belonged to them. He wasn't there, so he must be getting Chocolate Lad ready.

Lightfoot stood quietly as she lifted her saddle over his back and fastened the cinches. Josh wouldn't have dared trying it himself, though over the past week, man and stallion had come to a polite understanding. While Josh still couldn't touch him or get close, at least Lightfoot no longer behaved as if a rattler was stirring in the grass when he was present.

Kelly checked the contents of the saddlebags. She always rode with first-aid supplies and tools for fence repairs, but they'd need a container if they found old wire. Provided it wasn't a huge amount, an old leather sack would do; she tied one to the saddle.

She stroked Lightfoot's forehead. He made a snuffling noise and leaned into her. "Good boy," she whispered, appreciating the brief moment of peace.

Things had been easier before Josh had shown up.

He'd changed, which was to be expected. They were both older. He seemed more focused and contemplative than before, but even though he didn't know that Casey and Marc were his sons, he was annoyed by her determination to keep them from becoming rodeo crazy like their grandfather.

I shouldn't have said so much about it.

Josh loved his life and inevitably saw her attitude as a criticism of that choice. How could he not? He'd made a huge amount of money, become famous in rodeo and bull-riding circles and was on top of the world.

It was also a long way to fall.

She'd seen her father tumble from a more modest height and it hadn't been pretty. But it might be different for Josh. Plenty of professional rodeo cowboys were able to make their successes part of a good life, without making it their entire life.

Anyhow, it was his decision. And she'd made her decision when she left him all those years ago.

Happy chatter drifted through the air as Casey and Marc emerged from the house. They raced over and patted their respective geldings, fed them carrots and pulled on the reins to draw their heads down for a rub. It was tempting to ride out before Josh returned, but that would be pointless. Since arriving in Montana, he'd dogged her movements over the Galloping G and Kindred Ranch, so he wouldn't have any trouble catching up.

JOSH MOUNTED CHOCOLATE LAD and rode back to the main barn, pleased with how he was spending the afternoon. To allay Kelly's suspicions, he hadn't pushed to join previous outings with the boys. Anyway, it wouldn't be good for Casey and Marc to get the idea that he was courting their mother.

One thing was certain: Kelly had chosen good horses for her young sons. Ringo and Popcorn were compact, calm and gentle, but with enough pep to satisfy energetic six-year-olds. The thought made him realize that he was still looking for evidence of her fitness as a mother, which was ridiculous. He'd seen enough to know a judge would laugh him out of court if he claimed a concern about it.

Nonetheless, if he was the twins' father, he had a right to see them.

Josh abruptly made up his mind about what to do next.

He was done with sideways questioning and wondering—since Kelly wasn't volunteering any information about Casey and Marc, he would have to confront her.

CHAPTER SIX

"I FOUND THE PROBLEM," called Josh. "It's a tangle of ancient barbed wire. I'll start cutting it up."

Kelly looked up to the top of the gully where Casey and Marc were waiting with the dogs and horses while she and Josh searched. Barbed wire could be dangerous and she hadn't wanted to risk her sons getting injured the way Gizmo had done.

"Boys, stay there and keep hold of Lark and Gizmo," she ordered. "Move and you won't go riding for a month." It was her most effective threat; they loved horses and riding as much as she did.

"Ah, Mom, can't we help?" Marc begged.

"Absolutely not."

"But, Mom—" This time it was Casey protesting and she gave him a stern look.

"Your job is to keep the dogs safe. Remember how scared you were for Gizmo when I brought him home after getting hurt?

I need to be able to count on you both. So do Lark and Gizmo."

"That's right," Josh affirmed.

Two pairs of small shoulders squared. They bobbed their heads and took a firmer hold on the dogs' collars.

Kelly pulled cutters from her back pocket and crossed the gully to where Josh stood waist deep in undergrowth. "I've got it," he said.

"It's my responsibility."

"For Pete's sake, this isn't even your ranch. Can't you be reasonable for once?"

Kelly looked down and saw tufts of Gizmo's fur caught on the still wickedly sharp barbs. In all honesty, she was furious with herself for not getting back sooner to find the cause of his injuries. She'd planned to, but then everything—especially Josh—had caught up with her.

"We'll get it done faster if we work together."

He muttered something beneath his breath, but didn't argue further. Despite wearing gloves, they worked cautiously as they cut the wire into short lengths and stowed it in the leather sack she'd brought. Fortunately there wasn't a large amount, so they wouldn't have to come back to finish another day.

"I don't think Casey and Marc have moved an inch," Josh murmured, glancing up at them for the tenth time.

"Yeah, and it only took orders from their mother and a complete stranger to keep them there."

An odd expression crossed Josh's face. "Am I?" he asked.

"Are you what?"

"A complete stranger to them. I need to know, Kelly. Are Casey and Marc my sons?"

The air whooshed out her lungs and she glared. "This is hardly the time or place to discuss that. We can talk later where the boys can't hear us."

"All right, this evening in the foaling barn. I know you're spending the night there."

"Fine. Ten o'clock. Everyone should be asleep by then."

She rose and climbed the slope of the gully. Ultimately, she wouldn't be able to lie to Josh, but she didn't know what, if anything, he'd do with the truth.

JOSH HADN'T INTENDED to be so blunt with Kelly, but he'd lost his cool when she called him a complete stranger to the twins. The question had burst out of him like a bucking horse from a gate.

In his gut, he knew Casey and Marc were his kids.

He tried to act normally as they rode back to Kindred Ranch, doing better than Kelly, who was unusually quiet. On the other hand, Marc was so talkative, it would have been hard for anyone else to get a word in, regardless.

Much later, he watched from one of the bunkhouse windows as Kelly walked toward the foaling barn, a backpack slung over one shoulder and Gizmo a shadow at her heels.

Soon after, the last light went off in the main house. He waited, keeping an eye out, but spotted no other movement. A few minutes after ten, he headed to the barn and found Kelly in a camp chair at the back.

He sat opposite. "Am I the twins' father?" he asked without preamble.

A long silence followed. Then he heard a soft sigh. "Yes."

It was the answer he'd expected, yet anger rose in his chest. "I don't understand. Why didn't you tell me? How could you not tell me?"

Furious color flooded Kelly's cheeks. "Because you were married to someone else by the time I discovered I was pregnant. Do you get that, Josh? *Married.* I didn't know what you'd do. And since you'd used protection, I wasn't sure you would even believe the baby was yours. You were adamant about not having a family until you were financially set. What was I supposed to think?"

Josh rubbed his face. He'd had more than a week of stewing on whether or not he was a father, and the reality of what Kelly had faced still hadn't sunk in. Yet a part of him remained angry. He'd lost six years of knowing his children.

"I still had a right to be told." He paused and gathered his thoughts. "But we don't have to talk about that now. The most important question is, where do we go from here?"

Kelly pressed her lips together for a long minute, a myriad of emotions flashing across her face. "You should decide if being a real father is what you genuinely want. Casey and Marc don't need you acting all concerned about them as their dad, only to see you disappear for months with nothing but an occasional phone call or scribbled postcard. They already have a grandfather who pops in and out of their lives on his way to another rodeo.

Even though he's stayed home more lately, it won't last."

"It wouldn't be like that."

"Wouldn't it?" She tipped her head in challenge. "Remember, I have experience with this. I love Harry, but at best, he was a part-time dad."

Josh frowned. "Are you being fair? Even though Harry had his own spread in Alberta, he chose to live at Kindred Ranch. Surely that was for you and your mother's sake."

"My father has mostly lived on the road, not here. Even when he wasn't competing, he attended every rodeo and bull-riding event he could find. Weeks, even months could go by without a word from him. He's been seriously injured, rarely won enough to offset the costs and has mostly been a visitor in my life, not a parent. Maybe Mom and I weren't less important to him than climbing onto the back of a bull, but that's how it felt."

"So?"

She leaned toward him. "So until you've given thought to what kind of father and role model you want to be, the twins shouldn't be told. For that matter, don't say anything to the family, either. Harry knows, but my grandparents don't, and I'm not sure if Mom ever put two and two together. You know what she's like and how miserable her health was that summer."

Frustration rose, nearly choking him. "I want—"

"No. For once don't think about what *you* want. Think about what's right for Casey and Marc."

For once don't think about what you *want…?*

"Give me a break," Josh said harshly. "I've been thinking about what's right for them ever since I started wondering if they were my sons. But you've had six years of practice as a mother. I've had six minutes as a father. Catching up will take time."

The tension in their voices had alerted Gizmo, who'd gotten to his feet. He let out a low, warning growl.

"It's okay, Giz." Kelly put a soothing hand on his head. "Josh, you're here until the Shelton rodeo. You can stay longer if that's what you want, but please do what I'm asking. I don't believe you're a bad person, or that you'd intentionally hurt the boys. But being a parent is hard work. It's scary and you never stop worrying or questioning your decisions."

"You think I don't know that already?"

"Knowing something in your head is different than understanding it deep down. I'm not asking you to quit competing, just to think about the best way to handle this. Is that too much to ask before upending the boys' world?"

It was a hard pill to swallow, but Josh nodded. "Fine. I'll wait." He stood up. "I'm going for a walk. I need to clear my head."

KELLY WRAPPED A blanket around her arms after Josh left, cold from the inside, not from the night air. For over six years she'd second-guessed her decision to keep the boys a secret from Josh, and now fate had caught up with her.

Still, it was almost a relief. Now she could deal with the fallout, instead of endless worry about what *might* happen.

Restless, she went to check the mare closest to foaling. There was little indication that Lucy would have her baby in the next few hours, but you could never be sure. She stroked the drowsy mother-to-be, a sweet, easygoing girl with nerves of steel. A firecracker could go off in the barn and Lucy would blink with mild surprise.

But she got lonely, so Kelly kept the stalls

on either side of her occupied with other mares. Even so, Lucy's best pals were the barn cats. Topsy, a large gray tabby, was her favorite, and they shared a mutual affection. It wasn't unusual to see Topsy snoozing on Lucy's back, or riding on her shoulders around the corral. Right now the feline had made a straw nest for herself in the corner of the large box stall.

Kelly gave Lucy another check, then visited each of the mares, rather than stretch out on the narrow cot they kept available during foaling season.

She couldn't sleep, her mind going a mile a minute with the questions that had haunted her since discovering she was pregnant. What if Josh took her to court for a custody fight? He probably wouldn't win, but he might be given visitation rights.

A cold shudder went through her.

The thought of him taking her sons across the Canadian border was terrifying. What would happen if he got them under his own country's legal jurisdiction and decided to take action? Would she ever see them again? She didn't want to believe he'd pull something like that, but she couldn't be certain.

"Kelly?" called a voice.

It was Granddad, and she forced a smile as he walked toward her with barely a limp. His knee replacement had done wonders for his mobility. "Hey. What are you doing up?"

"I've been lazy too long. Go to bed. I'll keep an eye on the mares tonight."

"You haven't been lazy. You've been handling the ranch accounts and business contacts, and you're helping Mom and Grams get ready for the volunteers' barbecue at the rodeo grounds on Saturday. On top of that, you've done all the exercises and therapy the surgeon ordered."

Liam chuckled. "Your grandmother wouldn't let me do anything else. I appreciate that Josh has wanted to help while he's here, but I need to start pulling my own weight."

Josh.

She needed to talk to someone about the situation.

"Um, Granddad, let's sit down. There's something we should discuss."

Kelly waited until they were both seated, her pulse picking up speed. Liam raised his eyebrows when she didn't say anything right away. She finally cleared her throat.

"We, uh, we've never talked about the boys,

I mean, about their father, though you must have wondered."

Liam reached over and squeezed her hand. "It seemed best not to pry. You didn't date much here at home, but we assumed that you were socializing when you got older and traveled with your parents. After all, nobody could expect you to spend every single minute babysitting them."

His wry tone prompted a chuckle. Kelly had often felt as if she was the parent, instead of the other way around.

"Mom might have done better that summer if I'd stuck around more, but yeah, I was dating. It… It was Josh McKeon. I broke up with him just before I came home, and he married someone else a month later. Because of that, I didn't tell him about being pregnant. It seemed too complicated."

Her grandfather scowled. "Then why did Harry invite him to stay with us? He must have realized Josh was the boys' father."

"He did," Kelly said grimly. "But he decided he was doing the right thing by throwing us together again. It didn't take long for Josh to guess. He tackled me on it today. I've asked him not to say anything to Casey and

Marc for a while—he wasn't happy about it, but he agreed."

"What do you think he'll do?"

Kelly's stomach rolled. "I don't know. Naturally he was upset. He wants to be part of their lives, but how can he be a real father when he's spending all his time going from one venue to the next? What scares me just as much is that the boys are utterly enthralled by rodeos. I actually found Marc on the internet a few weeks ago, trying to see if there's a minimum age to become a professional bull rider. If they find out their father is a bona fide champion...?"

"I understand." The lines in Liam's face deepened. "Sometimes I want to jam a fist down Harry's throat when he claims the most exciting thing a man can do is climb on a bull's back and hold on for dear life. It's bad enough how he wanted you and your mother to follow him all over the continent. Isn't that enough for him?"

Whoa. Kelly's jaw dropped. She'd never heard Granddad be so blunt about his son-in-law.

"Mind, he's family and I'd never overstep," Liam said before she could respond, "but that's how I feel."

"Join the club."

They laughed together and Kelly wished they could have been this open in the past. Perhaps when something huge was revealed, the smaller stuff didn't loom as large.

"Anyhow," she continued, "I'll find a time to tell Mom and Grams, but I thought someone besides Harry should know in case Josh lets the cat out of the bag, or somebody in town sees the resemblance and starts gossiping."

Granddad patted her hand. "Good thinking. And try not to worry. You'll have everyone's support if Josh tries to make trouble. Folks in Shelton have their faults, but we stick together. However famous he is, it'll go against him if he tries something. Now get to bed. I'll wake you up if Lucy or one of the other mares goes into labor."

Kelly didn't argue. Granddad might have put her in charge of Kindred Ranch, but he was an expert rancher. She still had plenty to learn from him.

THE NEXT DAY Kelly listened as her grandmother took several early morning phone calls about the rodeo. Excitement about Josh registering to compete was racing out of control.

The committee was advertising throughout Montana and the surrounding states and they'd pushed information out on social media. Regional radio and television stations had also picked up the story.

There were continued pleas for volunteers to work on the rodeo grounds, both to do preparation work and to cover assorted shifts during the events. Tomorrow was the biggest day and local media kept reminding listeners that the traditional barbecue lunch for volunteers would be served.

The lunch was one of Kindred Ranch's contributions to the rodeo. Grams and Kelly's mom would be making yeast rolls, salads and brownies all day, and that afternoon, Harry and Granddad would get the coals ready, then bury them with bundles of seasoned beef for pit barbecue. Grilled chicken and hamburgers would also be served, along with baked beans and homemade ice cream. It was a big draw in getting volunteer workers.

Tension was thick when Josh came in for breakfast. Granddad immediately pushed his half-eaten food away and excused himself, saying he needed to take care of something. Kelly suspected he simply didn't know what to say to the man who'd fathered his great-grandsons and whose presence would affect everyone's future.

"I wonder what's gotten into Liam," Susannah mused as she handed a plate to Josh.

"Maybe he's restless," Kelly suggested, "not being able to do as much while his knee is healing. By the way, Josh is the one who located the downed barbed wire at the Galloping G."

Grams smiled at him. "We have a few ranchers in the region who aren't as careful as they should be with barbed wire, but don't think Dustin Gillespie was among them. He used to be one of the best. Something like that would never have happened in his heyday, but he struggled the last few years from poor health."

Josh winked at Casey and Marc. "Your mom told me that Mr. Gillespie's children don't want to be ranchers. Can you imagine that?"

"They're dumb," Marc declared.

"Totally," Casey agreed.

"I grew up wanting my own ranch," Josh said in a casual tone. "I was lucky to win enough money at rodeos and bull-riding events to buy one, but that doesn't happen very often. Most contestants lose more than they win."

He'd been so defensive of his career in professional rodeo that Kelly was floored.

Marc stuck out his chin. "Some cowboys win a bunch."

"A few, but it also costs a bunch to compete. A buddy of mine had to sell his horses to pay off his credit cards."

Casey's mouth opened wide and he exchanged a horrified look with his brother. *"No."*

"That's right. He was good. He just never seemed to break even."

"Boys, finish your cereal," Kathleen urged as she walked into the kitchen carrying her purse and keys. "You don't want to be late for school."

The twins ate the last bites of their oatmeal and got up from the table.

Kelly handed them their backpacks. "Have a good day."

"Thanks, Mom." Marc darted out the door, while Casey hugged her. Soon after Josh's arrival, Marc had explained that he didn't want to look like a baby in front of Mr. McKeon with all that kissing and hugging stuff. Casey—who was inherently more affectionate—had ignored his brother and gone his own way.

She sometimes wondered if Marc realized how much his brother didn't follow his lead.

Kathleen had stopped to confer with Grams over the revised shopping list for the barbecue when the phone rang again. Kelly answered it.

"For you, Grams." She held the receiver out to Susannah, who hurriedly advised her daughter to just triple everything she bought, to make sure they had enough supplies. Kathleen tucked the list in her purse and hurried out to her waiting grandsons.

Several minutes later Grams hung up with a rueful expression. "They're asking chili cook-off entrants if they'll make four times the usual amount for the public voting part of the competition. A wholesale grocer is donating ingredients to anyone who needs them and a restaurant supply store in Bozeman is loaning as many eighty-quart kettles and gas cook rings as we need. For promotional considerations, of course. Luckily the rodeo programs haven't been printed yet."

The cook-off was one of the most successful events of the rodeo—visitors got to sample each offering and vote on a favorite—but it was hard to believe they'd need that much more chili.

"Are they sure that many people are coming?" Kelly asked.

Grams bobbed her head. "I'm told online registrations are already well above the annual average and the phone is ringing off the hook with people asking about accommodations—including folks who want to come for the entire week." She smiled at Josh. "You're a popular fellow, Josh. We've never had this level of interest before. The committee will be scrambling to get ready."

"I didn't mean to cause trouble, ma'am."

"How many times have I told you? It's Susannah," she scolded. "And you aren't causing trouble. The town is thrilled to have you perform at the rodeo."

Kelly choked on a mouthful of coffee. She glared a warning at Josh, hoping he wouldn't snarl that he was an athlete, not a performer. Rodeos were commonly referred to as a performance. It was hardly something to be insulted about.

He shrugged and stayed silent as he ate.

"Oh, and can you believe it?" Grams asked indignantly. "Leonard Crabtree has already told the committee that he's calling his chili entry the 'McKeon Bronc Buster.' He probably wanted to get the name down before I had a chance. I'll bet he thinks he's going to win because he cooks in volume at the café."

Her rivalry with the owner of the Hot Diggity Dog Café was over two decades long. She'd won most of the time until Leonard had started competing; since then, they were about even in receiving the top honors. Leonard had won last year, so she was determined to get her title back. Luckily it didn't stop anyone else from entering the competition; the third- and fourth-place prizes were just as hotly contested.

"But he won't have Kindred Ranch beef," Kelly said lightly. "Or the roasted chilies you put up in the freezer." Each spring Susannah planted a huge vegetable garden. She planned ahead because the rodeo came before summer vegetables like Hatch and Anaheim chilies could mature.

"That's right. And he won't have my tomatoes. I'll beat his McKeon Bronc Buster chili with one hand tied behind my back. Not that I'm denigrating the power of your name, Josh, but I've been cooking since before Leonard was in diapers. Besides, this year I have a secret plan."

Josh had begun bolting his food, looking more and more uncomfortable. Now he muttered "thank you" for the meal and beat a hasty retreat out the door.

"What is it with the men today?" Grams said with a puzzled expression. "First your father didn't want breakfast. Then Liam didn't finish his, and Josh practically inhaled his steak and eggs."

"Josh is Josh, and Harry was miffed you wanted to use a low-cholesterol egg mixture for him," Kelly murmured.

She was alone with her grandmother, but was it the right moment to reveal Josh's relationship to Casey and Marc?

Grams looked excited and happy, thrilled to be plotting her big win against Leonard, so Kelly decided to keep quiet. The family had enough to think about today.

"Grams, what's your secret plan to win, or am I allowed to hear it?"

"Of course you're allowed." Susannah rubbed her hands together. "You know how Leonard serves his chili samples with chunks of fresh-baked buttered bread from the café?"

"Yes. It's very popular."

"Well, your mother offered to make cheese-and-green-onion corn bread to serve with mine. I'll also put out bowls of grated cheese, chopped jalapeños, salsa, sour cream and diced onions as self-serve toppings. Do you think Josh would work in the booth, helping to dish up the samples?"

"You'll have to ask him," Kelly muttered. "Uh, about Josh. I suspect it makes him uncomfortable to call you Susannah. He seems more of a 'sir' and 'ma'am' kind of guy."

A thoughtful expression crossed Grams's face. "You may be right. I'll speak to him."

"Great. I'll go now, unless you need help with the dishes."

Predictably, Grams shook a finger at her. "Since when do I need help in my own kitchen?"

Kelly restrained a grin. "What was I thinking? I'll see you later."

She was out in the main barn, adjusting the girth on Lightfoot's saddle, when the extension line there rang. It buzzed three times, so she answered, figuring everyone in the house was tied up. "Good morning, Kindred Ranch."

"Kelly, this is Simon Shaw." He was a member of the rodeo committee and an old friend of the family.

"Hey, Simon. I assume you're calling about the rodeo."

"Yeah. Isn't it great?" Simon asked. "We

received five more registrations this morning, including one from last year's top ten winners in the California cowboys association. Its members usually don't get to our little soiree. Mr. McKeon might have some real competition. We'll also be able to add more to the purse money with so many people in attendance."

Kelly wished she could share his enthusiasm. She enjoyed the Shelton Rodeo Daze. It wasn't just a rodeo; it was a week of community activities—everything from the chili cook-off, to a parade, to an American patchwork quilt contest. Essentially, it took the place of a county fair. Almost everyone in Shelton contributed something to make the festivities successful.

She pushed her shoulders back. "I'm glad everything is going well."

"Yeah, but it's a game changer. We'll need a whole lot of extra parking and seating for visitors. And that's just the beginning. We're already taking reservations for campsites that don't exist yet. Creating additional campgrounds will be one of our biggest jobs."

"Kindred Ranch has acreage along the highway," Kelly said. "It wouldn't take too much work to get it ready as primitive sites, though I'd want to throw up an extra row of fencing to ensure our animals are well separated from both children and adults. Or else move that herd temporarily."

"Thanks for the offer, but I'm afraid you're too far out of town. It'll be fine. The ranchers closest to the rodeo grounds have already volunteered."

"Then what can we do?"

Simon hemmed and hawed for a moment. "We have stock photos of Josh McKeon that we're using for publicity, but the committee would like to have local shots, showing him here in Shelton. Do you think he'd be willing to meet with a photographer? Nobody wants to interfere with his training, but it would help with our advertising."

Kelly resisted the urge to thunk her head on one of the barn's support posts. It appeared that Kindred Ranch's primary contributions to the rodeo were going to be four silver memorial buckles, cooking a barbecue lunch for the volunteers and hosting the newly crowned star of the event.

"That's entirely up to Mr. McKeon. He follows his—"

"What's up to me?"

Kelly turned and saw Josh at the open double doors, holding Quicksilver's reins. After a long night of wondering what he might do about the twins and how she would handle it, she still couldn't get away from him. The only good thing was what he'd told the boys that morning about the reality of rodeo competition.

"Call for you," she said.

She exchanged the receiver for Quicksilver's reins and tied him to the corral fence. He was a fine stallion, primarily white with brown spots, and a shade larger than Lightfoot. Of the two horses, Lightfoot was more agile and had cleaner lines, while Quicksilver had more powerful hindquarters. Nonetheless, they were close in quality. The top of their breed.

Kelly deliberately kept her attention focused away from the murmur of conversation inside the barn.

Quicksilver nudged her arm, so she stroked his neck and fed him an apple. He was a calm animal, an important quality for a horse used in competition, who needed to take loudspeakers, frequent travel, cheering and other unexpected noises in stride. The great outdoors was probably more unsettling to him than a rodeo.

Gizmo let out a whine and Quicksilver

touched noses with him. It was nice they got along since Kindred Ranch might be seeing a fair amount of Josh and his horses in the future.

The prospect filled her with renewed trepidation.

Should she be reassured about the way Josh had spoken to Casey and Marc? Maybe, but it seemed unlikely that he had changed his mind overnight about the grand life he led as a professional rodeo cowboy. Why should he? It *was* a grand life for him, at least right now.

A minute later Josh came out. "I've agreed to go into Shelton this morning so they can take the pictures they want."

"That's generous of you."

He stepped closer. "It isn't generous and I'm not trying to get attention, Kelly. There must be a publicity release included with the registration form. I should have read more carefully before I signed it."

Kelly remembered her second thoughts about Josh registering for the rodeo so early. Her concern had been that people would be disappointed if he changed his mind; now it would be a thousand times worse if he didn't show up. Disaster could be looming for the rodeo if all those people arrived, expecting to see him in the arena, only to learn he wasn't competing.

"Registering early was my idea," she admitted. "I knew everyone would be excited you planned to compete, so I should have guessed the committee would advertise. You're big news in rodeo circles."

"Then you don't blame me? I thought you'd be furious about the posters plastered across town."

Pain stabbed Kelly's temples.

Complications were stacking up, one upon another. She ought to thank him for being straight with Casey and Marc about some downsides of being a professional rodeo cowboy, but she didn't feel up to it. She also didn't want him to think that mouthing a few of the right words had made him daddy-of-the-year material. Parenting was more than a minimum eight-second ride on the back of a bull. It was a lifetime of days that could be both wonderful and terrifying.

Despite her instant headache, she managed a smile. "No, I don't blame you. The rodeo helps the town in more ways than one. Since you're going to be busy this morning, do you want me to unsaddle Quicksilver and put him in the corral?"

"Nah, I'll take care of it."

Though he looked ready to say something else, Kelly hurried to where Lightfoot was waiting.

Josh would probably find her later, but at least right now she could be alone with Lightfoot and Gizmo, doing what she enjoyed best about ranching, the quiet solitude of riding fences and checking on livestock.

Yet a small voice whispered inside, *Aren't you going to miss him?*

CHAPTER SEVEN

JOSH REMOVED QUICKSILVER'S SADDLE, wishing he hadn't agreed to the photography session. He would rather be out riding with Kelly, asking about the years he'd missed with his sons.

His sons.

Though he'd been convinced he was the twins' father, mixed emotions had filled him since the moment Kelly had admitted the truth. Apprehension. Uncertainty. Pride. Anger.

The anger was to be expected. A man had the right to know that kind of thing. Still...

You were married to someone else by the time I discovered I was pregnant. Do you get that, Josh? Married.

Kelly's passionate retort kept reverberating in his head, along with her reminder that he'd wanted to wait before starting a family— had expounded upon the subject frequently, in fact. It wasn't as if she'd deliberately gotten pregnant; her condition must have come as a shock.

He put Quicksilver in the corral with Chocolate Lad and Harry's four horses, who had accepted the newcomers without fuss.

Hmm. Harry was another question mark.

All those years of seeing each other at rodeos, and not a word about Kelly and the boys? So much for their friendship. Josh immediately berated himself. Okay, it wasn't fair to think Harry would choose friendship over family. Harry had been protecting his daughter and grandsons, but why extend an invitation to visit Kindred Ranch when he must have realized what could happen?

Josh checked his clothes to be sure they were reasonably tidy. He didn't have dressy duds to put on for a photographer, and wouldn't wear them, regardless. A rodeo cowboy should look like what he was: a working guy. By rights he ought to have dust on his jeans and a trickle of blood on his forehead.

Blood?

He scowled. Yeah, he'd gotten bruised, scratched and lacerated while competing, but Kelly was right that he'd never gotten a more serious injury. Few of his fellow competitors could make the same claim.

And what if one of those competitors was his own son?

Once again, the implications of being a father dropped on Josh's shoulders. It was one thing to joke about breaking his neck before getting into the chute with a bad-tempered bull, another to think about his kids taking that chance. No wonder Kelly worried.

Distracted, he collected his keys from the bunkhouse and headed for his truck, only to have Susannah come out on the porch and call to him.

"Josh, I thought you were riding with Kelly this morning."

"Change of plans. The rodeo committee wants me to pose for a few local pictures. I don't enjoy that kind of thing, but they think it'll be good promotion for the rodeo."

She smiled. "How nice of you to help. I… er…spoke to Kelly earlier about whether you'd be willing to serve samples of my chili during the contest. She told me to ask, but I've realized visitors might overwhelm the booth, wanting your autograph."

"I could stay in the background and see how it goes. Then leave if it becomes a problem."

"You're a dear. I also wanted to ask if

you'd mind me naming my entry McKeon's Choice, after your ranch."

"I don't mind, but do you think that's fair?"

Her eyes twinkled. "My biggest competitor is capitalizing on your name and reputation. Why not me?"

"And he didn't ask my permission ahead of time."

Susannah laughed. "True, but I'll give it more consideration. Anyhow, changing the name might confuse people—I've always entered as simply 'Susannah's Green Chili.'"

"Green?"

"Exactly. I don't make it with chipotle chili powder like my husband, or fresh cayenne like Leonard Crabtree. I use a combination of roasted Hatch chilies and Anaheim peppers."

Josh gestured to the extensive garden on the south side of the house, recalling what Kelly had said earlier. "Kindred Ranch grown, roasted and frozen."

"That's right. Well, I won't keep you. Oh, and, Josh?" she said as he started to turn around. "If you're uncomfortable saying *Susannah*, it's all right to call me 'ma'am.'"

Josh was grateful for her understanding. Whether she'd be quite as understanding about anything once she learned he was the twins' father was another matter.

BETSY ATE BREAKFAST with Mrs. Mapleton before walking across town to work her first official volunteer shift for the upcoming rodeo. Excitement gave an extra lift to her feet. A few puffy white clouds dotted the sky, the sun was shining, and the air seemed particularly clean and sweet smelling.

She was familiar with the rodeo grounds. She'd seen the site when she first chugged toward the city limits, her van wheezing more than a cat coughing up fur balls. Naturally she'd stopped to snap pictures and had taken more since then, fascinated by the transformation of a mostly blank slate of land to rodeo grounds. Today it was dotted with people, trucks and someone outside the exterior fence on a huge machine that mowed the long grass and deposited it into rows. She'd spent enough time in agricultural areas to assume it would be baled for winter use after it dried. Farmers and ranchers didn't let things go to waste.

She stopped at the coordinator's table by the main gate.

"Hi, I'm Betsy Hartner, a new volunteer."

"Morning, Betsy. Don't ya know me?" The man tipped his oversize cowboy hat backward on his head and she saw his face for the first time. He was one of the café regulars she'd privately dubbed the Retired Cowboys Coffee Club—the R Triple C for short. They were awfully nice, and generous tippers to boot.

"Hey, Lonny. I couldn't tell it was you under that tent you're wearing," she teased.

"Haven't you learned that a cowboy's hat is sacred, young lady? Why, I could use this hat for an umbrella if it starts raining. Or a blanket in the snow. I could even be buried in it."

"Let's hope that isn't for a good long time. What do you need me to do?"

Lonny scanned the list on his clipboard. "Do you mind gettin' paint on those purty clothes?"

Betsy chuckled. She'd intentionally worn a ragged pair of jeans and an equally disreputable long-sleeved shirt. Her hair was fastened back in a French braid and her small digital camera was zipped into an ancient backpack for protection. "Just give me a brush and tell me where to slap the paint."

"All right. Head thataway." Lonny pointed to where someone else was already working on the exterior wood fence. "You can do the inside, while he does the out. Don't worry about makin' it a fancy job. We aren't particular. Real pleased to have you, Betsy. We need all the helping hands we can get. I'll tote the paint bucket over there."

"Absolutely not."

Lonny was eighty years old if he was a day.

She grabbed a container of paint from the back of a loaded pickup, along with a brush and stirring stick, and heaved it to where the other volunteer was working. She nearly tripped over her feet when she saw it was Grant.

Yikes.

They hadn't run into each other since that scene she'd made in front of the Shelton Market.

"Oh. Hi, Grant," she said breathlessly. She was reasonably strong, but five gallons was a heavy load. "Looks like we're both painting fences today."

And maybe mending them.

He gave her a strained smile. "Looks like it. They think it's the best job for me since I'm on call. This way I can go without leaving anyone in the lurch."

"Makes sense. But aren't you always on call?"

"Pretty much."

Betsy opened the plastic bucket and stirred the viscous fluid before dipping her brush into the contents. She quickly began stroking paint onto the wood, which looked long overdue for a coat. The interior fence creating the arena was just aged wood, though a couple of men were inspecting it. Would they want that one painted, as well? Anticipation filled her. A lot of the rodeo prep wasn't something she'd be able to help with, but painting fences didn't require special skills.

Grant was working far enough away that she didn't have to worry about accidentally spattering him, yet not far enough that she had an excuse to keep her mouth shut.

"Um, Grant, I'm sorry about the other day. I overreacted."

He looked over at her. "Don't apologize. I get into my own world sometimes and can't see past the end of my nose. And I'm the one who owes an apology for calling you Becky. I know your name is Betsy."

"It wasn't the first time someone did that," she confided. "Or probably the last."

"You're nice to let me off the hook."

They worked in silence for a while. Then Betsy grinned. "Do you know what this reminds me of?"

"Tom Sawyer conning his friends into whitewashing Aunt Polly's fence for him?"

"Yup." Betsy shifted her paint bucket. "I wonder how many kids have tried to do something similar. Maybe with mowing the lawn or raking leaves."

"A few, I imagine." A glob of white flicked from Grant's brush and hit him on the cheek. He wiped his face and kept working. "But I doubt they're successful. Modern kids are savvy. Last year on National Lemonade Day, one of them talked me into paying three bucks for the worst lemonade I've ever tasted. Then I had to buy a cup from the lemonade stand across the street because it wasn't right to show favorites."

Betsy bit her lip to keep from grinning. Kids in Shelton must have Grant pegged as the biggest soft touch in town. "I'm sure you took a lot of convincing."

"It was a hard-sell situation—she had red pigtails, braces and cuter freckles than Little Orphan Annie."

A flatbed truck came through the open gate, loaded with a stack of disassembled benches.

"Are those part of the bleachers?" Betsy asked.

"I think so. They store everything in barns around the area, though they're building more this year because so many extra visitors are expected. They're also expanding the grandstand. You must have heard about the rodeo champion who's registered to compete. Josh McKeon is the reason for all this extra hoopla. This may be the only chance some visitors will ever have to see McKeon perform, or contestants to match themselves against him."

Betsy began applying her paintbrush again. "I understand he's really famous."

Grant frowned. "In the rodeo world, I suppose. I'd never heard of him before he came to visit, uh, Shelton."

She didn't say anything, but the expression on Grant's face was interesting, to say the least.

How could he have an issue with someone he barely knew?

GRANT HAD THOUGHT he was making good progress on his side of the fence, but Betsy was steadily catching up with him.

It had been gracious of her to apologize when he was at fault. He wished he could convince her that his distraction that afternoon at the market had nothing to do with her being a waitress.

If anything bothered him about Betsy, it was her footloose nature. His childhood memories were centered on being passed back and forth between his parents and of constantly trying to make new friends and starting at yet another new school. He'd seen all he wanted to see of the world. Now he wanted a settled life and home.

Betsy wanted the exact opposite.

He would have assumed that someone who moved to a new place every few weeks was a loner. The closest thing she had to a home was her van. But she was far from a loner. Instead she was great with people and enjoyed being with them. It didn't make sense;

it also didn't make sense that her lifestyle bothered him.

"What were you joking around with Lonny about?" he asked after they'd worked for a while.

"Oh..." She grinned. "His hat. The brim is so big that I didn't see his face until he looked up. He must leave it in his truck when he comes into the café."

Lonny's hat —large, even for a ten-gallon hat—was a sight to behold, but Grant had stopped noticing its exaggerated size after living in Shelton for a few months. "You probably won't be here long enough to get used to it."

"Maybe, but I'm staying for the rodeo, longer if I haven't saved enough money to repair the van. Uh, you're generous to help with the prep when you're also going to be working during the events."

"I enjoy being involved."

"Me, too."

He hiked an eyebrow. "From what you've said, it doesn't sound as if you stay anywhere long enough to get involved."

Betsy waved her paintbrush in the air. "How can you say that when I'm here, volunteering the same as you? Some people are more comfortable waiting to join in, but I have to leap into action if I'm going to take part. Irene Norville recruited me—she lives across the street from where I'm staying. She mentioned they take their dogs to your clinic, the same as Mrs. Mapleton with her cats."

"They're all longtime clients."

Betsy bent and applied paint to the bottom fence board. "You must enjoy the Norvilles' visits. Genghis and Khan are sweet—two giant, slobbery teddy bears."

Grant pictured the mixed-breed canines. Hounds from hell had been his first impression and his opinion hadn't changed. Luckily they were abundantly healthy, aside from Khan's penchant for gobbling overripe pears that had fallen from the Norvilles' tree.

"Actually, they aren't fond of veterinarians."

Betsy straightened with a sympathetic look in her eyes. "Of course not. You vaccinate them, poke and prod, and take their temperature in an unmentionable way. It must be tough to love animals and have them think you're a villain."

He appreciated her giving him credit as an animal lover. "Some of my patients don't hold grudges. I did a huge stitching job on

Kelly Beaumont's dog, with two follow-up visits, and he's still friendly to me. I can't say that for Genghis and Khan, however. They start growling the minute they walk through the clinic door."

Actually, *dragged* through the clinic door was a better description. Animals just seemed to know that it was a vet's office. Maybe it was something they smelled, or else they sensed something beyond human perception.

Betsy shifted her bucket—they were now working face-to-face—and Grant leaned over the top rail to see the section of fence she'd painted. She was not only fast, she was doing a better job than him.

She laughed. "You should have read the 'wet paint' sign."

"Huh?" Grant looked down and saw a broad streak of white on his chest and arms. "How are you keeping so clean?" he asked as a distraction to his idiotic slip. She didn't seem to be wearing a single fleck of paint from the tips of her toes to the top of her blond head—natural blond, too, if he was any judge of the matter.

"I have a pure heart and a low carbon footprint."

"What has that got to do with paint splatters?"

"I don't know, but it sounds good."

They continued in companionable silence, stopping occasionally to shift their buckets and stir the contents. Painting fences wasn't a precision task, simply repetitive, so Grant let himself relax and clear his mind. It was refreshing to have such a basic, down-to-earth responsibility.

Dip into the paint.

Sweep the brush back and forth.

Dip again...and try to keep up with Betsy without getting too caught up in her feminine appeal. He hadn't taken real notice of her attractive features when visiting the café, but they were harder to miss now.

The sun was climbing toward the midmorning mark when Lonny called to everyone through a bullhorn. "Time for a break. We don't want no volunteers' union complaint about unfair workin' conditions. As usual, we have coffee and fresh cinnamon rolls, courtesy of the Hot Diggity Dog Café. And remember, everybody who works tomorrow gets the traditional barbecue lunch cooked by the ladies and gents from Kindred Ranch. Families are welcome."

Laughter and cheers sounded.

Betsy pushed the lid down on her bucket.

"Put your brush in here to keep the paint from drying out." Grant handed her one of the plastic bags that Lonny had given him for short breaks.

RATHER THAN GET coffee and a cinnamon roll, Betsy pulled the camera from her backpack and walked around snapping pictures. She wasn't a great photographer, but she usually got some that were good if she took enough.

A remarkable amount of effort was going into setting up the rodeo grounds. The grandstand was already assembled, except the sides were open, probably because they were expanding it. At one time she'd considered going for a degree in engineering, so she took several shots, interested in how they planned to add to the modular structure.

Yet in the back of her mind, she kept remembering the warmth in Grant's voice when he talked about Kelly Beaumont and her dog. Not just "she's a client I like," but real warmth, the kind where something more might be involved.

Betsy pushed the thought away. It wasn't her business. She would be leaving soon enough, and if Grant Latham wanted to break his heart over someone who didn't want him, she couldn't stop it.

"Coffee?" Grant's voice interrupted, making her jump. For a woman on the move, she didn't have any business thinking so much about the guy.

She tucked her camera away and accepted the cup he was holding out. "Thanks."

"I didn't know how you drink it, but since you've teased about me taking mine black, I added cream and sugar."

Was that Grant's roundabout way of telling her that he'd actually paid attention to their conversations at the café?

"Whichever is fine. I'm not picky."

Together they headed back to the fence they were painting. It was satisfying to see how much they'd already done...until she remembered how much was left to do.

Oh, well.

The sun was shining, the grass was a brilliant green and wildflowers were starting to bloom. She couldn't think of a finer way to spend her time.

"Is there a reason you have so much wander-lust?" Grant asked after they'd resumed their task.

"I don't know if it's a reason, but my dad always talked about seeing the world. My parents married young and had me, and then my mom walked out. It's tough rais-ing a child by yourself. Sometimes there was barely enough money for trips to the supermarket, much less places like Venice or Machu Picchu."

"And?"

"And he died. A stupid accident at the fac-tory where he worked. I was eighteen and I promised myself that I would do all the trav-eling he could never do now." Betsy gulped. Even eleven years later it hurt terribly to think about her father's senseless death. It would always hurt.

"I'm sorry about your dad, but it sounds as if you're living his dream, not yours. Have you ever considered picking a place and making it home?"

She rolled her eyes. "Travel is my dream, too. I love seeing new places and trying new things. I've hiked parts of the Appalachian Trail, white-water rafted through the Grand Canyon, squirmed through caves and parachuted out of airplanes. Give me the chance to get on the back of a bucking horse, and I'll do that, as well."

Grant was silent for a long moment. "Doesn't the rest of your family worry about you living out of a van and risking your life so often?"

"I don't have any family, unless you count my mother, and I have no idea where she might be. Besides, it isn't about pushing the limits to see how close I can come to killing myself without actually doing it. I care about new experiences, not danger. I'll be just as excited to see the Shelton rodeo as I was rafting down the Colorado River."

He looked puzzled. "I still don't get it. Shelton is a great town, with great people. I can't imagine wanting to leave, and yet you leave places like this all the time."

"You don't need to understand. What's important is that it works for me. I told you before that when it's time to leave, I just go. Goodbyes stink and make you feel bad."

Betsy bent to dip her brush again in the bucket. The level of the paint had dropped considerably from where it had started that morning. She would have to tell Lonny that she'd come back tomorrow.

This was fun.

JOSH FOLLOWED THE directions he'd been given; they led him to the Shelton High School administration building. It turned out the "photographer" was the president of the school's camera club. Simon Shaw introduced the kid to Josh, then left, saying he needed to get back to the rodeo grounds.

"It's okay. I know what I'm doing," Dennis Ward said when they were alone. He was gangly and still growing into his parts, but his face was quietly self-assured. With many rodeo contestants starting in their midteens and younger, including himself, Josh would be a hypocrite to dismiss him based on youth.

"Is photography what you want to do for a living?" he asked.

"No, astrophysics. Dad says they should never have given me a telescope when I was eight."

"Aren't there good jobs in that field?"

"None in Shelton."

"I suppose nobody enjoys having their

children leave home," Josh murmured, realizing he was encountering yet another perspective as a parent. His learning curve was going to be steep for a while... Mount Denali steep.

Dennis made an adjustment to the camera hanging from around his neck. "It's more than that. Last fall the mayor came and talked to our class. He was, like, freaked that people are moving away and thinks the town could die. So we did our own survey and proved that Shelton has grown 8.9 percent since the last national census. Birth rates have actually dropped, so it isn't just from babies being born."

Josh was impressed, not with the statistic, but with the kid. He was smart.

Dennis took pictures at various locations, mostly where there was a sign showing "Shelton" in the background. He didn't ask Josh to smile for the camera, but he had a dry wit that often prompted a grin. They ended at the rodeo grounds, where a bustle of activity dominated the landscape. Dennis shot several additional photos before stowing his gear.

"I have a geometry final this afternoon,"

he explained. "Do you mind if I take off now?"

"No problem. Good luck with your exam."

Simon Shaw came over after Dennis had gone. "We appreciate the support, Josh. You're going to make our rodeo a major success. What brought you to Shelton?"

Josh kept his expression neutral; the last thing he needed was for everyone to start whispering behind Kelly's back. "Harry Beaumont. We've been friends for years."

"I should have guessed since you're staying at Kindred Ranch. Good man, Harry. Are you helping with the rodeo workshop he conducts for kids during rodeo week?"

Josh had heard about the workshop. Harry was preparing for it the way a general prepared for battle; when he was doing something he enjoyed, nothing could stop him. "I will if he asks, but it's his show and I wouldn't want to step on his toes."

"I understand. Let me give you a ride to your truck."

"Nah, I'm fine. It isn't a long walk and you're needed here. I'll be back tomorrow. I'm helping with the Kindred Ranch barbecue lunch for the volunteers."

Simon's smile broadened. "Excellent. We'll see you then."

Josh returned to where he'd parked in front of the school admin building. They had an electronic reader board on the front and he spent a while reading the various messages, including one about the upcoming graduation ceremonies. He hadn't gone to his own high school graduation, but he hoped to attend one for the boys. It was an important mile marker in a child's life.

The thought led him to his father. Pop had managed to see a number of his son's big rodeo and bull-riding wins, yet he and Kelly had never met.

Josh took out his phone. He'd agreed not to say anything to Kelly's family or the boys about being their father, but he hadn't made any promises about telling Pop.

"What's up, son?" Benjamin answered after three rings. "I don't have any news yet about hiring a cook. I've contacted that Nellie Pruitt you told me about. She sounds younger than I expected, but she also seems the type to handle cowhands with no problem. Nothing is decided yet."

"I wasn't calling about that. Are you sitting down, Pop?"

"I'm sitting on a horse. Where else would I be sitting in the middle of the day?"

Josh cast a practiced eye at the sun's location. It was around 10:00 a.m., which qualified as the middle of the day for Benjamin McKeon. He was generally up and working by 5:00 a.m. or earlier.

"Then I hope you're riding Blackbird, because he's nice and quiet," Josh told him.

"That sounds ominous."

"Not ominous. It's just—" He pulled in a deep breath. "I have some rather big news."

CHAPTER EIGHT

KELLY WAS TIGHTENING the wire on a fence when she heard hoofbeats approaching. The horse slowed and came to a halt nearby.

Gizmo let out a low sound between a bark and growl.

"Hi, Josh," she said without looking up from her task.

"How did you know it was me?"

"Quicksilver's gait. I can usually tell which horse is approaching and who is riding. But even without that, Gizmo's reaction was a dead giveaway."

He dismounted and came over. "Let me finish those repairs."

"No need. They're done."

Kelly returned the tools to Lightfoot's saddlebag. If Josh wanted to be chivalrous by constantly offering to handle something for her, then he was woefully misguided. Mending fences was her job, along with everything from performing first aid on range cattle, confronting the occasional trespasser and facing down any wild animals that threatened Kindred Ranch herds. This was her life, and would remain her life after he returned to his rodeo career.

"How did the photography session go?" she asked, hoping to keep the discussion pleasant.

"Pretty well. The photograper was a kid from the high school's camera club. Dennis Ward."

"Dennis is our local boy-genius. His father is the current president of the Shelton Ranching Association. The Wards own the largest spread in Shelton County."

Josh stared. "And he wants to be an astrophysicist?"

"Would you be this shocked if his goal was to become a professional bull rider?"

Josh jammed his hat down tighter on his head. "Dennis didn't mention his family's ranch, just that there's a concern about too many people moving away from the area."

"Shelton is holding its own. Anyhow, the Wards have four other kids who love ranching, so they'll have family to take over when Nate retires. You'll be competing against three of their sons at the rodeo. Their daughter is competing, too. Missy is the eldest and she's won several times in barrel racing and breakaway roping, although she's lobbied for years to allow women to compete in all events, right along with the men."

JOSH NODDED. "A kid at the saddle shop mentioned his sister will compete in several events in the junior rodeo."

"The junior rodeo is popular with everyone," Kelly said, apparently willing to drop the issue. "It's free for folks to watch and the cash prizes are reasonably good."

"You were a great barrel racer. Harry still brags about the prizes you used to win. I saw you practice a few times and was impressed. You could have become a champion on the professional circuit."

Kelly's face tightened and Josh wondered if he'd made a mistake by mentioning her history with barrel racing. Did she remember the way he'd urged her to practice and compete? Perhaps he'd gotten too insistent about it before their breakup, but he had wanted her to have a stake at the venues where they offered barrel racing as an event. A good number of the women who competed were married to professional rodeo cowboys, so it had made sense.

At the time he'd been convinced they would spend their lives together. He was starting to see his image of that shared life may have been vague, even a little self-centered, but he'd honestly loved her.

"I haven't done any barrel racing since before the twins were born," Kelly said at length. "I've had more than enough to occupy me since then."

"I realize that you've been busy managing Kindred Ranch, but I would have sent financial support," Josh told her urgently. "You know that, don't you?"

"Maybe, if you'd believed the boys were yours. But that wouldn't change me managing the ranch. It was always part of my plan. Not only that, I didn't want or need your support."

"Did you ever consider it was something that *I* would need to do?" he returned in a harsher tone than intended. "And don't quote deadbeat-dad statistics to me. A decent man takes care of his children, no matter what."

"Does that include changing dirty diapers?" Kelly asked wryly. "Or staying up with a colicky baby all night? Or walking them around and around, wearing a hole in the floor when they just won't sleep? I'd hate to tell you how many hours of sleep that Marc cost the family. He's a natural-born night owl."

Josh had given little thought to those aspects of childrearing, but he nodded. "Sure. It's part of the deal, right?"

A smile played across Kelly's face. "I believe you. But it might have been a problem with you married to Doreen and going to rodeos across the entire North American continent."

Chagrin instantly followed the elation Josh had felt at her admission. It was all too true that he would have had trouble being the kind of father who changed diapers and stayed up walking the floor with a cranky baby. For that matter, what if he and Kelly hadn't broken up? They would have gotten married and been living in the camper over his old truck when she had the twins. How did you walk a baby in a truck camper? *Two* babies?

Uneasiness crawled across his shoulders.

Kelly had spent part of her childhood on the road with her mother and father, and the rest at home with her grandparents on Kindred Ranch. She viewed Harry as a part-time parent. Maybe even Kathleen, as well.

She wasn't necessarily right about his career as a professional rodeo cowboy, but she probably had a point about its impact on a family.

KELLY AND JOSH rode back early to assist with the barbecue preparations. After fifty-plus years of doing it, the family had the barbecue down to a science, but because the scale of the rodeo had changed, so had the scope of the volunteers' meal.

"How many do you usually serve?" Josh asked.

"Close to two hundred, which includes families, but they're expecting a bigger crowd this year. Nobody can give us an estimate, which means we're shooting in the dark on how much food to prepare."

Thaddeus came over when they got back to the ranch center. "I'll take care of Lightfoot for you, boss."

"That would be great, Thad. How is everything at the Galloping G?"

"Pretty good, though if it's okay with you, I'll spend Monday morning doing repairs over there. Nothing major. I just don't like

how the barn door is swinging and the hay-
loft could use some maintenance. Best to take
care of things before they become a problem."

Kelly smiled at him. "Thanks for keeping
an eye out. I know Mrs. Gillespie appreciates
it, too. Put any supplies you need on account
at the hardware store."

"Will do. Oh, with spring coming so early
and the weather being so warm, it might be
a good idea to mow several of the fields next
week to spread out the work. The downpour
we got a couple of days ago should give it a
nice growth spurt without more irrigation."

"Glad to hear that. I'd love to just buy pro-
tein cakes this winter. Organic hay is pricey.
Use your judgment on the mowing. I'll let
Mike know the plan. He's eager to put in
extra hours since, as usual, he's entering the
steer wrestling competition in the rodeo."

Thad grinned and the corners of Kelly's
mouth twitched in response. The only reason Mike competed in steer wrestling was
because his girlfriend thought it was exciting to watch.

"Do you still want to cover basic ranch
operations during rodeo week?" she asked.
"You don't have to."

"I know, but I don't care for crowds, and

this year will be worse than ever." Thad flicked a glance at Josh, and Kelly knew exactly what he meant—visitors were expected to overwhelm Shelton. "Any which way, I prefer the peace and quiet at Kindred Ranch." He led Lightfoot away.

"Your ranch hands seem competent," Josh said when they were alone.

"Very competent. Thad has worked for us since before I was born, and I hired Mike five years ago. We went to school together, so we've known each other most of our lives."

"And he doesn't mind taking orders from you?"

Kelly blinked. "Why should he?"

"Nothing. It's just that you're close to the same age and sometimes… Never mind. Dumb thought. I'll come back after I've settled Quicksilver."

As he led the stallion toward the gray barn, Marc ran over carrying a pail. He was covered in greasy soot. "Mom, we're helping Grandpa Harry!"

"Helping him clean the barbecue pit, right?"

Marc nodded vigorously. "It was awesome.

Now me and Casey are getting sand for him from our old sandbox."

He ran off, the pail clanking against his leg.

Kelly smiled ruefully. Time moved on; it hadn't been that long since the boys were toddlers, playing in their sandbox. Now it was another source of amusement for them.

She headed for the barbecue pit, located away from the house to reduce fire risk. Harry believed a brick-and-concrete pit was best and had insisted on building one when she was a kid. Granddad still grumbled, saying he didn't think the meat tasted the same, but Granddad also thought hand-cranked homemade ice cream was better than the same recipe made with an electric freezer.

She found Harry spreading sand around the outside of the pit. "Problem?" she asked.

"The ground is still slick from the rain. Knew I should have put down a concrete pad or laid bricks when I made this thing," he grumbled. "Maybe next year."

The volunteer barbecue was one of the few Kindred Ranch traditions her father had truly embraced. That wasn't surprising since it was connected to the Shelton rodeo.

Kelly rubbed her arms. "Um, Dad, why

did you and Mom decide to make Montana your home base, instead of the Bucking B?"

Harry looked startled; she rarely called him Dad. "A lot of reasons. My folks were gone. Your mama's folks weren't. Liam and Susannah were really nice to me, even though I couldn't have been their first choice as a son-in-law. Living here just seemed best, especially after you came along."

"Why didn't you tell us about selling the Bucking B?"

He made a dismissive sound. "We both know I'm no rancher. I thought about keeping it for Casey and Marc, but Rory Fulton has always wanted to buy the place. Can't blame him. He's run it for more than thirty years and his son is grown now, working along with him. Didn't seem right to keep refusing. I hope you don't mind."

"Not at all, but how did Rory get a loan without any collateral?"

"He didn't. We arranged it between us, all legal and proper as a private contract, or whatever they call it. Rory and Taylor had a down payment saved and I gave them six months to start sending monthly checks for the balance. They'll do all right. The Bucking B is a good spread."

Casey arrived with his bucket of sand before Kelly could say anything else, like how decent her father's decision had been. Rory and Taylor Fulton deserved to own the Bucking B. They'd poured heart and soul into the ranch, even though it belonged to someone else.

"Just put the sand here," Harry instructed his grandson.

Casey diligently emptied his bucket. "Do we need more, Grandpa?"

"I think that would be best."

Casey raced away as his brother got there, his face red from lugging an overfilled bucket.

"Hi," Marc called to Josh, who was also arriving at the barbecue area.

"Hi, Marc. Harry, what can I do?" Josh asked.

"Help me with the barbecue pit. Once the fire is going, we'll keep feeding it to get the bricks hot and a deep bed of coals laid down."

"I wanna help, too," Marc declared, dropping his bucket. The contents spilled onto the ground.

Kelly locked gazes with Josh. It would be different if Granddad was out here as well, but energetic six-year-olds could get into trouble where fire was involved.

Josh stepped closer. "I'll keep an eye on them," he murmured. "Go do whatever you need to do."

She turned toward the house. The barbecue pit would be tended until late in the evening, when four hundred pounds of seasoned beef would be buried with the hot coals for slow cooking. She couldn't stay outside the whole time.

Susannah and Kathleen were peeling hard-boiled eggs in the kitchen. The scent of chocolate vied with the fragrance of baking bread.

"How is everything going?" Kelly asked. "And what can I do to help?"

"The coleslaw is done," Kathleen said. "Now we're working on the potato salad. Can you frost the brownies I just took out of the ovens? The pans are on the porch and the fudge is in a slow cooker."

"Sure."

Kelly went onto the long screened porch and ladled hot fudge over four jelly-roll-sized pans of her mom's Death by Chocolate brownies. It really wasn't a question of frosting them, but of making sure the warm brownies—also jammed with chocolate chips—were covered with a thick layer of fudge. Ten more pans were already cooling on racks.

The family's three ice cream freezers—along with seven they'd borrowed from neighbors—stood waiting to be filled in the morning. As many borrowed slow cookers waited for sweet baked beans. If they didn't have the high number of volunteers and families expected for tomorrow, an enormous amount of food would be left.

"What next?" Kelly asked after washing her hands again.

"Chop the eggs," Susannah said briskly. "Do them in the food processor. We don't have time for niceties."

The barbecue for the volunteers had originally been Grams's idea. She and Granddad had done the first one as newlyweds, continuing it annually ever since. Kelly worried that Grams was overtaxing herself between the barbecue and chili contest, but nobody could stop Susannah Flannigan from doing what she wanted.

Though Kelly didn't cook that much, she quickly fell into a pattern, doing smaller jobs to make the major prep easier for her mother and grandmother. With an effort, she forced herself to stay inside and trust Josh to keep the boys out of trouble.

However much she worried about the future, he needed to get acquainted with his sons.

BETSY DIDN'T MIND that Lonny asked her to paint fences again the next day. Her arms and shoulders were achy, but not too bad—working as a waitress was an excellent way to get into shape for a variety of activities. It also helped that she'd spent her previous Saturday helping at a car-wash fundraiser for the town's safe-and-sober program for teens. You needed elbow grease to remove bug splat from the windows of several dozen pickups.

She started painting with gusto.

Everything was going great. The magazine had bought an article she'd written about Shelton and the upcoming rodeo, and a second that would be about rodeo week itself. A payment had been deposited in her checking account yesterday, so now she could have the van repaired without waiting any longer. She'd already driven it—coughing and wheezing—to the mechanic.

A few minutes later Grant showed up, carrying a second bucket. She admired the way he lugged the thing without any trouble, the muscles bunching over his shoulders.

"Oh, hi," Betsy said casually, ignoring the heavy thumping of her heart. A veterinarian didn't have any business being so delicious. "I didn't know you were coming back today."

"I couldn't let you do the rest of the fence by yourself."

His easy smile didn't fool her. They'd chatted off and on the previous day and Grant clearly hadn't gotten over his discomfort with her mobile lifestyle. The look on his face when she'd talked about skydiving...? He must have wanted *any* work assignment except one located near her.

"You mean they asked if you'd be willing to paint again, the way they asked me," she said in a dry tone.

"Lonny claims I can't do any harm this way. He also says you get me to work faster," Grant admitted. "But I'm happy to help and it can't be fun painting alone."

Betsy gave a noncommittal shrug. Being alone didn't bother her. Neither did spending time with people. Surely one of the keys to happiness was the ability to be content within yourself.

"I've been thinking about the rodeo grounds,"

she said after they'd worked for a while. "The town owns this property, right? And it isn't being used for anything except the rodeo."

"Sure. What about it?"

"I'm not criticizing. It's just that taking everything down and putting it back up again seems a lot of effort. It's no skin off my nose. I'm having fun helping out. But why don't they make a permanent facility? You know, with more substantial structures and that kind of thing?"

Grant gestured to the people working around them. "Take a look. Everyone else is having fun, too. Winters are long here. And hard. Getting ready for rodeo week is a time to come together and catch up."

The concept of community building had sounded silly when Betsy learned about it in college. They'd done contrived exercises that hadn't changed a thing—in the end, they were still students with tests and lives outside the lecture hall, and they were still competing with each other for grades and recommendations.

But this?

Betsy looked around at the happy faces and heard snips of conversation and laughter drifting through the air. It was a real-life case of community building that worked.

"I get that," she said finally. "You're right. It's a nice town."

"We have our issues, but we do okay."

She cocked her head. "Issues?"

"Well, no place is perfect."

A grin tugged at Betsy's mouth. "Yesterday you tried to convince me that Shelton was perfect. Practically perfect, anyway."

"DID I?" GRANT ASKED. "I suppose it seems perfect compared to the way I grew up."

He yawned and dipped his brush into the paint bucket for the hundredth time that morning. He hadn't been called out on an emergency the night before, so he should have gotten enough sleep. Instead, he'd lain awake, trying to figure out why he was bothered by Betsy's gather-no-moss life.

Though they were polar opposites, she seemed like someone who could become a friend. But she was a free agent and it was up to her if she wanted to pursue her father's dream to travel. She'd denied that was what she was doing; he just wasn't sure he believed it. Why else would she toss a few things into a van and spend years wandering from place to place? Maybe it had something to do with her not having any other family.

Get over it, his brain told him.

Plenty of people hadn't understood why he'd become a veterinarian, instead of an MD. Or why he'd chosen to make Shelton a home, when he could have joined an upscale big-city animal practice with regular hours and a higher income.

A commotion at the main gate caught his attention and he saw that Kelly had arrived. A crew from Kindred Ranch always came early to get the barbecue grill going for the chicken and burgers. He watched as she lifted a loaded gunnysack from the truck bed. Josh McKeon grabbed a larger one and walked next to her until Gizmo pushed his way in between them.

Good dog.

"Is something wrong?" Betsy asked as she moved her bucket farther down the fence. Once again she was painting faster than him.

"No. I just noticed that some of the Kindred Ranch crew has arrived. They're providing lunch. That's Kelly Beaumont and Josh McKeon, the rodeo star, over there. He's staying with them. Kelly's father is also a professional rodeo cowboy."

BETSY TURNED HER HEAD; she'd yet to get a good look at Kelly Beaumont. The other woman's hair wasn't quite red and she wasn't particularly tall, at least not compared with the lean cowboy working with her, but she was strikingly beautiful.

As for Josh McKeon…?

The photos on the posters around town didn't do him justice.

With an economy of motion, he removed the grill from the huge barbecue unit someone had towed in earlier, then emptied sacks of wood into the cavity. Smoke soon rose into the clear air.

Betsy pulled the camera from her backpack and snapped a number of pictures. The McKeon guy was remarkably well coordinated—which must be a plus when trying to ride a bad-tempered bull or horse—and he was totally handsome. His focus also didn't stray far from Kelly Beaumont.

"I'm going to catch up if you aren't careful," Grant remarked, breaking Betsy's concentration.

"Sorry. I don't buy souvenir T-shirts or

other stuff. I take pictures to remember the places I visit." She decided not to tell Grant that she was also a freelance magazine writer.

She didn't want him to know, not right now, at least.

Anyway, the writing had happened by accident, rather than by design. She'd been sitting in a coffee shop, working on her computer, when she'd gotten into a conversation with another "plain" coffee drinker—no frills, just cream and sugar. Together they'd grinned as customers ordered things like double-tall, nonfat, sugar-free, decaffeinated lattes made with almond milk.

"Sugar-free, nonfat, decaffeinated… Why bother?" Abigail had whispered.

"I think that's what some baristas call it," Betsy had whispered back.

"Why Bother?"

"Yeah. Good name, right? Though I can't deny that it's healthier than getting the opposite."

When the line to the barista thinned, Betsy had grinned at Abigail and gone up to order a coffee-and-chocolate confection topped with whipped cream and a sprinkle of cinnamon. "But no lid," she'd said. "Just make it look pretty."

Back at the table, she'd taken a number of pictures and sent them to her computer.

"What's that for?" Abigail had asked.

"My travel journal. I illustrate it with photos so I can go back and remember the details better."

"May I see?"

Abigail had read the file, chuckling at various points, then offered to buy the piece for publication in the travel magazine she owned. They'd been working together ever since. Abigail kept urging her to submit more material, or to even consider a regular column, but Betsy was torn between recording her memories and making new ones.

"That's a handy little camera," Grant commented, breaking into her thoughts again.

"Thanks." Betsy zipped it safely into her backpack and grabbed her paintbrush. "I could have gotten a fancier model, but the zoom on this one is enough for what I want. I've taken terrific pictures of a black bear and her babies from a hundred feet away— you'd swear I was right in her face."

"A hundred feet doesn't sound very far. I doubt you could outrun it."

"Not at a running speed of over twenty miles an hour," she said, unconcerned. "But I was in my van and she was on the other side of a small ravine. I also left the engine going."

"I'm glad you take *some* precautions," Grant muttered.

Betsy rolled her eyes. "You sound like a stuffy older brother."

He glared. "I'm not stuffy."

"That's entirely a matter of opinion. But that's okay. I never had a big brother. It's kind of sweet." She suppressed a smile as he turned red.

"Uh, thanks. I think."

"Don't mention it. We both grew up as only children. Maybe we're looking for surrogate siblings," Betsy said lightly.

She didn't feel the least bit sisterly toward Grant, but it was safer to pretend otherwise. After all, her van was being repaired, she could leave Shelton after the rodeo…and there was no reason to think he'd gotten over Kelly Beaumont.

KELLY COULDN'T BELIEVE how much her feet hurt after the barbecue. Somehow, standing around, cooking chicken and hamburgers and helping to serve food and clean up afterward was more exhausting than a long day of work on the ranch.

But the event had been a huge success.

They'd fed more than twice the usual number of volunteers and their families. Kids from the high school had shown up en masse, and folks from all over the county were coming to help get the rodeo and new campgrounds ready.

To Grams's relief, they'd had enough food with some to spare—Susannah felt that if you didn't have sufficient leftovers, you couldn't be confident that everyone had gotten their fill.

Despite the pain in her feet, Kelly was restless. So once the family was in bed, she left a note and went out to the barn. The moon was bright in the sky and a night ride might help settle her nerves.

Josh appeared as she was opening the gate on Lightfoot's stall. "Can't sleep?" he asked.

"I haven't tried."

"Where's Gizmo?"

"Inside. He's doing well, but I want him to rest his leg."

Josh stepped closer to Lightfoot and the stallion let out an unhappy snort. He halted.

"Do Thaddeus and Mike ever have trouble with him?"

"No, but he's known them since he was born."

"I think it's more than that. Horses are sensitive. He's responding to how you feel. You don't like me, so he doesn't, either."

Kelly let out a harsh breath. "I don't dislike you, Josh. You're the boys' father. It's just that everything is confused right now. Maybe Lightfoot is picking up on my…" Her words trailed. It was hard to explain the turmoil going on inside.

"Mixed feelings?"

"Sort of."

She closed the stall gate and went to the sink to splash water in her face, not wanting him to see her expression. *Mixed feelings* was an understatement. Josh's hand on her arm made her gasp and wheel around.

"Sorry, I didn't mean to startle you," he murmured.

"I'm tired, that's all. This has been a long day. We appreciate your pitching in at the barbecue." He'd been a big help, diplomatically sidestepping requests for his autograph and doing whatever was needed. And he'd proved adept at finding things for the boys to do—tasks that six-year-olds could handle and still feel useful.

"It was a pleasure."

Josh trailed a thumb down her cheek and traced her jaw. She shivered, electricity sparking from his touch, her mind swimming with memories. She'd had boyfriends in high school, but nothing serious. The two summers they'd spent dating had been the most thrilling in her life.

"Don't. My face is wet," she whispered.

He took a folded hand towel from the shelf over the sink and dabbed the moisture from her skin. His eyes were shadowed, his head silhouetted by the light on the rafter behind him.

"Do you ever think about what would have happened if we hadn't broken up?" he asked.

Kelly had thought her heart was numb when it came to Josh, yet regret filled her. "We probably would have ended up with you on the road and me at Kindred Ranch with the boys. Maybe married. More likely divorced."

He leaned closer, his lips a breath away from hers. "Divorced? I don't think so. We had too much going for us."

Kelly brushed his chin with the tips of

her fingers, his dark beard stubble rasping against her nails.

"All I know is that I didn't want to turn into my mother," she said. "Distracted and withdrawn, struggling to cope with the constant worry, good health worn away, bit by bit. A man can get killed riding broncs and horses, yet Harry will compete in every single event at the Shelton rodeo. Mom's heart breaks a little every day knowing she comes second."

Josh shook his head. "Kathleen is a fine woman, but you're far too strong to become like that," he said, certainty ringing in his voice.

It was possible. Kelly mostly took after her strong-willed grandmother. Yet something else was niggling at the back of her mind, a sense that she was on the edge of seeing something important. Maybe she could figure it out when things were quieter, after the rodeo or when things were better settled with Josh.

Impulsively, she slid her arms around his neck and kissed him, the way she wished she had kissed him on the day they'd broken up...a sweeter memory to hold on to instead of a bitter argument.

Josh pulled her tight to his body, deepening the embrace.

It was different from before. He was now a strong, powerful man who'd learned to kiss infinitely better over the intervening years. The old tingles started in the pit of her stomach and spread outward until she would have sworn the barn was filled with exploding fireworks.

Then good sense intruded.

Kelly pushed on his shoulders until the message sank in.

Stop.

CHAPTER NINE

JOSH LET GO of Kelly.

Plainly the attraction between them was still there, banked by time and distance, but very much alive.

"Do you honestly think we would have gotten divorced?" he asked in a hoarse voice.

She nodded, looking composed except for the flush in her cheeks. "It was first love, Josh. Little more than a crush. You're a few years older than me, but we were both still young. You were trying to make it as a professional rodeo cowboy, while I was tired of the life. Even if we hadn't faced other challenges, such as having two babies at one time, the odds were stacked against us."

"First love, young love—what does it matter? I don't care about the odds. I make my own luck. We should have tried," he insisted.

She lifted her chin. "I may have been the one who left, but you didn't come after me, either. As a matter of fact, you didn't try that hard to convince me to stay. Why, if I meant so much to you? Because you needed to get to your next competition," she answered for him. "The Dawson Creek Stampede, right?"

"It was the Prince George—" Josh stopped. Each year he learned the Canadian rodeo and bull-riding schedule by heart, along with many of the events in the United States. Some of them overlapped and he had to choose which ones to attend. "Prince George was the next pro rodeo where I competed after we broke up, but needing to get there wasn't the reason."

"Then why?"

"You," he said simply. "You were clear that you didn't want to see me again."

"Hardly a surprise when I'd found you passionately kissing another woman." Kelly held up her hand to stop his protest. "I accept that Doreen initiated it and you hadn't met her before, but you also weren't resisting. Since the two of you got married a few weeks later, you must have felt something for her."

Josh thought about the man he'd been seven years earlier, trying to see things from Kelly's point of view.

What he saw was less than admirable.

He'd been cockily full of himself, certain

he was the best thing to hit professional rodeo since the invention of the saddle. He'd flirted with women at the various events as his due for being one of the upcoming "greats." Even after falling for Kelly, he'd enjoyed receiving attention from flirtatious autograph seekers.

But one thing was certain—nobody had ever affected him the way Kelly had, either before or since.

He winced as he recalled Doreen hugging his arm to her breasts as Kelly confronted him. Why hadn't he shaken her away? He'd seen his ex-wife's sly smile too many times not to know she would have been smirking at her rival—causing trouble had been Doreen's favorite hobby.

"Doreen was a colossal mistake, no matter how it stacks up," he admitted. "I should have done more to stop you, but I let my wounded ego get in the way. For a brief time, Doreen puffed me up. Pride is the only reason I didn't file for divorce within a month. It was an expensive mistake in more ways than one, but I learned my lesson."

Kelly pursed her lips.

When they were dating, Josh had seen the future as a glorious adventure, traveling from rodeo to rodeo, each destination crowned by his wins. But as the days and weeks of their courtship had worn on, she'd recognized the shape of their lives would be solely what *he* wanted. Maybe he would have finally bought a ranch and retired from competition, but maybe not. The risk of slipping into her mother's shoes had scared her.

Still, she couldn't deny that jealousy had also played a part. But Doreen had been a symptom, less than a cause. Josh was not only one of the most talented competitors in rodeo circles, he was also a strikingly handsome man. Women had thrown themselves at him. How long would he have resisted temptation? He obviously hadn't resisted Doreen for long.

"If we'd stayed together, you might feel the same way about *our* marriage," she said at length.

"You can't believe that."

"I believe we were too immature to succeed at raising the twins on the road."

Josh massaged the back of his neck. If the expression on his face was anything to go by, he was bothered by what she was saying. It was understandable. How could anyone achieve so much as a competitor without having an unshakable belief in his invincibility at anything and everything? You couldn't think about failing when poised over the back of a bad-tempered bull, or bareback riding a horse bred for wild bucking.

She let out a breath. "I didn't plan to talk about this. I was just going for a ride."

"Will you wait until I get Chocolate Lad ready?" he asked.

Company was the last thing Kelly wanted—especially *his* company—but she didn't want to refuse, either. "Why don't we just take a walk instead?" she suggested.

They headed out, the ground awash in silver moonlight. He didn't say anything for a long while, then looked toward her. "I called my dad yesterday and told him about the boys. He wanted to drive down here immediately. Don't worry—I talked him out of it."

Don't worry?

That was like telling the sun not to rise. She tried to slow her racing pulse. "Maybe Benjamin can come for a visit this winter."

"As one of Harry's old friends, or as a grandfather?"

"Some of that depends on what you decide…about what we talked about the other day."

A long silence followed, punctuated by the lonely cry of a coyote in the distance. "You don't have to be worried that I know about Casey and Marc," Josh said at length. "Yeah, I'm upset, but I wouldn't do anything to hurt them. Or you. You're their mother. They're happy, terrific kids, and Kindred Ranch is their home."

"It isn't as simple as that."

"Trusting me would go a long way to making it simpler."

Trust him?

Easier said than done.

KELLY WOKE BEFORE dawn the next morning.

Thoughts about the past were nagging her more than usual, because someone new had been added to the mix... Josh's father. Josh was Benjamin McKeon's only son, and presumably, the boys were his only grandchildren. It was natural that he'd want to meet them. Benjamin was probably just as upset with her as Josh was for keeping Casey and Marc a secret.

Sensing her mood, Gizmo whined softly and edged up from the foot of the bed to lay his muzzle on her stomach. His long, full tail whipped back and forth as she stroked his head. He was a magnificent animal with his mixed German shepherd and golden retriever ancestry.

It would be convenient to think his suspicion was a sign not to trust Josh, but Gizmo didn't trust anyone except her. The rest of the world was a giant question mark for him. She was sad to think he might never fully recover from being abandoned and hurt as a puppy, but at least he'd come to her for help after being injured by the barbed wire, instead of running away. He could have died, otherwise.

A few minutes extra in bed was all Kelly would allow herself and she finally threw back the covers. Gizmo eagerly leaped to the floor. Work on a ranch didn't disappear because it was Sunday, but she tried to keep tasks to a minimum so she could spend as much time as possible with the family. Right now that also meant spending time with Josh…as if she'd been able to avoid him the other days of the week.

GRAMS AND KATHLEEN spent part of the morning returning the borrowed ice cream freezers and slow cookers to their neighbors, getting home in time to share a lunch of left-overs from the barbecue.

"It always tastes better the next day," Harry declared, patting his stomach after a dessert of brownies and strawberry ice cream.

"Because we have time to enjoy the food, instead of eating a little here and there between serving everyone else," Kathleen told her husband.

Harry just chuckled.

"Who's up for a ride?" Granddad asked, pushing back his empty plate. "I need to settle that meal."

"Me!" Casey and Marc declared simultaneously.

"I have work to do on my rodeo workshop," Harry explained.

"And I'm going to take a nap," Kathleen said. Kelly wasn't surprised. Her mother didn't enjoy riding as much as the rest of the family and rarely went unless Harry was there, as well.

"How about you, Grams?" Kelly asked.

"I need to review my plans for the chili cook-off. The rest of you go and enjoy yourselves."

In the end, it was Granddad, Josh, Kelly

and the boys who rode out toward the higher hills.

"Josh, do you know there's a carnival this week, too?" Marc asked.

"I saw it on the schedule of events in the rodeo program."

"We don't care about the carnival rides," Marc added quickly. "But Grandpa Liam buys us corn dogs and cotton candy."

"And snow cones," Casey reminded his brother.

"Yup, snow cones loaded with lots of sugar and bright colors," Kelly said wryly.

"Mom gets funnel cakes," Marc volunteered. "They're fried and hot and yummy. She has strawberries and extra whipped cream on top. Oh, and chocolate syrup."

"Is that so?" Josh grinned. "Extra whipped cream and chocolate syrup. Sounds like Harry and the boys aren't the only ones with a taste for rich food."

Kelly gave him a reproving look. "Don't rub it in. I only eat funnel cake during rodeo week."

"I'm glad my knee is working better," Granddad said, rescuing her. He patted Thunder's neck. They'd seen over two decades together. In good weather the aging horse spent most of his time grazing in a field behind the barns, with only Granddad taking him out for gentle rides.

"Grandpa Liam hurt his knee jumping down a rabbit hole," Marc told Josh. "He was chasing a rabbit with a pocket watch."

The corners of Josh's mouth twitched. "A rabbit with a pocket watch?"

Though Granddad remained uncomfortable around Josh, he chuckled. "That sounded better than admitting I was clumsy. It wasn't the first time my knee got torn up, and the doc decided I should have a replacement. Modern medicine is a marvel. Boys, let's see if the homestead cabin got through the winter."

The twins eagerly urged their horses forward, leaving Josh alone with Kelly.

"I'm old news to them," Josh said resignedly. "They'd rather check on an ancient cabin than ride with me."

Kelly felt a strange impulse to comfort him. "They're still excited about you. They just have the normal short attention span of six-year-olds. Besides, don't you want them to like you as a regular person, instead of as a star?"

"Of course. I just want to catch up with the…er, get to know them better."

Catch up with the time we lost?

Kelly thought that was what he'd started to say. It was nice that he didn't try to flay her with guilt every second. Maybe she should have handled things differently when she discovered she was pregnant, but the thought of telling him and his new wife that his ex-girlfriend was having a baby…?

She shuddered.

It would have been ugly, no matter how it turned out. So between the ups and downs of pregnancy hormones, her mother's continued fragile health and her ire with Josh for marrying someone else so quickly, she'd stayed silent.

Ironically, having a grandchild on the way had given Kathleen a new lease on life. She still traveled with Harry during the summer, but she'd remained at home for over a year after the twins were born, helping out. And she insisted on being the one to take Casey and Marc back and forth to school.

"I need to get something straight," Josh said after a few minutes. "You used to do barrel racing, and your grandmother takes part in the chili cook-off every year?"

Kelly sent him a sideways glance. "Yes."

"And your mom enters the annual patch-work quilt competition during rodeo week. She showed me her ribbons the other day."

Kelly was suspicious, unsure of where Josh was going with his comments. Her mother took a quiet pride in her patchwork quilts and often won a ribbon at the annual contest. "Mom makes most of the patchwork quilts we use. The ones in the bunkhouse are hers. Patchwork is one of the few original American art forms, and she's an expert."

Josh shifted in his saddle. "That's how we got onto the subject. She brought out fresh towels and sheets and mentioned the name of the pattern on the bed I'm using. She's hoping for the Best of Show award this year."

"That's right. What are you getting at?"

"Just that Harry isn't the only one in the family who enjoys competing. Obviously the Flannigans have a competitive spirit, as well."

Kelly narrowed her eyes, annoyed. While Josh had a valid point, competing wasn't a driving force for the Flannigans the way it was for him and her father.

"There's a difference between enjoying a contest, hoping to win, and having it be the most important thing in the world, along with the next contest and the next and the hundredth one after that. Are you trying to convince me that it's normal for a father to travel forty or fifty thousand miles a year to rodeos, popping in once or twice a year to play daddy?" she asked.

"I told you, I'm not on the road as much as I used to be."

"You still travel plenty. And you have a ranch to look after, in another country."

"I can't move McKeon's Choice to Montana, Kelly."

"Of course not, but you have to take it into consideration."

Kelly focused on the familiar hills ahead of them, her heart aching. She couldn't stop thinking about their conversation the previous night. Josh was convinced they would have made it as a couple, despite the challenges. He might be right. The rush of first love could have turned into something deep and enduring.

If it had...?

She lifted her chin.

Thoughts like that were no different from wishing for the moon. They'd met because he was a rodeo contestant, the same as her father. And they had broken up for the same reason. Before getting involved with him, she should have paid more attention to the toll that she and her mother had both paid for a life with Harry Beaumont.

"Josh, there are so many things I admire about Harry, but putting family first isn't one of his virtues," Kelly said finally. "As his daughter, I know how that feels. Can you blame me for wanting to keep my sons from knowing they come last, the way I always knew?"

Emotions churned in Josh's face, but he didn't say anything else.

Kelly swallowed and looked away. She didn't want to hurt him. Her wounded feelings over Doreen had long since faded, but she needed to protect Casey and Marc. A stable childhood wasn't solely about having a home to count on. It was also about the people around them.

How would the boys feel going months on end without seeing Josh? It was doubtful he would be more attentive than Harry unless he made a real commitment to fatherhood. Life on the road was demanding.

An exciting, absentee dad might be all right for Casey and Marc, but what if it wasn't?

Betsy was looking forward to her next days off.

She and Grant had finished painting the exterior fence of the rodeo grounds, but the committee was still calling for volunteers. It was exciting to watch everything coming together. So after drinking tea with Mrs. Mapleton each afternoon, she went over to see how much progress had been made and to help if needed.

Twice Grant was at the rodeo grounds as well, and on both occasions someone asked if she'd lend a hand with the task he'd been given, claiming they made a good team.

The mechanic had only needed a day to finish the remaining repairs on her van and she'd been driving it to the rodeo grounds to get there faster. As soon as she arrived on Thursday, one of the coordinators waved her over.

"Are you interested in filling holes in the ground where the carnival sets up?" Simon Shaw asked.

She grinned. "Sure."

"Terrific." He handed her a baseball bat and she raised her eyebrows. "Use it to tamp the new dirt into the holes. Dr. Latham has a shovel and wheelbarrow of dirt. He's over there."

Grant looked startled when she walked over, swinging the bat. "What are you doing here?"

"The same thing you are, the same thing you were doing the other times I've been here. *Helping*. They asked me to pound the dirt into the holes after you've filled them."

"I've been doing that with the heel of my work boot."

"Now you don't have to."

Grant scowled. "You know what's happening, don't you?"

"Yes. They're matchmaking. It's sweet."

Betsy had suspected the rodeo organizers were trying to pair the two of them up. Obviously Grant didn't think it was a great idea, but what was the harm? *They* knew they were incompatible. Besides, she enjoyed teasing him.

His continued grim face made her smile. "Don't be so stuffy. This should be part of what you like about having a longtime home in a small town—folks wanting to play a part in your life."

"That's the second time you've called me stuffy."

"But it isn't the only time I've thought it."

His scowl deepened. "What other times?"

"For one, when you saw my van the other day."

"Oh."

GRANT HADN'T REALIZED his reaction to the battered van had been so obvious. How could someone travel the country in such a dilapidated vehicle? The wonder wasn't that it had broken down in Shelton, but that it hadn't quit working a long time ago.

Betsy crooked a finger at him. "You haven't seen the inside. Let me appall you further."

Though he wasn't sure what to expect, the interior of the van was an eye-opener. Outside the body was dented, with mismatched and chipped paint; inside it was tidy and organized. There were USB ports to charge her camera and other electronic equipment, along with a place to work and cook, a marine bath and a foldaway bed. It was a pleasant, modernized mini home.

"You must have gotten the USB ports installed aftermarket," he said. "Both my trucks have USB connections, but your van was made before they started putting them into vehicles."

"The ports might not be necessary with all the adaptive technology today," Betsy explained, "but I had a friend in college who enjoys trying new things as much as I do. We got a manual from the library and taught ourselves. I've had all the work checked by a mechanic, though. I didn't want my equipment blowing up or anything. This also isn't the original motor—it was rebuilt a couple of years after I started traveling around."

"You didn't do that, too?"

"If I knew that much about repairs, I wouldn't have needed a mechanic to fix my latest problems," Betsy said wryly. "I let someone else do the engine because I was learning to fly."

Of course.

"You have a pilot's license?"

"Just for small private planes, though I'm also instrument rated."

Grant fought the urge to scratch his head. Betsy had mentioned college and now he knew she had a pilot's license. She seemed able to do anything and was interested in everything, but she preferred an itinerant lifestyle, picking up whatever work came her way.

She also thought he was stuffy, which might be closer to the truth than he wanted to admit.

"I like your home," he said. "Where did you get the van?"

"It belonged to my dad." Betsy patted the side. "We'd take off on Saturdays and see how far we could get before having to turn around and go home. That usually wasn't far, because we'd see a museum or something and have to check it out."

"But you enjoyed the journey."

She flashed a brilliant smile. "It was always great. Dad also couldn't pass a bookshop without stopping. He loved holding a book in his hands. They're nice, but I prefer e-readers. That way I have thousands of volumes available and don't crowd myself."

"An e-reader is even smaller than most novels, much less one of my textbooks from veterinary school. It cost me a fortune to move my medical library to Shelton."

Betsy nodded. "A huge amount is available online, some for free. Even magazines are going electronic, though I still see plenty of them in grocery stores." She seemed to hesitate. "Uh, I sell freelance travel articles to the *A.C. Globetrotter*. That's a biweekly online travel magazine. My writing isn't high literature, but it helps with expenses and building my overseas travel account. I got a payment the other day and used it for repairs to the van."

The hint of vulnerability in her face made Grant ashamed of himself. She was so confident and vibrant, he hated knowing he might be responsible for dimming either quality, however briefly.

"That's amazing," he said. "I compose case notes, but no one would read them unless they're another veterinarian."

"Do you use big words?"

"Well, when I treat one of my patients for eating too much, or something they shouldn't have, it's called a 'dietary indiscretion.'"

He was relieved to see her brighten.

"Big enough, but still fun," she declared.

Plainly *fun* was Betsy's byword, along with learning new things and collecting experiences. He would have to look up the articles she'd written for *A.C. Globetrotter*.

"Medical terminology usually doesn't amuse people," Grant admitted, "but my clients love that one. By the way, have you ever considered getting a dog to travel with you? It would be both company and protection."

A longing expression filled her hazel eyes. "I'd love to, but what would I do when I go overseas? I couldn't bear to put a dog in a kennel for months and months or just give it away. That would mean I was abandoning family."

Grant instantly wanted to kiss her.

He'd rescued too many animals who'd been left behind when they became inconvenient. Not as much in Shelton, but in the places where he'd done his training. Most of his rescues had found other homes, but one of the dogs and two cats had moved twice with him. Chester, his black Labrador, was gone now of extreme old age. Luckily Scout and Carlo were still serenading him with purrs and happy meows.

"I should have thought of that," he said. "You're smart to think ahead."

"Hey, guys," someone called from the gate, "are you arguing or smooching over there? We're taking bets on which one."

"Neither," Grant shouted back as Betsy clasped a hand over her mouth, her eyes dancing now with merriment. "I guess we'd better get back to work," he told her.

"I guess."

POUNDING DIRT INTO holes was harder than Betsy had expected, but she understood wanting to even out the surface as much as possible. They wouldn't want anyone spraining an ankle walking around the carnival.

Rodeo week would begin in ten days and the excitement was building in Shelton.

Leonard was confident that he had a lock on the chili contest, partly because of the increased number of visitors expected—strangers who wouldn't know Susannah Flannigan. The grand prize was awarded when a cook won both a first-place ribbon from the judges *and* was voted most popular by the public. His tactic this year was to make a habanero salsa for the more daring voters.

Betsy wasn't so certain about the salsa. Once upon a time she'd eaten a raw habanero on a dare—a decision she questioned to this day. But at least he didn't plan to use ghost peppers or Carolina reapers, both of which were scarily hot.

"How many people enter the chili cook-off?" she asked Grant.

"Usually between fifteen to twenty. Maybe more this year. You won't want to eat chili for a month after sampling all of them. Will the Hot Diggity Dog Café be closed that day?"

"Leonard has already told us it's a paid holiday, along with a couple of other days that week. I can't believe how devoted he is to the cook-off and rodeo in general."

"Along with a whole bunch of other chili chefs. He and Susannah Flannigan usually take first and second place."

Hmm. Susannah Flannigan was Kelly Beaumont's grandmother, and the Flannigan/Beaumont family had provided the volunteers' barbecue last Saturday. The food had been delicious, but Betsy would have enjoyed it more if she hadn't realized her feelings for Grant were growing. It shouldn't matter. She was leaving Shelton sooner or later, but it was hard knowing there wasn't any chance he'd reciprocate.

She sighed.

Yearning practically *oozed* from Grant when he looked at Kelly Beaumont. Betsy didn't blame him. After all, she was a foot-loose wanderer, while Kelly belonged to a founding family of Shelton. She'd be the ideal wife for a man determined to plant his roots deep in Shelton County. Not to mention which, Kelly seemed like a genuinely nice person.

But Betsy had news for Grant—he should have sealed the deal before Josh McKeon had shown up. The electricity between Kelly and Josh was unmistakable.

ON SATURDAY EVENING before the start of the Shelton Rodeo Daze, Josh sat in the Kindred Ranch bunkhouse, stewing. He and Kelly weren't any closer to agreeing about his future with Casey and Marc, and it was turning him into an insomniac. Even at his worst, he'd never had trouble sleeping.

He knew Kelly was taking a turn in the foaling barn that night. School had ended the day before and she'd agreed to the twins bunking out there with her. Susannah had chuckled and called it a slumber party. In return, Marc declared slumber parties were for girls and that they were just helping Mom. Casey hadn't cared what it was called. He'd just run to get his sleeping bag.

Josh jumped to his feet. He didn't care what it was called, either; he wanted to be there, too.

A single, low light was on inside the barn. He stepped through the open door and, from the shadows, saw Kelly sitting at the far end on a pile of straw, talking with the boys. Casey was cuddled close, her arm around him, while Marc lay on his stomach nearby, knees bent and feet waving in the air.

Gizmo and Lark turned their heads in Josh's direction, alert to the faintest sound, but didn't bark. At least they'd gotten to know him well enough for that.

"Mom, tell us about Uncle Patrick," Casey asked. "Grandpa Liam was awful sad when he showed us the me…memral buckles."

"Memorial buckles," Kelly said softly. "The buckles are to remind people about his brother, who died in a war. They were twins, the same as you and Marc."

Marc rolled until he lay next to her, as well. "Grandpa Liam says his brother was a hero."

She smoothed his hair. "That's right. Grand dad was given a medal, too. He just doesn't show it to anyone."

"But Grandpa Harry shows us the stuff he wins at rodeos."

"War is different from a rodeo, Marc. Uncle Patrick was killed saving two other soldiers. Granddad misses him, and he wants other people to remember his brother and how special he was. So every year we have a silversmith make buckles for the top all-around Shelton County winners in the different rodeo divisions."

Marc stuck his lip out. "That means Josh can't get one."

Despite the low light, Josh could see the faint smile on Kelly's face. "No, but there are the All-Around Best Cowboy and Cowgirl Saddles sponsored by the Shelton Ranching Association. There's a good chance he'll win one in the adult division."

"Do the saddles remember somebody?" Casey asked, yawning.

She chuckled. "Nope, they're just saddles. Now crawl into your sleeping bags and close your eyes. I'll wake you up if Lady Sadie starts having her foal."

They reluctantly complied.

Kelly kissed them and Josh ached as he watched Casey hug her neck and Marc give her a quick peck on the cheek. One of his few memories of his mom was the nightly ritual of being tucked into bed...of feeling reassured that all was right in the world.

More of Josh's anger at not being told about the twins trickled away, along with the lingering distrust that such an important secret had been kept from him. Kelly had done what she thought was best at the time. The important thing was that his sons had a great mother, protective, but still able to let them be kids. It was something he'd have to learn as a father.

Kelly watched the boys for a few minutes, then stretched and went over to one of the stalls, Gizmo at her heels. A horse thrust its head over the gate and nuzzled her.

"Josh, it's all right to come in," she said softly, glancing over her shoulder. "Casey and Marc can sleep through practically anything."

He let out a rueful laugh. Little got past her. She must have spotted the dogs' reactions earlier. He walked over to admire the brown-and-white mare.

"I've been meaning to ask how you ended up with Lady Sadie," he murmured. "She's the only pinto on Kindred Ranch."

"Actually, she's a registered American Paint. I found her at an auction—a yearling in awful shape—originally bought as a hobby horse by people who knew nothing about equine care. The other buyers weren't interested in nursing her back to health, but

I wanted her to have a chance. This is her first foal."

Once again, Kelly's soft heart was revealing itself. Many ranchers wouldn't have taken the risk of buying a horse in poor condition, however low the price, but compassion tempered her practicality. And in the end, she'd gotten a fine animal.

"How did she test for genetic issues?" he asked.

Kelly rubbed Lady Sadie's nose. "Clean bill of health. I bred her with a neighbor's Paint, which has also been tested. She should have a beautiful, healthy baby. It's been an education. I've never worked with the breed before, but she's swift, agile, turns quickly—"

"Perfect for barrel racing," Josh interjected, though as soon as the words left his mouth, he wanted to groan. Since Kelly believed he didn't care about anything except competing, he shouldn't add fuel to the fire.

"I've never tried." Kelly's tone was dry. "But I'm sure she'd perform well with the right rider."

"And working cattle, too," he added belatedly.

"I already know that. Are you mentally gearing up for the rodeo?"

"To be honest, I haven't thought about it that much."

She cocked her head. "At least you'll have some real competition. Several well-known contestants have registered, though none with your win record. You're still the star of the event."

Josh didn't say anything for a long minute, unsure of how to take her comments. Being a star *had* been important to him for a long time—after all, it meant more prize money. But not here in Shelton. He wasn't sure it would ever be as important to him again.

What was it about Kelly?

She'd always challenged him, even as a skinny, half-grown kid with serious eyes and a book in her hands. And now she was making him take a hard look at his life. He'd gotten his dream, to own a ranch. Yet he was still competing, still winning big money, and his father ran McKeon's Choice, not him.

So how was he different from Harry, aside from the amount of prize earnings each of them had earned?

While the Kindred Ranch cowhands were friendly with Harry, they admired and respected Kelly. She was the boss. She worked as hard as they did and made good, even-handed decisions. Would his employees at McKeon's Choice feel the same about him? Sure, he'd debated the best way to balance his father's needs with his own once he was living full-time on the ranch, but when was he actually going to do it?

Josh reached out to touch a lock of Kelly's hair. It curled around his finger, soft as silk. She was a fascinating combination of rancher, mother and desirable femininity. Letting her go may have been the worst mistake of his life.

"What's going on in that head of yours?" Kelly whispered.

"The past and the present."

"The boys?"

"Partly."

Her eyelids flickered and she moved backward, almost imperceptibly, possibly sensing how much he wanted to kiss her again. "I shouldn't have asked," she said. "This isn't the time."

Josh glanced at his sleeping sons. However much he wanted them to know he was their father, he didn't want it to happen by accident. "Mostly I'm hoping the rodeo will be as successful as everyone thinks it'll be. It helps the town, which means it helps Casey and Marc. As for the rest? Being a celebrity isn't what it's cracked up to be."

"You used to enjoy the attention."

"Maybe I've grown up since then."

He wished he could tell if she believed him.

CHAPTER TEN

JOSH TRIED TO join in the festive mood as the Shelton Rodeo Daze week started.

On Sunday, Kathleen's patchwork quilt went to the Veterans' Hall for display and judging. For the first time, she took the Best of Show award and she glowed with quiet pleasure at her achievement.

Events devoted to children took over on Monday, with Harry's rodeo workshop crowning the evening. Josh did a roping demonstration at Harry's request, then stepped back and let the older man take center stage. Within a minute, Harry had both the youngsters and onlookers enthralled.

"Amazing, isn't he?" Kelly murmured.

"He has a great rapport with the kids," Josh agreed.

She rose up on tiptoes to whisper in his ear. "The prevailing theory is that he gets along with them so well because he never actually grew up himself."

Josh grinned. Kelly had long since recognized her father's faults, but it was encouraging to know she still loved and appreciated the good things about him.

"Your family is having a successful week," he said.

"Yes, and the twins are enjoying themselves. They'll be even more excited when the carnival opens on Thursday."

The brief, upward sweep of her blue eyes reminded him that Casey and Marc were also *his* family. Pride filled Josh. The boys were their grandfather's "assistants," and despite their young age, it was clear they'd already learned much of what Harry was teaching the other children.

Yet it also brought back a thought that had been haunting him. Kelly was right. For good or bad, he was going to be a role model for Casey and Marc —both as a man and a person. What did he have to offer *except* as a professional rodeo cowboy?

While many of his skills were applicable to ranching, nobody stood up to cheer when a cow was roped out on the range. And bucking horses were specially bred for the job; they weren't used for working stock. Basically, he had a name recognized in rodeo circles and a fine ranch where the cowhands took orders from someone else. That was all, aside from the proposals he'd received to be in commercials and ads for various products.

Was it enough to offer the two sons he'd just met?

"You have the oddest expression," Kelly murmured.

He forced a smile. "Do I? You know, despite all the rodeos I've competed in over the years, I've never paid attention to the surrounding festivities. Look at what I've missed. They're even selling raffle tickets for a ride in a helicopter."

"Not all rodeos are like this."

"Some are, though. I enjoy the sense of community here."

Kelly cocked her head. "Surely you have that at your ranch. McKeon's Choice is near a town, right?"

Josh shrugged. "Close enough."

Except to become part of a community, he needed to be there more. It was time to make real plans for the future and set them in motion, for his own sake, as well as for the twins. The question was what to do.

THE NEXT DAY, after a busy morning of ranch work, the entire family headed into town for the chili cook-off. Susannah was allowed to have helpers, both for cooking and serving samples, but she was in charge. The rules required the chili to be cooked on-site, though accompaniments such as bread or tortilla chips could be prepared elsewhere or purchased commercially.

"I'm going to win the grand prize. You should just pack your stuff and go home," Leonard called to Susannah as he stirred a gigantic kettle. He had a second kettle as well, and he was only one of twenty-four contestants, five of whom had never competed before. The amount of chili being prepared was phenomenal, but so was the growing size of the crowd.

"I'll go home the year *you* do," Susannah retorted. She was in high spirits, enjoying every minute.

Josh's mouth watered as he stirred one of the pots. The rich scent of beef and chilies rose from the contents, which were mostly meat, green chilies, a few tomatoes and other natural flavors. The rules called for beans, possibly an effort to level the playing field for entrants who weren't cattle ranchers, so Susannah had added just enough black beans to satisfy the judges. It would be delicious

with the cheese-and-onion corn bread Kathleen had baked early that morning.

Shelton, which had been so quiet during
his prior visits to the town, now had huge
crowds milling everywhere. Craft vendors
were stationed on the feeder streets, helping
to keep hungry visitors entertained before
the main event.

He stayed in the rear of the booth, trying
not to be recognized, as people began queu-
ing up for samples. Harry, on the other hand,
planted himself at the front, chatting with the
visitors, telling them about the rodeo and his
successes as a professional rodeo cowboy.

"Josh, could you and my father take the
boys to sample the different entries?" Kelly
asked after a few minutes.

He glanced at the restless line waiting for a
taste of Susannah's chili. Harry's gregarious-
ness was limiting the number of samples that
could be served, meaning Susannah Flannigan would be disadvantaged in the popular
vote, particularly with so many strangers in
town.

"No problem. *Harry*," he called in a louder
voice. "Collect your grandsons. We've been
cut loose to do our own taste tests."

With luck, the temptation of circulating

among even more people would be too much for him.

Harry looked torn, but finally nodded. "Okay. Casey, Marc, let's get out of here and eat chili."

The boys joined them excitedly.

They walked the small town square park, sampling the various entries, but Josh didn't think any of them came close to Susannah's chili. Flavors ranged from mild to hot, but most of the booths also had "child friendly" offerings that Casey and Marc could enjoy. The samples were generous and Josh got to the point he could barely swallow another bite.

It was actually a relief when some of the lines were too long and they decided to bypass them. He kept his hat pulled low, still hoping to avoid autograph seekers. It wasn't that he minded giving autographs, but there was a time and a place, and right now he wanted to simply experience the cook-off with his sons.

As they completed the circuit, he spotted paramedics at the edge of the square, along with Grant Latham, who seemed to be assisting them. A group of cowboys were seated on benches behind the Hot Diggity Dog booth, red-faced and gulping bottles of water, except for one who was pouring a quart of milk down his throat. From the amusement on Grant's and the paramedics' faces, their conditions weren't serious.

"I wonder what's up," Jake murmured.

Harry chuckled. "Looks as if they couldn't take the heat. Every few years a contestant decides they'll win by kicking up the spice to an atomic level. Inevitably, a few yahoos can't resist challenging each other to prove which one is tougher."

"And then somebody decides they're having a heart attack or stroke," Josh guessed. "Any guesses about who made the hotter-than-Hades chili? I haven't tasted anything that spicy myself, but we bypassed a few of the booths."

Speculation grew on Harry's face. "Maybe it wasn't the chili. I heard someone say there was a loaded salsa on Leonard Crabtree's condiment table. We had a couple of remarks last year that some of the chili entries lacked authority, so Leonard may have kicked things up a notch with his toppings. I feel for the guy. My mother-in-law is a force to be reckoned with."

Josh agreed.

They went over and he saw a prominent caution sign on the Hot Diggity Dog's salsa; beneath it was a roughly drawn skull and crossbones. Anyone sampling the salsa was being given fair warning of what they were getting into.

"You aren't going to try that, are you?" Grant asked. "It's practically lethal."

Josh looked at the veterinarian. "Nope. I enjoy spicy food, but I'm not a masochist. Don't your patients usually have four legs?"

Grant shrugged. "A few of them have feathers, but I saw a commotion and came over to help." He looked down at the twins. "Hey, guys. Are you enjoying yourselves?"

Casey bobbed his head vigorously.

"It's *awesome*," Marc declared. *Awesome* had become his favorite word over the past few days.

Kelly smiled at Grant from inside her grandmother's booth and Josh tried to decide if it contained a special warmth. Then kicked himself. His feelings toward Kelly were getting more tangled by the day. She was a former girlfriend and the mother of his children. The hypocrisy of being jealous was beyond understanding.

Then Josh abruptly realized he wasn't jealous. He simply envied the uncomplicated way she was looking at another man.

He wasn't sure she'd ever looked at him that way.

On Thursday morning after the parade, Kelly crossed her fingers as the mayor began announcing the chili cook-off awards at the official opening of the rodeo. Nellie Pruitt was given fourth place by the judges and an honorable mention in the popular vote. Emmy Carson took fourth in the popular vote, while a first-time contestant, Jorge Mendez, won third in both categories.

"We had so many tasty entries that this was a tough call for our judges," the mayor said through the loudspeaker. "But they finally came to an agreement—Leonard Crabtree of the Hot Diggity Dog Café wins second place, also in the popular vote, and Susannah Flannigan receives the grand prize for getting first place in both categories."

Kelly cheered as Grams and Leonard went up together to accept their awards. After Leonard spoke, Susannah stepped to the podium. "Thank you to everybody," she said into the microphone, "especially to my family and Josh McKeon, for all their help. I couldn't have done it without them."

Another loud round of applause and cheers sounded. A glance suggested at least three-fourths of the audience members weren't from the Shelton area, so some of their enthusiasm could be from hearing Josh's name.

The reality of his celebrity had been coming home to Kelly all week. It was one thing to hear Harry talk about Josh being a champion, another to understand what it meant to have so many people willing to travel huge distances, just to see him compete or to compete against him.

"Your grandmother looks pleased," Josh said.

"She has a right to be."

They were standing side by side, keeping the twins in front of them. The crowd was large enough, with so many people she didn't know, that she wanted to keep a particularly close watch. Granddad was over by the platform, looking as proud as if he'd won the prize himself.

He put out a hand to help Grams walk down the steps, then gave her a tender kiss. Onlookers applauded again.

Kelly blinked away a sentimental tear. Her

grandparents were living proof that two people could spend a lifetime loving and supporting each other. She wasn't as sure about her parents. It wasn't that they *didn't* love each other, but she wasn't sure they were always happy the way her grandparents were happy.

"You okay?" Josh murmured in her ear.

"I'm fine."

His grin widened. "I think your soft side is showing. I'm glad that part of you hasn't changed. Not that I thought it had after hearing about the retired horses you keep at the Gillespie ranch. Or the way you rescued Lady Sadie."

She shrugged. "I'm not the only rancher who won't sell off horses too old to work. I bet you don't, either."

Josh's face turned serious. "I haven't owned McKeon's Choice long enough to face that decision, but you're probably right."

She knew she was right.

Josh had his faults, but he'd be loyal to horses that had become friends. She wanted to stay focused on his faults, but it was hard. The other day at the chili contest was a good example; he'd quickly understood the traffic jam Harry was causing. No need to explain. He'd simply gotten Harry and the boys away from the booth. Would Josh have done that seven years ago, or would he have joined Harry to chat up the visitors? Intuition hadn't been his strongest quality when they were together, but it seemed to have developed since then.

Kelly's grandparents made their way through the crowd and Grams held up her trophy—a giant pewter chili pepper mounted on a polished wood base.

"Congratulations," Kelly said, giving her a hug.

They'd talked a few days ago about Josh, the same day Kelly had spoken to her mother. She'd told both of them that Josh hadn't known about Casey and Marc, so he couldn't be blamed for not being part of their lives. Kathleen had seemed puzzled at the news— she really *did* live in her own world most of the time —but Grams had suspected for a while. She shared her granddaughter's concerns, at the same time wanting to believe that Josh would do the right thing when it came to the boys.

Problem was, Kelly was no longer sure what the "right thing" might be.

ON SATURDAY JOSH positioned himself over a snorting bull, wrapping the bull rope around his gloved hand.

The thought crossed his mind that if the worst happened during the ride, he'd never get to truly know his sons and be part of their lives.

Stop.

He forced the thought away, as he'd forced it away during the first go-round, along with other hazardous events like saddle and bareback bronc riding. Being too aware of his own mortality was a liability.

Yet he wasn't afraid; it was simply the knowledge of how much more now that he had to lose.

He put his free arm up and nodded to show he was ready.

The gate opened and the bull charged forward. Time seemed to slow as Josh's instincts and experience kicked into place. Up, down, whirling madly, the animal got angrier the longer the human irritant on his back remained, matching him move for move.

The eight-second buzzer sounded.

Josh stayed on another couple of seconds, then jumped away in the unbroken motion he'd practiced countless times. The judges scored on style, as well as the quality of the ride.

Screams and cheering from the audience filtered into his head as he moved one way and the protection "bullfighter" athletes steered the bull in the opposite direction. He lifted his hat to the crowd, but there was only one face he looked for in the grandstand.

Kelly's.

It was reminiscent of old times. Her hair was fiery in the sunshine, and while he was too far away to read the expression on her face, she was clapping, along with her mother, grandparents and the boys. As his score was announced, the twins shot to their feet with the rest of the audience, pumping their small fists in the air.

Determined to avoid any appearance of showboating, he waved and exited the arena before the cheers died away. He shook hands with several of his fellow contestants, some of whom had opted for a re-ride because their bull had performed badly. A re-ride was chancy since you might lose out on getting any score, but it was a risk Josh had always taken.

Harry was there, as well. He'd been thrown before the required eight seconds on both go-rounds. Kelly had mentioned that he refused to join the rodeo association for senior competitors. Now Josh wondered if he was seeing his own future. He was at the peak of his performance, but it couldn't last.

Watching Harry and the strain his lifestyle had put on Kelly and the rest of the family had been an education. More and more he agreed with Kelly that the boys needed a balanced view of rodeo life. He knew rodeo cowboys who'd hung on, destroying their marriages and becoming strangers to their children, even when they had no hope of being successful. He wanted his sons to be happy, and he didn't want them getting hurt unnecessarily.

"You okay?" Josh asked, spotting the bandage on Harry's forehead, stained with a blotch of red.

"Nothing important got broke. You did terrific. Nobody *ever* gets that high of a score in the Shelton rodeo."

"I've been fortunate to draw a couple of feisty bulls."

A roar rose from the audience as another contestant was announced and Josh recognized the teenager he'd met at the Shelton Saddle and Boot shop. Bull and rider shot from the chute. He did well and received a respectable rating from the judges.

"Congratulations," he said when the kid returned. "You have a nice technique."

Owen Corcoran's face lit up. "Gee, thanks, Mr. McKeon."

"Hey, it's Josh."

They chatted for another few minutes and he could have been talking to a younger version of himself, except Owen didn't want to become a professional rodeo cowboy. Not that he needed to go on the professional circuit unless competing was his passion; his family already owned a ranch.

You own one now, too, Josh reminded himself. But somehow, a ranch compared with his sons was becoming less important, the same way stardom had lost most of its appeal.

FROM HER POSITION on the edge of the grandstand, Kelly could see little of the activity behind the chutes. She looked anyway, trying to spot her father and Josh.

Though he'd downplayed the showmanship side of competition, for each event Josh had worn a snug light blue Western shirt, long sleeves rolled to his elbows, with twisted red and blue bandannas around his neck. She'd seen enough pictures of him to know it had become his signature look. He also didn't wear a protective helmet, just a plain tan cowboy hat that matched his chaps.

She tried to suppress the memory of how she'd once tied bandannas around his neck. Combining the two colors was something she'd started, as if she was branding him with her own special touch. Did he remember, too?

Women of all ages in the audience seemed to sigh with longing whenever he appeared. Kelly didn't blame them. Josh was unusually tall for a rodeo cowboy and rode a horse as if born to be there. He was strong and coordinated and always looked in control, even on a wild bull or bronc.

That doesn't mean he can't get hurt.

Kelly's stomach clenched. Even after all these years, she was still torn between admiration of Josh's skill and the old fear that he'd be injured.

"I'm going for a cup of coffee," Granddad said. "Anyone want to come with me to stretch their legs?"

The boys shook their heads, but Kathleen

and Grams rose to their feet. They eased along the crowded row of seats to the staircase.

"Mom, why doesn't Grandpa Harry come out to watch with us?" Casey asked when two other bull riders had finished their turn. "The loudspeaker guy said he got 'liminated."

She pushed the small cowboy hat up her son's forehead to see his face better. "He stays with the other contestants so he can encourage them and offer advice," she said gently.

Marc shoulder-bumped his brother, a superior expression on his face. "Yeah. Don't you remember from last year? Mom wouldn't let us see the bull riding, but Grandpa didn't come out during the other events."

"I remember." Casey glared at his twin. "But he told Grandma Kathleen that things are gonna be different now. Remember?"

Kelly was glad the rest of the family had stepped away. Kathleen didn't need to hear her grandsons squabbling about their grandfather.

"That's enough," Kelly said before Marc could respond. "Grandpa Harry didn't go to several of the spring rodeos he usually attends, but the Shelton Rodeo Daze is extra special."

They recognized her tone; it meant the dispute was over. *Period.* She often let them settle things between themselves, just not in the middle of a large crowd wanting to enjoy the rodeo. And certainly not with her mother returning, coffee cup in hand.

Kathleen's expression was more relaxed now that her husband had competed in his last event. The audience had been kind, despite Harry's poor showing, but it made Kelly sad. For years he'd been the unofficial star of the Shelton Rodeo Daze and now someone else was center stage. He had to be feeling displaced. Still, her father was also responsible for Josh being in Shelton in the first place.

Was that karma, or just poor timing?

"Who did I miss?" Kathleen asked as she sat down.

"Owen Corcoran and a cowboy from the professional rodeo association in California. Both got decent scores. Depending on how Owen does tomorrow in the final short go, he'll probably win the memorial buckle. That'll almost be like keeping it in the family."

Casey tugged on Kelly's arm. "What d'ya mean, Mom?"

"Once upon a time your great-great-uncle Patrick was going to marry Owen's grandmother. If Uncle Patrick had lived, she would have been your great-great-aunt."

Casey settled down, digesting the relationship. "So Owen is kinda like a cousin, 'cept he isn't, 'cause Uncle Patrick died."

"That's right," Kelly said.

Another contestant was announced, drawing their attention. The bull charged from the chute, twisted once, throwing his rider. His hand remained tangled in the bull rope and a collective gasp came from the onlookers as he was dragged by the spinning, kicking animal.

The bullfighters raced to assist.

Kelly tried to cover Casey's eyes at the same moment Kathleen reached for Marc, but the boys ducked away, watching excitedly as the rider was finally freed. It seemed horrific, but somehow he stood, waved at the audience and walked unassisted from the arena.

Kelly's heart was still pounding when she looked back at the twins. They didn't seem fazed. Casey was swinging his legs, chewing on the short straw from his snow cone, while Marc was pulling the last tufts of his cotton candy from a bag. Perhaps they were too young to understand how bad it could have turned out.

She'd struggled with the decision to let them watch the bull riding, but how could she have kept them away? This might be the last chance they'd have to see Josh compete, at his peak, at least. He wasn't likely to be in the Shelton rodeo again; there were bigger venues, with much bigger purses. Besides, even Grams, who was notoriously protective, had pointed out that the chances were minimal of Casey and Marc being there when a serious injury occurred.

"Mom, where are Grams and Granddad?" she asked.

"Here we are," called Grams, coming down the row of seats. "The lines are long and we were getting treats for you and the boys. We don't have enough opportunities to spoil you the way grandparents are supposed to."

Kelly grinned as she accepted a cup of coffee and a plate covered with a funnel cake, topped with strawberries, whipped cream and a drizzle of chocolate. This year the vendors had upped their game and added mini chocolate chips, as well. The twins were thrilled to see Granddad had gotten them batter-coated deep-fried candy bars—a first—and another bag of cotton candy each. Nutrition went out the window during the Shelton Rodeo Daze.

Kelly put the cup next to her, balanced the funnel cake on her knees and ate a bite.

Mmm. Culinary heaven.

"I see that," Josh's voice murmured close to her ear.

She looked and saw him standing next to the grandstand. He put a finger to his lips, but she wasn't sure if he was telling her to stay quiet about his presence or promising not to tease about her decadent dessert. She broke off a chunk of the funnel cake and gave it to him, along with the coffee.

"I understand why you like this stuff so much," he said after munching it down. Kelly handed him a napkin and pointed to the corner of his mouth. He wiped the fleck of whipped cream away with a grin.

"Hi, Josh." Casey abruptly leaned over her knees, almost upending her plate. She rescued it just in time. "When did you get here?"

"A couple of minutes ago. Are you having fun?"

"Yup. You were real good on the bull and Grandpa Liam got us fried candy bars. They're yummy. Wanna bite?"

"Uh, no, thanks. I'm fine." Josh seemed disconcerted and Kelly bent closer.

"They were excited to see you compete, but that was a half hour ago and Granddad just brought them deep-fried chocolate to eat," she whispered.

A thoughtful expression filled his eyes. "That's okay. It was just a ride. Not even a very long one."

She ate more of her funnel cake, wishing she knew what he was thinking. The twins finished the latest indulgence and asked her to guard their bags of cotton candy while they went with Grandpa Liam to wash their hands.

"Faces, too, please," she said. Their mouths were stained with snow-cone syrup and mustard from the corn dogs, and now chocolate had joined the color palette.

They rolled their eyes, but Granddad winked. "Will do."

Grams and her mother decided to go along again.

After a minute, Kelly handed Josh the second half of her funnel cake. "Can you finish this? I'm full."

He quickly ate it between gulps of coffee and went to deposit the plate and cup in a trash can at the front of the grandstand. "Isn't that Dr. Latham?" he asked upon returning.

She looked toward the arena and spotted Grant with Betsy Hartner by the fence. It was nice to see him with Betsy...and a relief. Kelly still felt bad about refusing Grant's proposal, even though she'd known he didn't really love her.

"Yes, with Betsy Hartner. She's new in town. I met her at the barbecue and we've run into each other several times this week. Twice with Grant, and once with her landlady. Betsy must be a force of nature to get Maya Mapleton out in a crowd. Maya is notoriously shy."

"Grant and Betsy look as if they're discussing something intense."

Kelly gave Josh a glance, remembering when he'd tried to find out if she and Grant were involved. In retrospect, she suspected it was his attempt to discover if another man could be the twins' father. Would he have been relieved to discover he hadn't committed parenthood after all?

"Grant and Betsy seem to spar a lot," she said lightly. "When I saw them on Thursday at the carnival, they were in a heated debate as to whether Shakespeare's comedies or tragedies are the best. The other time it was something else."

"Sparks, then."

"I suppose, but Betsy is a travel writer who moves from place to place every few weeks. It doesn't bode well for them having a future."

Kelly just hoped that Betsy's friendship with Grant would remind him that there were other possibilities for romance beyond a woman who kept giving her heart to the same wrong guy.

Kept giving her heart...?

A chill ran through Kelly.

Surely she wasn't falling for Josh again. It would be a mistake. He wasn't a terrible person, but they couldn't make a relationship work now, any more than they could have made one work seven years ago.

Josh quirked an eyebrow at her. "The future isn't the only reason that two people date."

Kelly gulped, trying to regain her composure. "Actually, it may be more of a frenemy situation. I gather the committee had fun throwing them together during the rodeo prep."

"Like watching gladiators in the arena?"

"Along those lines."

Thankfully, movement in the aisle grabbed her attention and she saw the others were returning. The boys led the way, followed by her mother and grandparents. She should have gone with them to avoid being alone with Josh.

It was getting dangerous to her heart.

CHAPTER ELEVEN

LATE THAT EVENING Josh sat on the hood of his truck, taking in the star-studded Montana sky. The main house was dark and he knew it would be wise to sleep as well, but he had too much to think about.

The weeks he'd spent at Kindred Ranch had been an education. Harry's determination to keep competing had put a terrible strain on his family, both emotionally and financially. Kelly was getting the ranch back on a solid footing, but she was having to work harder than was right. While she seemed to thrive on the challenge, Josh could see how tired she was at the end of each day, and it frustrated him.

How much worse would it be if they'd gotten married seven years ago? Would he have recognized what he was doing to her, or just gone his own, self-centered way?

He didn't know and the question haunted him.

Josh looked up, sensing activity in the

large house. A light came on in the upstairs window that belonged to the twins. When he saw Kelly pass the window for the third time, he couldn't sit still any longer. The boys might be sick.

He jumped to the ground and found a small pebble to toss. It hit with a faint clink and Kelly reappeared. She opened the window and leaned out.

"Josh?"

"Yeah. What's going on?"

"Upset tummies."

"May I come up?"

Even in the faint light, he could see the hesitation in her face. "Um, all right. The front door should be unlocked. Be quiet. I don't want to wake anyone else."

Josh hurried inside and up the stairs. Kelly was sitting with Marc, rubbing his stomach in a slow, circular motion. On the other twin bed, Casey had a pillow clutched to his midriff. He looked miserable, but he still managed to roll his eyes at each of his brother's theatrical groans. Lark lay at the end of Casey's bed, her worried gaze going back and forth between her two charges.

"Kelly, what can I do?"

"Take over here and I'll go downstairs for saltines. They might help."

Before leaving, she bent over Casey and kissed his forehead, murmuring something Josh couldn't hear.

He rubbed Marc's tummy, trying to emulate Kelly's gentle rhythm, but even as his mother disappeared through the door, the six-year-old bolted upright, leaned to one side and heaved.

"Moooommmm," he wailed. "I got sick on Josh's cowboy boots."

Kelly rushed back and grabbed towels from their bathroom. Josh accepted one, but was less concerned about the state of his boots than his son's clammy skin. He changed the bedsheets while she got Marc into a fresh pair of pajamas and ran a damp washcloth over his face and arms.

Josh frowned. "Maybe we should call the doctor. Wycoff, right?"

She shook her head. "I'm sure it's just sugar and fried-food overload. I'll be right back."

He admired her composure. He finished cleaning the floor and the tips of his boots while she was gone, then checked on Marc again. Color had replaced his pallor and he was already curled up asleep.

"How are you, pal?" Josh asked, turning to Casey.

Casey stuck his bottom lip out. "Okay."

Josh sat next to him. "It's all right to admit when you feel sick."

"Mom has enough stuff to do. I didn't think we should wake her up, but Marc said he was dying and wanted her."

An ache grew deep in Josh's soul. Though Casey was only six, he was determined to protect Kelly. "I'm here. I'll help."

"'Cept she's *my* mom."

Pride joined the ache inside Josh. His quiet, stubborn son was going to take care of his mother, come what may.

Soft footsteps came into the room and Kelly looked back and forth between the boys, then sat on the other side of Casey's mattress. "Try these," she said, giving him a bowl of saltines and putting an open bottle of ginger ale on the bedside table.

Still holding the pillow to his tummy, he squirmed upright and ate a few of the crackers. He drank some of the ginger ale, burped, then ate a few more as Kelly rubbed his back.

"I don't want 'nymore fried candy," he muttered finally as he settled down again, eyes drooping. "It makes my stomach icky."

"I know. Do you think you can sleep now?"

"Uh-huh."

They waited until his breathing slowed into slumber before leaving. In the hallway outside their room, Josh leaned against the wall, drained. The boys weren't seriously ill, but he'd practically panicked. "How do parents survive this stuff?" he muttered.

"It gets easier," Kelly said softly. "Though you always worry and hate when they feel bad. Sorry about your boots."

"They aren't important."

"Perhaps, but you should get to bed, too. You need rest for tomorrow."

Tomorrow?

Josh looked at her blearily, then remembered the bull-riding finals. Taking his chances, he leaned over and gave her a quick, hard kiss.

Kelly stepped backward. "Wh-what was that for?"

"All the times someone should have kissed you after something like this. Let me know if I'm needed."

He returned to the bunkhouse and kicked

off his clothes. His last thought before dropping off was that mothers deserved a medal.

THE BULL-RIDING finals were the last event of the rodeo and Kelly remained on edge as each contestant was announced.

The twins had bounced back quickly, eating their morning oatmeal and blithely asking if they could have corn dogs again for lunch.

"We'll see," she'd said. Memories were short when you were six and had a chance to eat carnival food.

Josh had seemed okay at breakfast, too, but she remained concerned. Everything affected an athlete's performance, including not getting enough sleep.

She tried not to think about his spontaneous kiss, mostly because it couldn't mean anything. He was still finding his place as a father, and seeing the boys sick for the first time had disturbed him. Perhaps it was also a case of sorting out how he should relate to her as their mother.

When Josh's name was announced, Kelly's breath caught.

A short time later the gate opened and the bull exploded from the chute. The audience sprang to their feet as Josh's body moved with each spin and twist. It was as if he could read the animal's mind, yet his persistence just seemed to aggravate the bull, who kept upping attempts to throw off his rider.

Dust rose around the bull's legs and his gyration intensified.

She was distantly aware of the eight-second buzzer going off. For another endless few seconds Josh stayed with the bull, then leaped away. Screams thundered through the arena and the grandstand shook with stamping feet and applause. He waved his hat and walked to the gate.

Kelly sank back down on the bench, feeling drained, though everyone else remained standing, their response growing even louder as his near-perfect score was announced. Her conviction kept growing that she was falling for Josh all over again, but this time she suspected it would be a lot harder to get over him.

No, she told herself.

She had to stop thinking that way. Kisses aside, he was the boys' father, and that was all.

The announcer was having trouble being heard over the continuing applause and he finally asked Josh to come up to the judges' tower.

"Hello, everyone," Josh said a short time later over the loudspeaker. He leaned out so his face was visible and made a gesture to quiet the crowd. Slowly the noise lessened. "Thanks for making me so welcome here in Shelton, but we have three fine bull riders still waiting to compete. Please give them the same warm reception you've given me."

Another round of clapping followed, but it quieted quickly when the name of the next contestant was announced.

The remaining riders were good, but not in Josh's class.

To no one's surprise, he took first, the same as in the other events, and was awarded the Best All-Around Cowboy Saddle from the Shelton Ranching Association.

"Josh is awesome," Marc said, plopping down, breathless from cheering after all the announcements and award presentations. "Super...fan...fantaboolous."

"Where did you get *that* word?" Grams asked.

"From one of the carnival guys. He wanted us to go on the Ferris wheel." Marc scrunched his nose. "He said it was better than a riding horse or anything."

"A slight error in salesmanship," Kelly murmured.

Grams chuckled. "Right. He should have known better in this part of Montana."

With the action over, the crowd dispersed quickly, some to enjoy the last few hours of the carnival, and others for home, campgrounds or travel. The rodeo was an important fundraiser, but the town would take a breath of relief now that it was over. Two months ago nobody could have anticipated that the event would turn into such a monster, drawing cowboys and visitors from across the United States and Canada.

Josh and Harry joined them as they were deciding what to eat for lunch. The boys asked for corn dogs again, then changed their minds when everyone else wanted tri-tip sandwiches. Most of the service organizations in town had opened booths to help feed the visiting crowds, offering everything from hot buttered scones with huckleberry jam to barbecue of every variety.

"I'll bake hot dogs in corn bread for you next week," Kathleen promised them. It wasn't quite as much fun as getting food from a carnival booth, but it was a favorite dish they didn't get very often.

The tri-tip was hot and juicy, but Kelly barely tasted the sandwich. She was restless after spending so much time in town. There wasn't any reason. The last of the mares had foaled and Thaddeus would have called her if a problem had cropped up. But unlike her father, she didn't need people to be energized. The rhythms of life on Kindred Ranch suited her best.

Surely it was the uncertainty hanging over their lives making her uneasy, rather than the uncertain state of her heart. Josh knew about the boys. And now the whole family knew, except the twins themselves. Nobody talked about it; they were simply waiting to see what happened next.

GRANT WAS PLEASANTLY tired from his veterinary shifts at the rodeo. Even when not there, he'd often been on call for the veterinarian who was on duty, or else taking care of his own patients.

Still, he'd found time to read Betsy's online articles in the *A.C. Globetrotter*. They were humorous, insightful and filled with appreciation for the places she visited. It was impossible not to admire her bright, daring spirit.

He sighed. Next to Betsy he felt like a sleepy groundhog, refusing to admit that spring had arrived.

"Dr. Latham," called one of the contestants. "Can you check my horse's eye? It's irritated and we have a long drive home."

The problem turned out to be a piece of chaff under the lid, causing excessive tearing. Grant removed it and gave them eye drops, with advice to contact their own vet if signs of an infection developed.

Now that the rodeo was over, everyone was rapidly loading their horses or cattle onto trailers. A few of the contestants had already left, but most had stayed to see Josh McKeon in the bull-riding finals. Grant's responsibility wouldn't end, however, until the last animal had departed. Any contestants and their families wanting to stay the night in Shelton needed to move to another camping area.

"Look what I found," said Betsy. He turned around to see her with a thin black Labrador-mix dog. "He has a sore paw. I've gone all around trying to find his owner, but I'm not sure they deserve to have him back."

Grant frowned. "You could be right, though lost dogs can lose condition quickly." He leaned over to check the animal, who was huddled against Betsy's leg. In a short time, she had become his protector.

"Let him see your foot, baby," she soothed.

It wasn't a surprise when the Labrador lifted his leg and allowed it to be examined— Betsy seemed to have a reassuring effect on people and animals alike. The sad pleading in the Lab's eyes reminded Grant of his old dog, Chester, when first rescued.

He probed and found a small cut, which he disinfected and wrapped with supplies from his medical bag. The animal's nails and foot pads were worn and he suspected it had walked long miles.

"This doesn't seem serious," he murmured, "but when I'm done here, I'll take him back to the clinic and do a full exam. It's possible he got lost by sneaking onto a horse trailer or off of one, either at home or at a rest stop."

"I'll go with you. What about a microchip?"

"I'm going to check for that." Grant took out the microchip reader he kept handy and ran the wand over the dog—it was rodeo

SOP that the veterinarian on duty was contacted when a lost pet was involved.

"No chip," he murmured.

"I gave him water and some chicken breast," Betsy explained. "He acted as if he wanted more, but I didn't know if he should have a large amount of food all at once."

"Small meals are best for the moment, though he doesn't look as if he's in starvation mode, just poorly fed. I think he's not quite a year old and still growing. Why don't we call him Rosco for now?"

"Sounds good."

Betsy waited with Rosco while Grant inspected two more horses, then finally watched the last vehicle drive out of the contestants' parking and camping area.

It seemed fitting that Betsy would show up with an abandoned dog. A black Lab, no less, like Chester had been, though considering the length of his fur and shape of his head, Rosco had a touch of something besides Labrador retriever in him.

Back at the clinic, Grant lifted the dog to the exam table and looked him over. Aside from being underweight, his injured foot seemed to be the worst of his problems. His basic blood work was all right as well, though more extensive tests would need to be run in the morning.

"Will he be okay?" Betsy asked anxiously.

"I believe so." Grant rubbed behind Rosco's ears and the dog's tail thumped on the table. He was a good-natured dog, despite everything he'd gone through. "I'll give him a bath once he's gotten more rest. In the meantime, we'll put him somewhere quiet."

Not knowing Rosco's health history, an isolation kennel seemed best, so they made him comfortable with water, a soft bed, blankets and another small meal.

"Don't worry. He'll be fine here," Grant promised as they left him, already asleep on the cushy dog bed. Hopefully that meant he felt safe. "I'll give you a ride to your van."

Betsy shook her head. "The traffic has been so heavy that I've been walking to the rodeo grounds. It isn't far and I'll just hoof it back. I still haven't ridden the whirligig ride. We didn't go to carnivals when I was a kid, so I'm checking everything out."

Of course.

Despite Grant's admiration for Betsy, the risks she took still bothered him. Not that carnival rides were dangerous, but skydiving and white-water rafting held a certain amount of jeopardy. She'd even tried to convince the rodeo committee to let her get on a bronco, only to receive an emphatic no. As much as they liked her, they wouldn't break their rules for anyone.

"Let's go to the carnival together," he suggested, though an hour earlier he'd wanted nothing more than to relax at home.

"Do you want to go on the whirligig thing, too?"

He made a noncommittal gesture. "I'll decide when we get there."

Back at the small carnival, they wandered around, playing the ring-toss game and throwing darts at balloons before getting a cinnamon-and-sugar-crusted churro. It was delicious, but he had doubts about the ride Betsy wanted to take. Basically, you were buckled into a seat that was suspended by cable from a mechanical arm, then got spun around and around in a wide circle.

"I have enough tickets for both of us," Betsy said with a mischievous expression.

"Oh, okay."

Against Grant's better judgment, he found himself strapped into a seat, his back to the center apparatus so that he was looking skyward as centrifugal force lifted him in the air.

When the ride ended, Betsy got off first and waited for him, bright-eyed and laughing. "Are you sorry about eating that churro first?" she asked as the attendant unbuckled the safety restraints.

"Why? Is my face green?"

"Not exactly." She hooked her arm in his. "But let's take the Ferris wheel next. It's tamer."

Great. Now he was both stuffy *and* tame. He should have admitted that he'd enjoyed her whirligig ride. Nevertheless, Ferris wheels were a historically convenient location for guys to sneak a kiss, and Grant wasn't above hoping to sneak one with Betsy.

"Sure. Let's go."

He bought a handful of tickets and they waited their turn. They were the first on and their seat slowly moved higher and higher as the ones below were loaded. Yet he began to second-guess his plan. After all, she *had* called him a surrogate brother, and brothers didn't kiss sisters the way he wanted to kiss her.

"Are you going to try to kiss me or not?" Betsy asked, breaking into his thoughts. "That's what happens in the movies when someone is at a carnival. Dad warned me about boys like you."

"Boys like me?" He grinned, wondering if mind reading was one of her talents. "Do you always follow your father's advice?"

"Sometimes. Will Hartner was a wise man, probably because of the wild oats he'd sown as a teenager. I've always suspected that I was the result of those wild oats."

Grant loved the sparkle in her eyes. She could be sad when talking about her father— understandable considering his early death— but now she seemed happy, rather than melancholy.

"In that case," Grant said, "to make you never miss an experience…"

He put his arm around her shoulders and pulled her close. Her lips were sweet with sugar from the churros they'd eaten and he deepened the embrace. It was innocent and pulse jolting at the same time.

Everything suddenly moved around them and Grant realized the Ferris wheel was shifting again to take on another set of riders, or maybe the world was moving because of the kiss. He wanted to hold on to Betsy forever.

Forever?

Uh-oh.

Betsy wasn't a forever kind of woman. She spent a few weeks here and there before moving on. It was a life she loved.

Besides, they'd known each other only a short time and he couldn't possibly have the kind of feeling that led to forever. It was just the madness of the moment.

The Ferris wheel began turning steadily now and he forced himself to let go. "How was that?" he asked.

BETSY FLICKED THE tip of her tongue across her tingling lips. Her skin was hot and there was a rolling in her stomach that had nothing to do with food or the rides she'd taken.

"H-how many girls have you kissed on a Ferris wheel?" she asked, trying to keep her tone light.

"Would you believe me if I said you're the first?"

"Maybe, but you must have experience kissing in all sorts of *other* locations."

Grant cocked his head. "How can you say that? I'm a staid, responsible doctor of veterinary medicine. You even called me stuffy. Calling a man stuffy is like waving a red flag at a bull."

His arm remained around her shoulders

and she wished it was nighttime, with the stars above in the wide Montana sky and the lights of the carnival sparkling below. If only she could be certain he wasn't thinking about someone else.

"Are you trying to start another argument?" she asked.

He chuckled. "Maybe I'm trying to prove you're wrong. Nonetheless, I don't deny being too old-fashioned for some women."

Just then the ride ended, and since they'd been the first to board, they were the first off.

"Being old-fashioned is all right if it's kept in check," Betsy told Grant as they went down the platform's few steps. "You don't seem to have a problem with women ranchers like Kelly Beaumont."

"Traditionally ranching has been male dominated, but that's been changing for quite a while. There are several women running ranches in Shelton County, and they're as good or better than their male counterparts."

Betsy had expected a reaction from Grant at hearing Kelly's name, but his expression remained unchanged. A hopeful sign, though not conclusive. He could still be wishing it was Kelly he'd kissed on the Ferris wheel.

"By the way," Grant said, "I checked out

your travel articles for the *A.C. Globetrotter*. You have a gift for getting readers to see through your eyes. I also told the committee about the one you wrote on the rodeo preparations and the upcoming article about Shelton Rodeo Daze week."

"Oh." Betsy was immediately uncomfortable. As a rule, her articles were published when she was already on her way to somewhere new. She never said anything negative about a place, but her sense of humor could be misunderstood. "I didn't tell you about them to get readers."

"I know. But folks are interested because no one expected a national travel magazine to publish something about Shelton. You and Josh McKeon have put us on the map."

"Shelton is already on the map," Betsy said quickly. "It doesn't need me or anyone else to put it there."

Grant cocked his head. "Does that mean you're leaving now that your van has been repaired?"

Betsy shrugged, wishing he sounded upset at the idea. "I haven't decided on a date."

The customers at the Hot Diggity Dog Café were generous tippers and most of the money for the articles about the rodeo was still in the bank. Originally she'd planned to stay long enough to see the rodeo, then move on, providing she'd been able to fix the van.

But the van had been repaired now, the rodeo was over…and she was torn.

There was a lot of the world left to see, but the rest of the world didn't have Grant Latham. It shouldn't matter. It was just that he had a warm, kind twinkle in his eye and was a good sport about getting teased. He was also smart and hardworking and loved animals.

A woman could get her heart in a real tangle over a man like that.

THOUGH KELLY ENJOYED the Shelton Rodeo Daze, she was always happy to have life settle into the normal summer routine. It was a pattern that usually saw her parents leaving for rodeos across Canada and the northern United States, but this year Harry and Kathleen didn't seem to be making immediate travel plans. Perhaps they were waiting to see how things worked out with Josh.

On Wednesday, Kelly got up and headed for the foaling barn, Gizmo at her heels as usual, only to find Josh already there, cleaning stalls, the way she'd found him working somewhere on the ranch almost every morning.

"You should be sleeping in," she said.

"I could say the same about you."

"Why me?"

"You work hard, Kelly. There's no reason you can't ease off with me here."

Kelly eyed him. She was no longer particularly concerned Josh intended a custody fight over the boys, but that didn't mean she was willing to surrender care of Kindred Ranch.

"I don't want to 'ease off,'" she asserted.

"Casey worries about how much you have to do," Josh told her quietly. "He didn't want to say how sick he felt Saturday night because of it. I promised that I was helping. You don't want to make me into a liar, do you?"

She let out a breath. Casey was more introspective than his brother. The small injustices at school rolled easily off Marc, but not with Casey. He determinedly defended what was right, so it wasn't a surprise to hear that he worried about her.

"It's ironic wanting to protect our children from everything, and knowing they need to learn about life to succeed as adults," she murmured. "Marc is headstrong, often rash, which can get him into trouble, but he doesn't internalize the way Casey does."

"I've been amazed at how different they are."

Kelly smiled. "Some people think identical twins have identical personalities, but Casey and Marc are individuals. Even as babies they were different from one another."

"In what way?" Josh asked eagerly.

"For one, they had unique cries. I knew when Marc was hungry or needed a diaper change, or Casey wanted cuddling, just from the sound."

Josh nodded. "I've noticed Casey is more affectionate."

"Marc is affectionate, too, but not in the same way. Casey was the first to walk. I think Marc was upset that his brother succeeded first, which could explain why he's so competitive. He doesn't want to ever get beaten again. It may not be a conscious decision, more of a reaction."

"Maybe that's simply Marc being Marc. Still, I also think he gets frustrated, because deep down he knows Casey doesn't care that much about beating him—he just does his own thing."

Kelly was impressed. A lot of people couldn't

see the complex aspects of the twins' relationship. "Right. I hope to help Marc understand that it's okay if he's better at some things, and his brother is better at others. He doesn't have to make everything into a contest. And I mean *everything*. Marc even has to be a foot or two ahead of Casey when they're out riding or walking. You should see Casey roll his eyes about it."

Josh didn't say anything for a while, then cleared his throat. "Maybe I could talk to Marc. When I was starting out, one of the other professional cowboys told me not to worry about the standings and to just compete with myself, because someday, somebody will come along who's better."

The small crunch of footsteps registered the same moment Marc interrupted, "Nobody is better than you, Josh!"

Uh-oh.

Kelly looked over at the barn door and saw both Casey and Marc had arrived, along with Lark. They were still wearing pajamas, feet stuffed into their small cowboy boots. One thing about kids: you never knew when they were going to show up. Now that the boys didn't have to be pulled out of bed for school, they were getting up early to enjoy their freedom.

"Sure they can beat me," Josh said. "Anybody can get thrown, or have a bad day, or just not be as good as another rider. It took me a while to understand that it's just eight seconds on a bull or bronc, and eight seconds out of a day isn't that much. The big question is what to do with all your other seconds and minutes and hours."

Kelly blinked, remembering what Josh had said after one of the bull-riding go-rounds—something about it not being a very long ride. She'd wondered what he was thinking… Was this his conclusion after all these years, or was he just mouthing sentiments he thought she wanted to hear?

Marc stuck his lip out. "I bet Mom told you to say that."

"That's a bet you'd lose."

Marc kicked the wood plank floor, then looked up with a curious expression. "Okay. I've been wondering something. I asked Mom before, but she said I wasn't old enough to understand."

A prickle of warning crept through Kelly. There weren't very many things she didn't speak openly about with the twins. Illness, injuries and death couldn't be kept out of sight on a ranch. In fact, there was only one thing she could recall saying they were too young to understand.

Marc squared his shoulders. "So, are you our dad, or what?"

Yup, that was the one thing.

CHAPTER TWELVE

JOSH EXCHANGED A glance with Kelly.

Wow.

Nothing subtle about a six-year-old. As much as he wanted Casey and Marc to know he was their father, he couldn't think of what to say.

"Boys, come over here," Kelly said. She waited until they were seated on one of the nearby hay bales. "Josh and I dated each other a long time ago, when I used to go to see Grandpa Harry compete at different rodeos. Remember I told you about Grandma Kathleen getting really sick before you were born? Well, Josh and I broke up that summer."

"But why?"

"It was my fault," Josh interjected. "I thought I wanted to compete more than I wanted anything else. Your mom realized that meant things weren't going to work out between us, which is why she came back to

Kindred Ranch. She didn't know about you then, and she had a good reason not to tell me when she found out she was pregnant."

"So you're our dad." Marc seemed determined to hear the words.

"Duh, of course he's our dad." Casey rolled his eyes. "Only a dummy would have to ask."

"I'm not a dummy."

"Yes, you are. I guessed Josh was our dad right away, but you thought he was just Grandpa Harry's friend. *Dummy.*"

Marc jumped to his feet. "Take that back."

"You're just mad 'cause it's true."

"Am *not.*"

The argument took Josh off guard. He wasn't sure what he'd expected from the revelation. Hugs? Excited approval. Anger because he hadn't been there for any of them? Anger would mean they cared.

He glanced at Kelly and saw wry amusement in her eyes.

"Why don't we go for a ride after you get dressed and have breakfast?" he suggested before she could stop the escalating quarrel. "The four of us."

"Yippee," shouted Marc. He ran out the barn, followed closely by Casey and their faithful Australian shepherd.

"I don't know how you feel about it, but I thought that was anticlimactic," Kelly murmured in the silence.

Josh let out a humorless laugh. "I figured they'd have more questions, at the very least."

"I suppose they're still young enough to accept what they've been told. But the questions will come. Marc has always been more curious about his father, so I'm not surprised that he's the one who said something first. You were generous to accept the responsibility."

"It wasn't generous," Josh said intently. "It was honest. Much as I want to believe we could have had a life together, I realize now that you and the boys would have gotten the short end of everything. I can't help wishing I'd known about them, though maybe it's just as well. You said it yourself. I might have handled the news badly. I could even have ended up never knowing them."

"At least you're getting to know them now."

"Yeah, but Pop isn't." He hesitated. "Once things settle down, how about all of us drive up to McKeon's Choice? Just for a short visit. I know you wouldn't want to be away from Kindred Ranch for long."

"No," Kelly said quickly.

Josh wasn't surprised. She was fiercely protective and this wasn't even a question of taking the boys to another state; he was asking to take them to another country. He knew little about the custody laws in the United States or Canada, but it must be extra tricky when *two* countries were involved.

"Right, summer is a bad time to be away from a ranch," he murmured. "Even for a short period."

Some of the tension in Kelly's body eased. "Yes. I was impressed that your father offered to leave McKeon's Choice to come down here for a visit."

"He'll still come, whenever you give the word."

Kelly walked restlessly around the barn, rubbing her arms as if cold. Recently he'd realized it was something she did when stressed or worried, remembering also how often she'd done it in the weeks before their breakup. She'd sit in the stands on a hot day, shivering as if freezing. There had been other clues, too, that she was unhappy. He just hadn't seen them.

Clearly she had lingering trust issues, but how could he change that?

Perhaps he could consult a lawyer and have paperwork drawn up as reassurance that he wasn't going to seek custody. Kelly was a good mother and his sons' happiness was more important than anything else. If he showed trust, she might reciprocate. But one thing he was determined to do was make child-support payments, including back amounts. If Kelly was reluctant to take the money directly, he could start by paying off what was owed on the foaling barn.

"Hey," Josh said, hating to see her so uneasy. "It's okay. Pop understands we need time to sort everything out. I've sent him the pictures and videos I've taken on my phone. He's doing the proud grandpa thing and showing them to anyone who will stand still long enough."

Kelly frowned. "He isn't posting anything to social media, is he? You're well-known in rodeo circles and it wouldn't—"

"No chance of that," Josh reassured her quickly. "I even had to talk him through how to pull them up on the phone. Pop isn't technology savvy. It took forever to talk him into carrying a satellite phone when he was out riding. He still snorts and calls it techno ranching. He'd be perfectly happy keeping everything the way things were done in the 1880s."

She smiled faintly. "It's amazing how the modern world has intruded on ranching. Luckily Grams maintains the Kindred Ranch website and our social media presence. It seems crazy that we need to do that for a cattle ranch, but it genuinely makes a difference in our sales. Still, I'm like your father. I appreciate the old ways."

"Yeah, he's going to like you."

"I would have expected him to be angry at me for keeping the boys a secret."

Josh shook his head. "If anything, I'm the one he blames. He's told me for years to stop acting like a—" He stopped abruptly.

"A what?"

"Nothing I can repeat in mixed company," Josh admitted. "Needless to say, it wasn't complimentary. He felt I should retire once I bought McKeon's Choice, so you should get along great together. *Retire*. What a word for someone in their late twenties."

Yet Josh's feelings had changed. The weeks of watching Harry interacting with his family had brought home how bad it could be, not knowing when to stop. And the truth was,

Josh would rather retire at the top of his game than on the downhill side of it.

KELLY SWALLOWED. "JOSH, it's your life and your decision. I wasn't asking you to quit when I said to consider what kind of father you want to be. At least, I didn't intend to ask or make it a condition of telling the boys. If that's what I implied, I'm sorry. I was just afraid of seeing them get excited about you being their father, spending lots of time together with you, and then have weeks or months go by with little or no contact. The contrast would be hurtful."

"I realize that."

Did he?

Since the night they'd kissed in the barn, she'd tried to sort out her sense that she'd missed something important. Gradually it had dawned on her. While it was true that she'd worried about turning into her mother, the biggest reason she'd broken up with Josh was because she hadn't wanted to ask him to stop competing just for her. She still didn't want that. Even if he agreed, he'd end up resenting her and the twins.

It had to be something he chose for himself. How could he be happy otherwise?

Still, Josh was right that she wouldn't have turned into her mother. But her bitterness at coming second to his rodeo career would have eventually torn them apart. The pressure would have been worse once children were involved.

"Come on," Josh said. "Let's have breakfast and go on that ride with the twins."

Shivers sang through Kelly as he took her hand, though she was no longer an impressionable girl falling in love with the boy of her dreams. They were adults now, with a complicated past that made the future even more complicated. At the very least, she hoped they could be friends. It would be best for Casey and Marc if their parents weren't at war with each other.

"Josh, tell your father he's welcome to spend Christmas with us," she said as he tugged her to her feet. "Or whenever he wants to come. We also celebrate the Canadian Thanksgiving in honor of Harry."

"What about me?"

"You're welcome, too, of course."

He gave her a wry look. "But you expect me to be at a rodeo somewhere."

Kelly shook her head. "I didn't say that. Harry is always here for the holidays. He attends the National Pro Rodeo finals after Thanksgiving and returns before Christmas— our Thanksgiving holiday in the States, that is. Maybe I could bring the boys if you qualify. Or to the Canadian finals."

JOSH WAS STUNNED.

Kelly was offering something he'd never expected. He brushed a strand of hair from her forehead. "The finals are the last thing on my mind, but I'll talk to Pop about the holidays. He's regretted not having more family, particularly at Christmas. We serve a Thanksgiving meal for our ranch hands at McKeon's Choice—any who aren't spending it somewhere else. We do a Christmas meal, too, but somebody else can head it up if we aren't there."

She smiled faintly. "Who cooks?"

Josh chuckled. "No one at the ranch. We want it to be special, not the usual chow. There's a small grocery store nearby that offers take-out Thanksgiving and Christmas meals for whatever number of people you expect to feed. They do a brisk business during the holidays. They're generous, but Pop orders extra, so we'll have leftovers."

"Don't tell me he's a fan of turkey cro-
quettes, turkey curry, turkey—"

Josh held up his hand. "Nope, but turkey-
and-ham sandwiches are popular. The rest of
the stuff is heated in the microwave, which
is one of the few modern inventions Pop has
embraced. Things may change when he gets
a full-time cook."

"No progress yet on that front? Getting a
cook, I mean."

"Actually, Pop is considering Nellie Pruitt.
They've talked and he likes her no-nonsense
attitude. He thinks she could keep the cowhands in line. There's a mother-in-law suite
in the house that we can close off to give her
a private apartment."

A smile played across Kelly's mouth. "I
didn't know you were considering Nellie."

"I got her number from the phone book
and gave it to Pop. You may have been teasing when you mentioned her, but I decided
it could work."

"The high school will be unhappy with me
if they have to hire a new head dietitian. Nellie can be crusty, but she's an excellent cook
and nowhere near retirement age."

"I won't tell."

Josh cupped Kelly's face and stroked the

soft skin of her cheeks. Should he confess that he still dreamed about her sometimes? Dreamed about the laughter they'd shared and the brilliance of her eyes and smile. He'd never quite succeeded in getting her out of his head. Now he wondered if the same was true of his heart.

He bent closer for a kiss, only to have her back away.

"We can't, Josh. It will just confuse things, especially the boys if they see us. They could start expecting something that isn't going to happen."

Knowing she was right didn't help.

It had been much easier when he was still furious with her for keeping Casey and Marc a secret.

"HI, JILL," BETSY said as she breezed into the Shelton Veterinary Clinic on Friday morning. With the rodeo over and the crowds dissipated, she'd returned to walking almost everywhere, including her visits to see Rosco. She and Jill Shavers, Grant's office manager, were fast becoming friends, and Chuck, the vet technician, was teaching her how various lab tests were run.

"Hey, Betsy," Jill replied.

"Has anybody called or emailed about Rosco?"

"No, nothing. We're also monitoring various online lost-pet sites and have contacted other vets in the county. Nobody has posted anything."

Betsy felt a secret relief, knowing she should want a loving owner to come forward with a believable explanation about how Rosco came to be skinny, tired and lost. Still, she was certain Grant hoped to give him a home. He'd even mentioned how hard it was for black cats and dogs to find adopters, but Rosco wouldn't have to worry about that. Like her, he had fallen instantly in love with the stray.

They'd returned to the clinic after the carnival to give the Labrador a bath. Rosco had wriggled with pleasure, enjoying the warm water and gentle sponging. Betsy had laughed and said he was practically purring.

"Cats purr, not dogs," she was informed.

Betsy had just laughed again and lifted an eyebrow at Grant. "Are you always so literal?"

"I... Well, pretty much," he'd admitted. "Don't forget, I was raised by military parents. Creativity wasn't a priority to them."

Thinking back on the conversation, Betsy

felt sorry for Grant. Her father had nurtured her imagination, along with a love for nature and history and people. "The world is an ever-expanding painting," he'd declared. "Isn't that wonderful? We can explore it all and add our own bits to the picture."

The clinic door opened, pulling Betsy away from her memories. She turned and saw Grant carrying a large flat box of flowering plants. "Hi. What are those?"

He looked embarrassed as his gaze fell to the plants. "Well, at some point you mentioned the empty flower beds made the clinic seem uninviting. I don't have another appointment until later this afternoon, so I decided to do something about it. I have more in the truck."

"That's great," Jill said. "Nobody has touched those beds since Dr. Pierson's daughter and her husband moved to Great Falls. She has an amazing green thumb. The Shelton Garden Club practically fell apart when she left. Well, not really, but it was a shock for them."

Betsy instantly thought what an adventure it would be to dig up the ground and fill it with plants…and to watch the flowers grow and bloom. Except she couldn't think about the last part. It wasn't that she was totally opposed to staying in Shelton, but Grant hadn't offered an invitation, either. Just because he'd made his feelings clear about her travels, it didn't mean he had a personal interest in seeing her remain in one place.

She didn't know what to do.

The road still beckoned, along with all the places she had yet to see. At the same time her heart kept reminding her that adventure could be something besides new places and people.

She had considered Grant's idea that she was just following her father's dream. That might be partly why it had started, but mostly it was knowing that life was short and she didn't want to miss out on anything.

"I'll help with the flowers," she said casually, "but I need to say hi to Rosco first."

She headed to the rear of the clinic, where Rosco yipped the moment he saw her. He rose on his hind feet and put his enormous front paws on the door of the kennel. He still had a ways to go before growing into those paws.

"Hello, baby," she said, rubbing under his jaw and around his silky ears. In just a few days he'd put on weight and the sad, hopeless look in his eyes had been replaced by the perky curiosity of a healthy young dog. It would be awful leaving him when she had to move on.

"He loves seeing you," Grant murmured from behind her.

"The feeling is mutual. But in case you're wondering, I haven't changed my mind about adopting a dog for my travels, so assuming nobody responsible claims him, he's all yours."

"I see."

Betsy wondered. Grant had declared he was old-fashioned, but she was discovering she was old-fashioned about some things herself, and one of those things was wanting a hint from a man that he was interested in her as a woman. A kiss on a Ferris wheel didn't mean anything, particularly when she was the one who'd invited the kiss.

She didn't know the answer. Loving someone and building a life with them wasn't necessarily exclusive to seeing the world… provided that someone was willing to travel part of the time.

But that someone wasn't Grant.

According to Jill, he hadn't left the Shelton

County limits since taking over Dr. Pierson's veterinary practice six years ago.

"ARE YOU SERIOUS about working on the flower beds?" Grant asked. "The garden center at the feed-and-seed store said it could be a huge effort getting them into shape for planting."

"I wouldn't have offered if I wasn't serious."

The eager sparkle in Betsy's eyes was a constant amazement to him. She enjoyed life, whether it was painting a fence, getting on a carnival ride or digging up sorry flower beds that hadn't been touched in years.

"Yeah, dumb question. There's gardening stuff in the storage area around back. The store loaded me up with organic fertilizer and other supplies, so we should have everything we need."

He shouldn't have asked if she was serious. The time Betsy had put into the rodeo preparations had demonstrated how hard she was willing to work. The owner of the Hot Diggity Dog Café thought the world of her, along with the folks on the rodeo committee. She fit into Shelton, or maybe it was more accurate to say that she'd made Shelton fit her.

Betsy was uniquely herself and folks liked her that way.

"When does your magazine article about the rodeo come out?" he asked as they headed around the building.

"Next week. I asked a kid from the high school to take pictures at the rodeo—the one who took those photos of Josh McKeon. My little camera is handy, but Abigail wanted quality action shots with high resolution."

"Abigail?"

"The owner and editor of the *A.C. Globetrotter*. Anyhow, she's putting one of Dennis Ward's pictures on the cover. Or what passes for a cover on an online magazine."

Grant unlocked the storage compartment. "That means you have the lead article, right?"

"I suppose." Betsy didn't sound particularly interested, which fit. She wasn't ambitious in the way most people thought about ambition. "Oh, good, there are two shovels."

The storage area was filled with gardening implements. He'd inspected the building when buying the clinic, but had paid little attention to the contents of this particular compartment. If anything, he would have expected Dr. Pierson to take the gardening tools with him, but he hadn't. Randall and his wife were nice people. They'd even invited him to stay in their spare room while he was looking for a house to buy.

Out of loneliness?

Possibly. Their only child lived two hours away and they didn't have grandkids. But Grant enjoyed the occasional Sunday lunch with them and often benefited from Randall's advice. They were considering a move to Great Falls to be near their daughter and he'd regret seeing them go.

"Any preference?" Betsy asked, pulling out the shovels.

Grant grinned and took one. "They look identical to me."

"It's a good thing the ground isn't totally dry," Betsy said as she turned up the first shovelful of dirt. "Though I don't remember it raining for a while."

Grant nodded. "It hasn't, but when I mentioned my plan to Dr. Pierson, he suggested flooding the beds. I pulled the weed mat out, along with the decorative bark, and ran water a few days ago so it would soak in, but not leave things too muddy."

"Good thinking. I noticed the bark was gone, but if anything, I figured you were going to plant grass for your doggy patients."

Betsy dug her shovel in again. "You know, I'm a novice when it comes to gardening, but this dirt seems sandier than the stuff at the rodeo grounds. Does that sound crazy?"

"No, they sold me bags of sand at the garden center, saying it helps soil drainage. But maybe we don't need it. Since Dr. Pierson's daughter took care of these beds, she probably added sand a long time ago."

"Yeah."

They worked in comfortable silence until Jill came out to say Fritz Peters had a horse with an injured flank. Though he'd put compression on it, the cut was still bleeding and likely needed stitches.

With an apology, Grant hurried to his truck. Fritz might overreact where his prize bull was concerned, but not with his horses or other cattle.

When Grant returned a few hours later, the flower beds were neatly spaded and he found Jill and Betsy inside, chatting.

"Is everything okay with Mr. Peters's horse?" Betsy asked.

"It took a fair amount of stitching, but luckily there wasn't any deep damage. I feel guilty about leaving you here. You shouldn't have kept working."

She lifted an eyebrow. "Why should you feel guilty? Anyhow, it's my day off. I mixed all the mulch and fertilizer stuff into the ground according to the instructions on the bags, but didn't want to plant anything without you. That's probably the best part."

Grant didn't know if he appreciated her consideration. Spending time with Betsy was too enjoyable. Everything was fun with her, whether it was pounding dirt into holes or giving Rosco a bath. Considering the way water had splashed her T-shirt during the bath, making it semitransparent, he'd also had difficulty restraining the desire to kiss her again. It wasn't just that she was physically beautiful; she had an inherent optimism that was utterly addictive.

"I usually have tea with Mrs. Mapleton in the afternoon," she said, glancing at the office clock. "Why don't you come with me? She can give us gardening tips."

"I wouldn't want to impose."

"She's told me to invite anyone I want. But it's okay if you're too busy."

He didn't say anything for a moment, then nodded. "I have time. My next patient won't be here until four. Besides, Rosco could use a walk. I've been taking him home at night and my cats love bossing him around, but we'll tie him outside since Bootsy, Miss Priss and Spurs might not feel the same way."

"Then you can both do the planting after your last appointment," Jill said cheerfully. She had a merry expression in her eyes that Grant tried to ignore.

After all, matchmaking was a popular indoor sport in Shelton and he'd rather not encourage it—especially when the woman in question might leave at any moment.

CHAPTER THIRTEEN

OVER THE NEXT week Josh spent a few hours each morning with one of the twins, riding or doing other work, while Kelly stayed with the other. In the afternoon, they switched places.

Since Gizmo refused to go anywhere without Kelly, Lark went with Josh. It was hard on the Australian shepherd. Casey and Marc were her "herd," so she was torn whenever they were separated.

"You'll get to know the boys better if you have one-on-one time," Kelly had explained. "Especially Casey. He talks more when his brother isn't around."

Some of the tired tension had eased from her face, but Josh knew she was still working too hard and losing sleep.

Over him?

He didn't like to think so, but he was realistic. Trust took time to build. His own doubts had eased, largely from seeing Kelly's devotion to the twins. She'd had good reasons not to tell him about her pregnancy, and in the six years since their birth, she had simply been protecting Casey and Marc in the way she'd felt best. Maybe it hadn't been ideal, but life didn't always have neat, easy choices.

"Josh, is it okay if I call you Dad?" Casey asked as they rode toward the north herd one afternoon.

"Sure," he agreed, elated.

It was the first time either of the boys had brought up what to call him. If anything, he would have expected the question to come from Marc first, but it made sense that Casey would ask since he'd had more time to think about it.

"That would be great," Josh added. "I call my own father Pop, so maybe you could call him Grandpop. I'll show you his picture when we get back. We can call him, too, if you'd like."

"Sure. Can I tell my friends about you?"

Josh hesitated. "I don't mind, but let's talk to your mom first."

"I already asked. She says it's okay with her if it's okay with you."

Josh could imagine the storm of gossip that would ensue once the news got out. But there wasn't a good way to tell people something like this. They were long past putting a birth notice in the local paper, though he had a brief longing to see exactly that.

How were those things worded, anyhow?

Kelly Beaumont and Josh McKeon announce they're the proud parents of twin sons named Casey and...

He stopped and told himself not to be ridiculous.

Then another thought struck him; in all of their discussions about the boys, Kelly had never said anything about saving face in front of Shelton. The Flannigans were highly respected, and even in today's more accepting climate, it must have caused a stir when she gave birth to the twins with no father in sight. Yet she'd deferred the decision of telling people to him.

He and Casey guided their horses up the narrow path to the north end of the ranch. As they threaded the gap in the rocks, they could see the herd spread out across the valley.

A hawk suddenly took flight from a nearby rock, causing Quicksilver to rear; he was more accustomed to loudspeakers and milling crowds than large birds exploding at his feet. As Josh brought the stallion down, his attention remained riveted on Casey. What if Ringo threw his rider or took off in a frenzy?

Casey and his horse, however, were calmly watching the hawk soar in a circle, then rise skyward on a warm current of air.

Josh puffed out a relieved breath.

For the hundredth time he recalled Kelly's comment about parenting being scary and hard work. He was getting a crash course on the subject, but she was helping and had reassured him that he'd eventually find a balance. He hoped so; otherwise he'd died of heart failure inside of six months.

"Mom says all the cows in our herds have had their calves," Casey said matter-of-factly. "Two in this herd were born really late, so they'll have trouble growing up enough in time for winter."

"I see." It was an issue they faced on McKeon's Choice as well, though they tried to breed their cows for an early delivery. A calf normally put on a hundred pounds a month, weight they needed to get through the winter months. Late calves had less time to gain needed pounds.

"Mom hates losing late calves," Casey continued, "so she puts them in a special pasture where they can go into a barn when it's extra cold. Grandpa Liam laughs about it, but she even has heaters in the barn when it's really bad. We lose less cows than any other ranch in Shelton County."

Warmth went through Josh. Kelly had a temper and was as stubborn as a badger, but everything about her charmed him these days, even her faults. Two nights ago they'd had a rollicking row when she discovered that he'd paid off the mortgage on the foaling barn.

"The bank had no right to accept that money from you," she'd declared furiously.

"Banks generally take money from anyone willing to give it to them. But don't worry. I made the payment through a holding company, so nobody knows it was from me."

"That isn't the point."

"I don't care about the point. I expect to help financially. That isn't negotiable."

"I'm totally capable of supporting Casey and Marc."

Josh had crossed his arms over his chest, more amused by her obstinate vehemence than angry himself. "That isn't the point, either. I'm not impugning your ability to take care of Casey and Marc. I'm just doing my part."

"You—"

She'd stopped, glared and stalked away. He would have preferred her to stay and discuss why she was so stubbornly independent...not that it needed discussing. Kelly had grown up with parents who were nice people but who lacked reliability. Liam and Susannah would have looked after her when she was at the ranch, but when traveling with her parents, she'd been forced to take care of herself. And she'd had over six years to worry about proving she was a fit mother in case of a custody battle.

At least she was talking to him more. Opening up and letting him see the complex woman he should have seen when they were dating.

"Your mom is a good rancher," he told Casey.

"Mom is *super*," Casey returned staunchly. "She knows all about horses and other important stuff. She just doesn't like rodeos much. Is that why she didn't tell you about us?"

Josh sighed. "It's complicated." Even as the words left his mouth, he groaned. Growing up, he'd hated people telling him that something was too complicated for him to understand.

"Everybody says that when they don't want to talk about something." Casey sounded disgusted.

"It's just that I don't know how to explain. Your mom and I loved each other, but I was ambitious. I thought about winning most of the time and I didn't see how much that was hurting her."

Casey cocked his head. "What d'ya mean?"

"When you love someone, they need to know how important they are to you," Josh said. "And they can't know, unless you tell them. I'm bad at that because I get busy and focused on what I'm doing. Then I don't take care of things that are more important. Earning enough money to buy a ranch wasn't a bad goal, but I made your mom feel as if she was less important than winning and being a big star."

"Was she?"

Josh sighed again. He'd quickly discovered that Casey didn't accept half explanations.

"I don't know," Josh told him honestly. "Not now, but back then I was really bigheaded and figured everything should go my way."

Casey giggled. "Bigheaded?"

"That's another way of saying I was full of myself. Which means I was conceited," Josh admitted. "Do you know what that is?"

"I guess."

"Anyhow, I let something happen that made your mom angry and I didn't try hard enough to fix it. Then by the time she knew she was pregnant, I was married to someone else."

Casey's eyes widened. "You're married?"

"Not any longer. It was a mistake. Not as huge a mistake as letting your mother go, but a big one. The basic truth is, when people don't know how much we care, we risk losing them."

Casey's chin went up. "Marc says you'd think I'm a baby for hugging Mom, but I told him that I didn't care if you did. I was gonna hug her anyhow."

Josh's heart thudded with emotion. He gripped the reins with one hand and leaned over to give Casey's shoulders a quick, hard hug. "Everyone has to choose their own way of showing love, but I like hugging, too."

His son's face scrunched up. "Does that mean you love us?"

"It means I love you and Marc, very, *very* much, and you're much more important to me than rodeos or winning."

"Does Mom know that?"

"I hope she does," Josh said carefully. "But whatever happens between your mom and me, it won't change how I feel about you and Marc."

Josh hoped his explanation would be enough. He'd fallen in love with Kelly again, but what happened next wasn't just up to him. Even if she felt the same, she might not be willing to take the chance of history repeating itself.

He couldn't blame her. Right now he was still formulating ideas for the future and hoping he could convince her that even if his priorities had been screwed up seven years ago, they were on target now.

A big idea had occurred to him while watching Harry lead his children's rodeo workshop. Namely, to buy his own ranch in the Shelton area and start a training facility for rodeo contestants.

But no matter what, he needed to be near Kelly and his sons. If she didn't accept his first proposal, maybe she'd finally accept if he stayed around and kept asking.

A WEEK AFTER Betsy had first helped with the veterinary clinic flower beds, she drove over to the feed-and-seed store to get more plants. It was her third trip. Shelton was a small town, so businesses had multiple functions, and she was fascinated by the farm store's variety.

They didn't sell just animal food and farm seed. They also sold tractors, yard equipment, animals, trees, water troughs and a bunch of other stuff. Some of it needed to be special-ordered because it wasn't practical to keep everything on hand, but there was still a huge amount in stock.

According to Jill, the farm store's prices were competitive, but the cost of a tractor had still made Betsy's eyes pop. It wasn't any wonder that she'd seen ancient tractors still being used, not just around Shelton, but through her various travels.

"Hi, Betsy," called the warehouse manager as she got out of the van.

"Hey, Mack."

"We have a new batch of baby rabbits if you're interested," he said, grinning. He'd been patient with her questions about warehouse operations and knew how much she loved visiting the animals. Particularly the babies. She didn't think it meant anything special; she'd always loved them. Well, animals of any age. They were so basic and honest about their responses and needs. Anyway, she wasn't old enough for the ticking from her biological clock to be keeping her up at night.

"Of course I'm interested," she told Mack.

Betsy went to the rabbit hutches near the warehouse doors and cooed over the tiny babies. The amiable warehouse cat lay on top of the hutch, watching them as well with a benevolent expression on his whiskered face. He wasn't being predatory, just protective; his job was to catch the pesky rodents that got into the building. Apparently when chicks occasionally escaped, usually assisted by a curious toddler, he even helped round them up like a harried uncle whose charges were being uncooperative.

She petted the ginger tomcat and his purr rumbled out.

"You're spoiling that animal," Mack said.

"As if I haven't seen him riding around on your shoulders," Betsy teased. "Or don't know you keep a bag of treats in your pocket for him."

"Guilty as charged." He looked past her at an arriving vehicle. "Say, Dr. Latham just got here. I wonder what he needs. As if I didn't know." Mack grinned.

Betsy's breath quickened. Everyone seemed to think something was going on between her and Grant, but he'd been annoyingly proper since their kiss on the Ferris wheel. True, he'd taken her with him on an emergency veterinary visit on Saturday, but that didn't mean anything. They'd been working on the flower beds together when the call came in and she had asked if she could go along. The chance to see a working ranch had been irresistible.

It wasn't totally picturesque, at least not in the way movies often portrayed ranches, but better because of that. The Wards had a huge spread and she'd already met some of the family while helping with the rodeo preparations. The quiet strength and self-assurance of ranchers intrigued her. It was as if the world could get knocked on its ear one night and they'd go on riding fences and checking cattle the next morning.

"Good morning, Grant," she called.

"Don't tell me—you're here to get more flowers," he guessed.

"And learning how a feed-and-seed farm store operates."

IT WAS NO surprise to Grant. When Betsy threw herself into something, she did it wholeheartedly, like helping with the rodeo and taking care of her customers at the café. He just didn't know how she had the energy to be interested in so many different things.

"That's why I'm here, too," he explained. "The garden center claims we're planting everything too close together, but I think it would be nice for you to see the beds looking good before you leave."

"Are you trying to scoot me past the town limits?"

Grant kicked himself. He didn't want to push Betsy away, but for some reason he kept referring to her departure. Admittedly, he was also looking for signs that she was restless. She'd said she didn't stay anywhere for more than a few weeks, and she had been in Shelton for well over two months.

"Not at all. It would be great if you stay," he said. "In fact, the Shelton City Council may even give you the keys to the city."

She laughed. "Just for staying? Shelton can't be *that* desperate for new citizens."

"Of course not. But at the chamber of commerce meeting they mentioned getting inquiries because of your article in the *A.C.*

Globetrotter. More tourists have been coming to town—the motel has been booked continuously and the permanent campgrounds are full. Also, a filmmaker from Hollywood wants to make a rodeo-based movie here because of the article. That's why they haven't called for volunteers to take the grandstand and other stuff down again."

"I heard about that," Mack exclaimed. "Some of us might get to play extras. Nice going, Betsy."

"Oh. That's nice. About the movie and having more tourists, I mean." She didn't seem interested in the praise. Her travel articles were published under the byline *B. A. Hartner,* and her reluctance to talk about them suggested she didn't want name recognition.

"I'd better get to work," Mack said, winking at Grant.

"I just remembered that I've never asked what the *A* in B. A. Hartner stands for," Grant said when they were alone.

"That's a state secret."

"If you're going to be that way about it, I won't tell you my middle name."

"I already know. It's Douglas," Betsy returned promptly. "I saw it on your veterinary certificate in the waiting room."

"Oh, right."

He looked at her laughing face and the final defenses in his heart crumbled. She was the most amazing woman he'd ever met. But would she consider sharing his life? While she was enjoying Shelton now, there was no telling how long that would last.

There had to be a way they could work out being together. Maybe he could start making changes that would give him more time to travel with her, and go from there.

Because the alternative was too awful to contemplate.

JOSH HAD SPENT the past eight days laying the groundwork for his rodeo training facility, though he still hadn't mentioned it to Harry. There were consultations back and forth with lawyers, and he made a number of calls to the Western clothing company that had asked him to represent their clothing line. For just a few days of work a year, he'd earn a hefty income. He set up a meeting with their representatives down in Dallas, where they expected to immediately shoot the first series of commercials and magazine advertisements.

When he was finally ready to take the first step locally—approaching Mrs. Gillespie about purchasing the Galloping G—he told Marc that he had an appointment and they wouldn't be able to go riding together the next morning.

Marc stuck his lip out. "Why not?"

"Because I have things to take care of. Adult things. Maybe all of us can take a ride tomorrow afternoon."

"What kind of adult things?"

"Marc, that's none of your business," Kelly interjected. "Josh doesn't have to explain himself to you."

Marc's pout grew even more pronounced. "Ooookaaay," he said in a long, drawn-out way that announced he wasn't the least bit okay with it. He stomped out of the barn.

"Don't worry. He's just—" Kelly started to say, only to be interrupted by Harry.

"Josh, the boys need to be able to count on you," Harry scolded.

Frustration rose in Josh. He didn't intend to take parenting advice from a man who knew nothing about the subject. "Let me be clear, Harry. I'm not the one who's let them down. You practically bankrupted *two* ranches to keep competing, and most of the time you left your daughter to be raised by her grandparents instead of raising her yourself. Even when Kelly was with you on the road, you paid little attention to her or what she needed."

"You don't und—"

"I don't want to hear it," Josh said sternly. "You've been a good friend to me and hundreds of rodeo cowboys, but Kelly is the only one who has the right to make comments about my relationship with the boys. For that matter, have you even noticed how hard she's had to work at getting Kindred Ranch back on solid financial ground after all the support you accepted from the Flannigans?"

Looking shaken, Harry turned to his daughter. "Was it really that bad?" he appealed. "I tried not to ask Liam and Susannah for too much, and I was always going to pay it back when I started winning more often."

Kelly's expression was strained. "Harry, you can't continually take more out of a ranch than it earns. The reserves Grams and Granddad had saved were gone by the time I was eighteen. After that, they started going into debt. I wish I could put it more gently, but that's the truth."

Harry's face went haggard. "I didn't realize. That's why you said you couldn't give me more money to compete. You told me it was to protect the boys, but I thought it was mostly because you didn't approve."

"I had to cut it off," Kelly said gently. "Otherwise we risked losing everything. We're doing better now, but it's a slow process. I'm delaying most of the improvements until we have some reserve again."

He straightened and put his shoulders back. "Then I guess it's time to stop being proud and explain something. Taylor Fulton sent the first scheduled payment for the Bucking B this month and I've signed it over to Liam and Susannah. The down payment went to pay off the Bucking B mortgage I took out a few years ago. I couldn't have sold the ranch otherwise."

"Oh, Dad..." Kelly went over and hugged her father.

Josh's chest tightened and he marveled at how forgiving she was to Harry. She might have some lingering resentment about her childhood, but she wasn't living in the past.

She saw Harry for what he was, a good, if flawed, man, and loved all of him.

It gave Josh hope that she could look past his own less-than-stellar qualities and see value in him, as well.

He cleared his throat. "I'll go talk to Marc."

Kelly turned, her remarkable eyes moist with emotion. "Don't worry. He'll sulk for a while, but he'll get over it. They can't expect all of your time, any more than I can give them every minute. It's healthy for children to understand that their parents have lives, too."

Josh thought about it all evening. The twins and the rest of her family were Kelly's unquestioned priority, but she also had to take care of Kindred Ranch. If she didn't, they'd lose their home and livelihood. So even if the ranch wasn't as important as the family, it had its proper place in her concerns.

What Kelly hadn't done was take good care of herself. He intended to change that.

THE NEXT MORNING at the Galloping G, Josh knocked on the door and smiled at the silver-haired woman who answered. "Hello, ma'am. My name is Josh McKeon."

"I recognize you from all the rodeo publicity. Please come in. I'm Dorothy Gillespie."

The ranch house was newer than the Flannigan home, though not as large, and it was decorated in a simple theme of Native American art and pottery.

"Please sit down," Mrs. Gillespie said, gesturing to the wood-framed couch.

Josh sat, but immediately leaned forward. "Ma'am, thank you for agreeing to meet with me. I don't know if you've heard, but I'm Casey and Marc Beaumont's father," he announced, coming right to the point.

Her gray eyes widened. "No, I hadn't heard. That's…" Her voice trailed. Clearly she wasn't sure how to react and Josh suspected it would be a common issue until people got used to the idea.

"I didn't know about the boys until a few weeks ago," he explained. "My relationship with Kelly was a mess when we broke up, and she didn't know how to tell me she was pregnant. But the boys are telling their friends about me, so the news will get around fast."

"Well…yes. Well." Mrs. Gillespie folded her hands on her lap. "It must have been a shock to discover you had two sons."

"We've sorted it out," Josh said, reluctant to get into more personal details. He wouldn't have said anything about the boys, but he didn't think Mrs. Gillespie would sell the Galloping G to him if she believed he'd been an absentee father. "As a matter of fact, I'm more in love with Kelly than ever. She and the boys are the most important thing in the world to me. I haven't told her how I feel, but I hope to propose soon," he added hastily.

The rigidity in Dorothy Gillespie's face eased. "I think of Kelly as another daughter. She rides over every week to check on me, even though her ranch hands live in our bunkhouse and I see them at meals."

"She mentioned your children have careers that have taken them away from Shelton."

Dorothy laughed, a small, silvery laugh that matched her hair. "How tactful. Yes, my children, while dear to my heart, simply don't care for country living. I don't blame them. They have terrible allergies, one to bees, another to pollens, and the third can't touch a horse without breaking into hives."

"That's unfortunate."

"They're happy, which is what counts. After their father died they wanted me to sell the Galloping G, but my arrangement to have the Kindred Ranch employees live in our bunkhouse has reassured them."

Josh leaned forward. "That's, uh, sort of what I came to talk to you about."

"Oh?"

"I understand you hope to sell the Galloping G to Kelly one day, with the condition that you can continue residing on the ranch. Is there any way you'd consider me as a buyer? With the same terms, of course."

Josh had done his research on the property. Even if it hadn't been adjacent to Kindred Ranch, it would be a smart buy—with more than adequate water and mineral rights, located near the highway, and no unreasonable use restrictions. It was also a ranch with a long history of unbroken ownership by a family respected in the community. He'd ridden over every inch of it the past few weeks, so it also seemed unlikely that an environmental assessment would uncover a private dump, uncontrolled noxious weeds or hidden fuel tanks.

Mrs. Gillespie stroked the black-and-white cat who had leaped onto her lap, giving the feline her full attention. Josh suspected it was a delaying tactic while she digested his proposition.

"I would prefer selling to Kelly, but I'm realistic. What would you do with the Galloping G?" she asked finally. "And I'm not talking about the name. Changing that would be fine. Dustin didn't care for it himself, but the Galloping G was his great-great-grandfather's choice and one tends not to change that sort of thing."

"It would remain a working ranch, but I also want to start a training facility for rodeo contestants," Josh explained. "It doesn't matter if there isn't much money in the idea. My primary focus would be breeding horses."

"And a rodeo training facility could give Harry Beaumont a purpose," Mrs. Gillespie said shrewdly. "One that might keep him at home if he has the sense that God even gave a chicken."

"I hope Harry will be a part of it," Josh admitted, hoping the conversation wouldn't go beyond the confines of the living room. Harry might have begun seeing the light about his professional rodeo career, but he was a proud man. "Kelly's father was a great help when I started out as a rodeo cowboy. He has a wealth of expertise to share."

Mrs. Gillespie watched him for a long moment and Josh had the feeling that little escaped her notice. "Would you continue competing in rodeos yourself?" she asked at length.

His smile grew. "No, ma'am. I expect to be raising children, horses and cattle for the rest of my life. With Kelly. That'll be more than enough to keep me happy and busy. I just hope she loves me as much as I love her."

"There's only one way to find out."

"I know, but I want to put certain things into motion before I ask her to take a chance on me."

"I think we can make a deal," Mrs. Gillespie said slowly. "Dustin and I supported Kelly's organic efforts on Kindred Ranch, so you should know that we've been certified, as well. I'll show you the documentation."

"That's great to hear."

Josh had given little thought to the organic movement over the years, aside from thinking it made sense. But once he'd seen Kelly's research and spreadsheets, he'd become a firm believer; he'd already asked his father to look into what was needed to get McKeon's Choice certified.

Pop wasn't thrilled by the prospect. He was going along because it was something his son wanted, but Josh hoped that once Pop and

Kelly met, she'd do her magic and his father would see the benefits.

Josh reviewed the material from Mrs. Gillespie and mentally bumped the ranch's value in his mind. This *wasn't* the time for sharp real-estate dealings, and having the ranch already certified was a plus. Mostly he needed to get a good enough deal that Shelton didn't see him as a fool, and pay a fair enough amount that nobody believed he'd taken advantage.

Luckily they'd both researched property values around Shelton and Mrs. Gillespie seemed well aware of the Galloping G's monetary worth. They quickly came to a mutually agreeable figure, and he promised to have paperwork sent from the real-estate broker he'd consulted in Helena. He would have gone local, but in a small town, keeping something like this confidential could be next to impossible.

"You won't, er, tell anyone about this, or what we've discussed, right?" Josh asked as he was leaving. "I hope to make an announcement within the next few weeks."

"Of course, but expect to do it no later than when the land transfer is recorded," Mrs. Gillespie said. "Ranches don't change ownership in Shelton County very often. It will be big news."

"I understand."

Josh headed back to Kindred Ranch, satisfaction zinging through him. Running a rodeo training facility wasn't an ideal solution—it would still expose the twins to the rodeo world—but nothing could work between him and Kelly if they weren't both willing to compromise. Besides, wasn't this the best way to teach Casey and Marc the balance she wanted for them?

He wanted it, too.

Life as a professional rodeo cowboy could be good, but it needed perspective. Plenty of his fellow contestants had that perspective; it was the ones who didn't who got into trouble.

For the first time in a long while, Josh was excited about the future. Something had been missing in his life, and now he knew what it was.

Winning at rodeos and bull-riding events was great, but they were short-term goals. Keeping up with a woman like Kelly Beaumont and raising their children was worthy of a lifetime challenge.

CHAPTER FOURTEEN

BETSY HURRIED INTO work at 5:00 a.m. on Monday and was surprised to see a new employee standing in front of the cash register.

"Hi, I'm Jacki," the woman said. The newcomer wore a Hot Diggity Dog apron with an order pad in its pocket, which was puzzling. Leonard didn't need another waitress. Or cook. Or any other employee, as far as Betsy knew.

"Good morning, I'm Betsy Hartner. You worked here before, didn't you?" she asked.

"That's right. I quit when I got married, but my husband and I are having trouble making our house payments. Our moms are going to take turns watching the baby."

Betsy tried to catch Leonard's eye, but he was resolutely focused on cooking. The morning went slowly. With less to do, it was always slow.

It wasn't until Didi came in for the afternoon shift that Betsy got the full scoop in whispered asides. Leonard *didn't* need anyone, but he hadn't been able to turn Jacki down when she'd asked for her old job back.

Since Betsy had told Leonard that her stay in Shelton was temporary, she kept expecting him to explain that her services were no longer needed. Jacki had been born in the area and had started working at the café in high school, and it was where she'd met her husband. It was natural that he'd want to keep her over someone who'd told him she was just passing through.

Betsy stewed about it that evening and the next day, knowing she should make it easier on Leonard by just quitting. Normally she was okay about leaving a place, no matter how much she liked it. Shelton was different, though.

Nonetheless, she couldn't remain.

Having Leonard hire Jacki was the same as a sign on the wall; it was time to move on.

At a quiet moment, Betsy went up to the order window and waited to get Leonard's full attention. "Hey, boss, I've loved working here, but you obviously don't need me any longer."

Leonard stuck his jaw out. "Nonsense. You can help in the kitchen when we aren't busy."

He'd shown her how to operate his giant commercial dough mixer and she had learned how to make both cinnamon rolls and loaves of bread. The rolls were hugely popular in town and he did a brisk side business selling them to customers for home consumption. But that didn't mean he needed her any longer. Leonard had a night baker, along with enough cooks to cover the evening and morning shifts when he had days off. Restaurants were a margin business; you didn't hire more staff than was required.

"You don't need me," she repeated. "I'll finish my shift, but this will be my last day."

"You belong in Shelton. What will Dr. Latham do if you aren't here? We all know how much time you spend at the vet clinic and other places with him."

Betsy's determined smile wobbled. Grant wasn't the only reason she liked Shelton, but he was the most important one. "Dr. Latham will be fine. I've mostly been at the clinic when he's out on calls. He won't care if I'm gone."

"You know that isn't true."

She wasn't so certain. If Grant had feelings for her, he'd carefully kept them to him-

344   TWINS FOR THE RODEO STAR

self. And it hadn't been that long since he was hankering after Kelly Beaumont.

"Nobody wants you to leave," Leonard said.

Betsy gulped. "Thanks, but it's time to start my next adventure. Please don't tell anyone until I'm gone. It's easier that way."

He didn't look happy, but she was firm and finished her shift. It was hard to keep smiling, particularly when she thought about Grant and Mrs. Mapleton. Well, also Jill, Leonard, the Retired Cowboys Coffee Club...and a whole bunch of other people. She would go by the clinic and say a private farewell to Rosco, but nobody else. Goodbyes just made leaving harder.

Then tonight, when nobody could see her, she'd probably indulge in a few tears.

Really, she ought to have left before her heart started telling her to stay.

WHEN GRANT WENT into the Hot Diggity Dog Café for breakfast on Wednesday, he was confused to see one of Leonard's former waitresses, instead of Betsy. He also noticed that the elderly cowboys who hung out at the café were sitting in their corner with uncommonly glum expressions.

"Are you okay?" Grant asked Lonny.

"Coffee just don't taste right this morning," Lonny muttered as he pushed his cup aside.

Since Lonny was one of those cordial people who didn't complain, Grant was worried that something big might be wrong.

He went to a table by the window and waited while Jacki poured him a cup of coffee.

"Is something up? I hope Betsy isn't sick," Grant said casually. "She didn't mention that her shift was changing."

Jacki looked miserable. "Betsy isn't sick and her shift didn't change. She quit on Monday. I think it's because I asked Leonard for my old job back. He won't say so, but I'm sure that's why she left. I feel awful about it."

Alarm replaced Grant's hunger.

He knew that Betsy hated goodbyes. She could be hundreds of miles away by now. How would he find her? The highway patrol didn't put out an all-points bulletin as part of a lonely hearts service.

"I just realized I'm not hungry after all," Grant said as he got up and threw money on the table.

"Do you want some coffee to go?" Jacki asked.

"Uh, thanks, but no," he muttered and rushed to his truck.

He'd been looking for the right moment to ask Betsy to marry him and his delay may have blown everything. How ironic that a footloose wanderer had shown him that there was more to making Shelton a home than planting himself and refusing to leave. Being with Betsy was all the home he needed. Everything else was just window dressing.

Grant sped to Maya Mapleton's house, his alarm escalating when he didn't see Betsy's van. He ran up the steps and was relieved to find her sitting on the porch, though the screen door was propped open with a backpack and duffel bag. Plainly she was getting ready to go.

"Thank heaven you're here," Mrs. Mapleton blurted out. "I've run out of excuses to keep her from leaving. I need reinforcements."

Betsy set her cup down. "Shame on you, Mrs. Mapleton."

"You want to stay. You just don't know it yet," her landlady returned stubbornly, though a light blush brightened her cheeks.

"She's right. You can't leave," Grant said. "It's what I do. Remember?"

He crossed his arms over his chest. "Then you can't leave without me. I'm in love with you, and if you won't stay, then we're going together. We just have to pick up Rosco and the cats first."

It was a rash declaration, but he was beyond caring. Places didn't matter, people did, and nobody meant more than Betsy. Once they were on the road he could look up what was needed to start a mobile veterinary clinic or something of the kind.

"That isn't what I want," Maya exclaimed in dismay. "Who will drink tea with me? Who will take care of Miss Priss, Bootsy and Spurs when they get sick? Neither one of you can go."

BETSY LOOKED FROM GRANT, to Mrs. Mapleton and back to Grant again. She was thoroughly enchanted by his admission. She got up from her chair and kissed him soundly.

"Do you hear that?" she asked. "I guess we have to stay. What kind of proper veterinarian would abandon Miss Priss, Bootsy and Spurs?" she murmured against his lips.

Behind them, Mrs. Mapleton sighed her relief.

"Just for the pampered pusses?"

Betsy tipped her head back and regarded Grant's face. He was the dearest man in the world and she adored him completely.

"Also because I love you. I guess you're my next big adventure. But not if you still have feelings for Kelly Beaumont," she said firmly. "I expect to be the *only* woman in your life. Unless we have a daughter or two. Then it's all right."

Grant chuckled. "That's coming right to the point."

"I don't believe in pussyfooting around."

"Your candor is just one of the million things I love about you." He looked into her eyes, sincerity blazing in his face. "Honestly, I mistook friendship for romance with Kelly. On the other hand, *you* drive me to distraction. I'm certifiably over the moon about you, now and forever."

"That's nice."

They kissed a second time and tingles went through Betsy from head to toe and back again. She wouldn't be cold this winter, not with Grant Latham to snuggle up to under the blankets. Of course, he probably spent a fair amount of time going out on emergency veterinary calls, but that was okay… She could warm him up when he got home.

"But what about your dream of seeing the world?" he asked after another endless kiss. "Are you sure you want to live in Shelton?"

"Positive. I've given the possibility a great deal of thought over the past few weeks," she said. "You just have to promise to take a vacation each year with me. A *long* one. Not an overnighter to Helena, but a real vacation, and a three-day weekend every month. You can see a lot in three days."

"I will, I promise. Jill has been urging me to get a veterinary resident to help cover the practice and make things easier during calving and foaling season. We started sending letters out to veterinary colleges last week, and already have several answers back."

Betsy gave him a long, deep kiss. She knew Grant disliked change, and yet he was embracing a whole lot of changes, just for her.

"Great idea," she said against his lips. "In the meantime, I'm thinking about running for that vacancy on the city council." She waved her left hand in the air. "And I have to say, a wedding ring would look so much better on my campaign posters than a bare finger."

Grant grinned and gathered her close. "That won't be a problem. I don't believe in long engagements."

AS EACH DAY PASSED, Kelly saw how hard Josh was trying to be a good father. He spent time with the boys together and individually, and was working to strike an equilibrium between wanting to give them whatever they asked for and knowing when to say no.

She understood it was hard. He wanted them to love him, so setting limits was difficult; her own parents had indulged her when they came home after months of absence.

Yet Josh seemed distracted, as well. It wasn't anything she could put her finger on. He was attentive to Casey and Marc, but he was on his cell phone often and spent more time with Harry poring over paperwork. She didn't want to know if it was rodeo schedules. What difference did it make now? The boys knew Josh's identity, and whatever happened, she would do her best to make them happy.

Still, his successes at the Shelton Rodeo

Daze must have reminded him of how exciting it was to be the focus of a crowd's attention. Since coming to Kindred Ranch, he'd
missed a number of events in both Canada
and the United States. Was he wondering if
he'd lost his chance at the finals after staying
inactive for so long? Maybe he was tracking
the win totals of his opponents and figuring
out the possibilities.

"You're quiet this morning," Josh murmured as he sprayed down the corner horse
stall in the foaling barn, directing dirty water
into the drainage system.

Sanitation was easier in the new barn than
in the older buildings, though it still entailed
wheelbarrows and good old-fashioned shov-
eling. But Kelly didn't want to tear the older
barns down. They were built from historic
chestnut timber that could never be replaced.
Eventually her plan was to redo the founda-
tions, adding more plumbing and a drainage system.

"Are you bothered by what I said to Harry
the other day?" Josh asked. "You seemed
okay with it at the time."

Kelly shook her head. "He was being a
hypocrite, though he didn't see that until you
pointed it out. As for the other part, the fam-

ily should have been more up-front about the way Harry was draining Kindred Ranch resources."

Josh looked puzzled. "Liam and Susannah are so strong, I would have expected them to put an end to the financial hemorrhage when you were a kid."

"It's complicated." Kelly turned off the water and dropped to a bale of hay where she could keep an eye on the open door; she didn't want anyone to show up and overhear the conversation. Josh sat next to her, his warmth radiating from her ankle to her shoulder. It was a decided distraction.

Men shouldn't be so nice they tempted you in inappropriate directions. She'd actually come to the conclusion that she was willing to marry Josh, even if he never quit competing. All she needed to know was that she and the children would come first.

"Kelly?" he prompted.

"Uh, it's partly based on Flannigan family history," she explained. "My great-grandparents had big plans for the future, which is why they bought the north arm of the ranch. That way there'd be more than enough land to support both Liam's and Patrick's families when they had them. Before that, the eldest surviving son inherited."

"And since Liam's twin brother was the eldest, traditionally Kindred Ranch would have been left to Patrick, but that wasn't what they wanted to do."

"That's how a lot of families kept ranches in one piece in the old days. Now, too, for that matter. But Nanna Mary and Grandpa Sean wanted to leave Kindred Ranch to their sons equally. They also gave a chunk of money to Grandpa Sean's younger sister, supplementing what her parents had already given her. Since we have such strong Irish roots, I suppose it was similar to providing a dowry, except she never married."

"Essentially your great-grandparents felt bad that she hadn't inherited a share in the ranch and were trying to make up for it," Josh guessed.

"That's right. Aunt Eileen didn't care. She traveled and had a career. She was very happy and successful. She only passed three years ago, as feisty as ever, leaving half of her estate in a trust for Casey and Marc, and the other half to an artists' colony in Vermont."

"That still doesn't explain Harry."

A sad smile curved Kelly's lips. "My grandparents couldn't have more children after my mother was born—Granddad came down with mumps when Grams was pregnant and there were complications."

"Didn't they have a mumps vaccine by then?"

"Yes, but he thought he'd had them as a kid. They'd hoped for a large family. Then it turned out that their only child, my mom, wasn't, um, outdoorsy."

Josh chuckled. "A diplomatic way of saying that ranching didn't suit Kathleen."

"Not in the slightest. You can't force a child to love something you care about. It has to come naturally. I'm fortunate that the boys are passionate about horses and cattle. It could have been computers and online fantasy role-playing games."

Kelly regarded the worn denim on her legs. She didn't enjoy mucking out stalls, but it was part of running a ranch and it wouldn't be fair to keep the best jobs for herself, like riding fences and surveying the herds. Besides, she was able to work in the barns before dawn and after sundown when needed.

"Come to think of it, I've never seen Kathleen on a horse," Josh mused.

"She only rides with Harry these days, but you should see the pictures of her as the Shelton Rodeo Daze princess. She's on horseback, decked mostly in red, white and blue fringe over a silver vest and skirt."

Josh looked intrigued. "I don't recall a rodeo princess, just a Cowgirl and Cowboy of the Year."

Kelly stretched and wiggled her toes in her boots. "That's because Shelton had a belated encounter with the twentieth century. They decided to stop having a beauty contest, and to evaluate entries based on an essay and community service."

"Sounds fair."

"Anyhow, my parents met when she presented the Best All-Around Cowboy Saddle to him at the Shelton Rodeo Daze. It was love at first sight."

JOSH DIDN'T KNOW what to say. While it might have been better for Kathleen if she'd never met Harry, they wouldn't have produced such a remarkable daughter.

"Uh, how did your grandparents feel about the romance?"

Kelly got up and looked out of the barn again. "We haven't discussed it, but they probably thought things would work out since he had a ranch himself."

"Then they realized Harry wasn't a rancher at heart, either."

"Yes, but by then I'd come along. According to Granddad, I was riding before I could walk and they couldn't keep me away from the cows, big or small, so they were reassured that Kindred Ranch would have a future."

Josh wondered how Kelly had withstood the weight of so many dreams and hopes. Perhaps it was the same with any other single child, but Kindred Ranch's long history of unbroken ownership must have added to the pressure.

She brushed her fingers over her jeans. "My grandparents saw the situation as similar to the one with Aunt Eileen. Granddad and Grams decided Kindred Ranch should go to me, and in turn, they decided to pay off Harry's debts, which were substantial, and to support him on the rodeo circuit while he got established."

"Except he never really got established and the need for support never ended."

"I think he broke even for a couple of years, but that was all." Kelly stuck her pitchfork into a fresh load of straw. "Granddad knew I'd take care of things when he put me in charge, but even so, I wasn't completely up-front with Harry about the financial hole he'd landed us in. After seeing the accounts, I simply told him Kindred Ranch couldn't give him any more, that I had to think of the boys' future."

"He should have realized the ranch was in trouble without being told."

She spread straw around the stall and Josh went to help. So far it had been a capricious summer, often with sudden, sharp cold coming on top of warm days, so Kelly was keeping the mares and their foals inside at night.

"Harry is an eternal optimist," she said. "It's a quality I admire, but some of us have to live closer to the real world. He must think I have a cash register in my chest instead of a heart. You must think so, too."

Josh put a hand on her arm. "That's the last thing I believe," he said softly. "And don't worry. Harry understands, though it may take a while for him to adjust to seeing things in a new way. Besides, you're an optimist in a different sense. You wouldn't have rescued Lady Sadie otherwise."

"I suppose." Clearly still on edge, she

pulled out a grooming cloth and began running it over Fiona Chance. The mare's foal, Black Galaxy, nosed in, trying to get his share of the attention. Kelly laughed and spent several minutes playing with the colt, yet she was also teaching him.

"This is a bad time to bring it up, but I should warn you that another scene with the boys is on the way," Josh said finally.

Kelly turned and lifted an eyebrow. "Oh?"

"I've put it off for as long as possible, but I need to go on a trip to handle some business. It could be for two or three weeks. Will it be a problem if I leave Quicksilver and Chocolate Lad here?"

"No, of course not. Going away for a while isn't a bad idea. We haven't talked about the future that much, but you don't live here and the boys need to get used to you being gone."

Josh knew what Kelly was thinking—that he was going back on the rodeo circuit. She was wrong, but he also wanted to have more of his plans in place before he explained. By the time he returned, the sale of the Galloping G should be well into escrow. Every inspection had gone perfectly and the paperwork was all signed. It would soon become McKeon's American Choice ranch. And the other plans he'd put into motion would be far enough along that she should feel reassured he was happily embracing a new life in Shelton.

"I'll explain to the boys," he assured her, "but I want you to know that I wouldn't leave if it wasn't necessary. Don't worry. I'll stay in touch with Casey and Marc. Maybe that will reassure them about me being away."

"I'M SURE IT WILL," Kelly said, trying to keep her expression neutral. Everything Josh did lately seemed to give her hope. Maybe it was pure nonsense to start thinking he'd fallen in love with her again, but sometimes the way he looked at her...

Her heart turned over.

Common sense said that a future with him wasn't likely. People couldn't always get back to where they'd been, no matter how hard they tried. But he loved the boys and seemed to be fond of her. Was it unrealistic to think there was a chance they could be together?

It was a thought that kept her occupied after he left on his trip. She missed him desperately, more than she could have ever thought possible. The single bright spot was when she learned that Grant had gotten engaged to Betsy Hartner. Admittedly, she was also grateful the couple's romance would give her neighbors something to think about besides the identity of her sons' father. The silence had been deafening when she'd walked into the Shelton Ranching Association meeting two nights earlier. She understood that people didn't know what to say, but after all, Casey and Marc hadn't been delivered by the stork. Somebody had to be their father.

"Congratulations on your engagement. I'm so happy for you," Kelly said to Grant when he came out to Kindred Ranch to do a wellness check on the foals.

He beamed. "Betsy is incredible. She's going to write a regular column for the online magazine that published her articles about the rodeo. She also wants to get certified as a lab tech for the clinic. And we'll travel every fall."

Kelly's eyebrow went up. "That's a switch."

"Yeah, but I don't think traveling was my problem as a kid. It was feeling that I didn't have a real home. Betsy is my home now. It has nothing to do with an address." Grant seemed to hesitate. "What about you and Josh McKeon? I hear that Casey and Marc are his sons, or is that just a bit of misplaced gossip?"

Kelly sighed. "Not misplaced. He's on a business trip right now, but he calls and talks to the boys every night."

Josh also made a point of speaking with her, asking about her day and what was going on at the ranch—little, ordinary things, but enough to make her think she meant more to him than just being the twins' mother.

Grant frowned. "Is he competing?"

"He didn't say and I haven't asked. But he didn't take his horses with him, so maybe not. I don't know if the boys understand that Josh isn't going to live in our old bunkhouse forever. I keep reminding them that he has a ranch in Canada, but it doesn't seem to get through. Um, are you and Betsy going to have a family?" she asked, hoping Grant wouldn't try to find out if she and Josh were getting together.

Her feelings were too deep and raw to air in public, and she didn't want to confess her fear that if Josh *was* competing again, he wouldn't be able to resist the adrenaline and excitement. The boys were surprisingly okay with his absence, though. Mostly they seemed excited about something and she hoped he hadn't made any promises he wouldn't keep. Even Harry seemed to be brimming with a secret.

"We both want kids," Grant explained, dragging her attention back to the conversation. "And we'll keep taking trips, even after we start a family. We want our children to see the world."

"Is that your fiancée talking, or what you want, too?"

"It's both of us. I may have resented being constantly shuffled back and forth between my parents, but I saw some great places because of it. Betsy has made me recognize that."

Kelly couldn't recall Grant ever looking so happy and relaxed. "That's wonderful. When is the wedding?"

"A week from Saturday. We wanted to do it sooner, but my dad had a cruise scheduled. He offered to cancel, but Betsy declared she wouldn't allow her future father-in-law to miss a trip to Alaska on her account. Anyhow, Leonard Crabtree insists that he's doing the food and he probably needs time to plan."

"Chili and cheeseburgers, with a cinnamon roll cake?"

Grant laughed. "I wouldn't be surprised.

Betsy doesn't care, so I don't, either. It will be an informal ceremony out at the rodeo grounds. Everyone is invited."

Kelly was thrilled for him. Betsy was a breath of fresh air, not only for Grant, but for the whole community. And if a man and woman with so many differences could work things out, then maybe she and Josh stood a chance.

CHAPTER FIFTEEN

"THAT'S A WRAP," called the photographer.

Josh drew a sigh of relief and went over to the catering cart for a last cup of coffee and to fill his thermos. After six long days of posing for photographs and spouting lines for commercials, his face felt frozen in a smile. But it helped that he liked the clothing he was promoting and had actually been wearing the company's jeans and shirts and other goods for years.

"Josh, thanks for such a great job," said Deacon Wainbridge as they both stepped away from the cart with steaming cups. "The board is very happy about everything they've seen. They're jumping on the ad campaign even faster than I expected, so you'll start seeing yourself on television and in magazines before long."

Josh rubbed his sore jaw. "I'm glad they're satisfied, though I may need to get a new smile. I've discovered that posing for pictures is harder work than riding a hundred broncs."

Deacon chuckled. He was the head of advertising and had been the primary contact during their negotiations. He was also a good guy, born and raised in ranching country, and a fan of all things rodeo. He'd even flirted with the idea of becoming a professional rodeo cowboy himself before discovering he'd rather ride a desk chair than be thrown by a bucking bull.

"Sorry about that," Deacon apologized, "but maybe getting back to Kelly and the boys will help. She sounds special. I was blown away by that photo you have of her with Casey and Marc. You're a lucky man."

"I can't argue with that." Josh grinned, knowing he probably looked like a lovesick calf. He hadn't been able to resist telling Deacon that he planned to propose to Kelly as soon as he returned to Montana.

"By the way, I brought a few gifts for your kids," Deacon said. "From the company. Shall we put everything in your truck?"

"Sure. Thanks."

They went over to Deacon's SUV and Josh discovered a "few things" translated to two finely crafted saddles, cowboy hats, a pair of personalized belt buckles and a small mountain of clothes made by the company, including a generous selection for Kelly and himself. He was impressed, though he also knew they were anxious to keep him happy. While he was being paid well, he hadn't held them up for the amount of money that his lawyer had said was possible. Not even close.

"Are you leaving this afternoon, or can I buy you dinner?" Deacon asked as Josh closed the door on his camper.

"Definitely leaving. Texas is great, but I'm ready to head north."

"I was surprised you drove here instead of flying."

Josh laughed. "Maybe I'll fly the next trip, but I've spent so much of my life driving from one rodeo to the next, it seemed normal to simply get in my truck and go. Anyhow, Shelton doesn't have a commercial airport, so I would have needed to fly out of Helena or Bozeman regardless, and I don't know if there are any direct flights from there to Dallas."

"Maybe next time we can do the photo shoot on your new ranch. I'll look into it."

"That would be ideal."

They shook hands and Josh got behind the

wheel of his truck. The time away from Montana had underscored the rightness of his decision to retire from competition. He ached to be with Kelly, to go riding with his sons…to be a normal man taking care of his family. It wasn't that Kelly couldn't handle things; he just wanted to be there, doing his part.

The drive seemed to take forever. He slept in the camper when he got tired and continued when he was rested enough to drive safely. As he approached Shelton, he realized it was like coming home, more than he'd ever felt about returning to his ranch in Canada.

Because while McKeon's Choice had his father, it didn't have two sons and the woman he loved waiting for him.

IT WAS MIDAFTERNOON when Kelly rode toward the Kindred Ranch barns. She'd spent most of the day checking fences with Lightfoot and Gizmo. The boys hadn't gone with her because they were attending a birthday party for one of their friends, but she knew they'd be back soon, if not already.

Summer meant she usually didn't go out this long at one time. Casey and Marc were too young to spend an entire day on horseback, though they'd object loudly if she said so.

A cloud of dust was coming from the road leading into the ranch and she leaned forward in the saddle. It wasn't one of the Kindred Ranch vehicles.

Her pulse jumped.

Josh.

"I'll take care of Lightfoot, boss," Thad said as she rode in and dismounted.

She handed over the reins as Josh pulled into the same spot where he'd parked the first day. She might have broken down and thrown her arms around him right then and there, except the door of the house opened and her sons came out, yelling his name.

"Hey, guys." He laughed and dropped to one knee, hugging them both.

They asked a series of excited questions, not even waiting for an answer before the next one tumbled out. He laughed again and said he would tell them everything later, but that he wanted to talk to their mother first.

Casey, then Marc, shot her a glance, and to Kelly's surprise, they went back into the house without an argument.

She swallowed as Josh reached into his truck and took something out. "Come on. Let's take a walk," he suggested.

Kelly injected steel into her wobbly knees

and nodded. "All right. Did you have a good trip?"

"It was okay, but I'm glad to be back."

"Your dad called last night after we spoke to you. Grams talked him through getting on Skype, so he was able to videoconference with Casey and Marc."

"Pop was on Skype?" Josh said as if he didn't quite believe his ears.

"Shocking, I know. He wants to do it every week, too. You may have a technology convert on your hands."

Kelly had enjoyed her first "meeting" with Benjamin McKeon. He was an older version of Josh, just as handsome, with silver at his temples and a sad, serious expression on his face. Her invitation to spend the holidays in Montana had been eagerly accepted, and more than once he'd said how much he looked forward to seeing her and the boys in person.

"He truly doesn't seem to be holding a grudge against me for keeping Casey and Marc a secret," Kelly added.

"That isn't Pop's style. Besides, like I told you, he blames me," Josh said. He looked both tired and excited.

They were walking down a trail that went

out from the back of the foaling barn. At the lowest level of the valley a small creek flowed, lined by black cottonwoods and pines. When they'd gone around a clump of trees, out of sight from the main buildings, he stopped and held something out.

"I have something for you. It's an advance copy, not on the stands yet."

Kelly blinked.

It was a popular magazine on Western living and his picture was on the cover, but she couldn't figure out why it was important until she focused on the large caption.

Rodeo Champion, Josh McKeon, Announces Retirement.

For a moment she couldn't breathe or even think.

"I…I didn't ask for this," she choked out, torn between thankfulness and dismay.

"I REALIZE THAT," Josh said quietly. "This is what *I* want. I've bought the Galloping G and am renaming it McKeon's American Choice ranch, with Mrs. Gillespie's approval. I'm going to breed horses there, along with raising cattle. I'm also starting a rodeo training facility with your father."

Kelly seemed dazed. "Harry knows?"

"Yes. He's agreed to stop competing and work with me. He's always had a gift for mentoring. This will give him a chance to put that gift to better use. And together you and I can make sure that Casey and Marc get a balanced view of life as a professional rodeo cowboy. I sure don't want them growing up like their grandfather."

"They've seemed to know something was up."

"Not the details, just some of the broad outlines. I thought it might help them to know that I was going to move here. They loved the idea of keeping it a secret until I could get more of my plans in place."

"No wonder they didn't take me seriously when I kept pointing out that you had a ranch in Canada," Kelly muttered. She stared at the cover of the magazine, then flipped to the article and pointed to a section of enlarged print. "The author is right—you're at the top of your profession. You could still have more successes."

Josh gently tugged the magazine away from her. "I don't care about that. Listen to me. I had two reasons for my business trip. I needed to do the interview for this story, and I also signed a contract to represent a clothing company in their ads and television commercials. They've already done the initial filming. I may have to attend a rodeo or two as part of future photo shoots, but only as a visitor. If so, I hope we'll go together as a family."

AS A FAMILY?

It took a second for the words to sink into Kelly's mind. "Wh-what?"

"You heard me," Josh retorted with a smile. "But to make myself perfectly clear, I'm in love with you and I'm asking you to be my wife. I did all of this before proposing because I want you to know that whether you say yes or no, I'm going to live in Montana and be a part of Casey's and Marc's future. But I'll feel a whole lot better if you marry me."

Sincerity blazed in his dark eyes and Kelly flung herself into his arms. "Of course I will, you idiot. I would marry you even if you hadn't retired. I decided that before you left."

JOSH LAUGHED. "So you love me?"

"With all my heart."

"Great. I understand you can apply for a license and get married the same day in Montana. Pop told me he can leave to come down here on a moment's notice. So how about the day after tomorrow?"

"Grams and my mother will want more time to plan."

"They can have an extra day. That's all." Josh gave her a lingering kiss. "I don't think I can wait any longer than that," he murmured in her ear, then took something from his pocket. "By the way, I brought you another gift. Harry helped out with the size, so I hope he got it right."

Kelly smiled as he slid the engagement ring over her finger. "Perfect fit, but why get a ring for such a short engagement?"

"Because I wanted to do things right this time around."

He kissed her again, finally at peace with himself...maybe for the first time since he'd let Kelly walk away, instead of fighting to keep her.

Life was great, and it would only get better with her at his side.

Eleven months later...

JOSH YAWNED AS he pushed the double baby stroller across the grassy parking area of the

Shelton Rodeo Daze. The rest of the family was walking ahead of them with Benjamin, who'd driven down from Canada to meet his new granddaughters and had stayed to experience the Shelton Rodeo Daze week.

Kelly hid a grin.

Her husband was learning what sleepless nights really meant now that he had twin daughters a few weeks old. It was good that he *wasn't* performing at the rodeo, or else a bull might turn tables on him and smack his sleep-deprived rear end.

Josh had been true to his word.

He no longer competed and he turned down any requests for bull- and bronc-riding exhibitions. The rodeo school had quickly become a reality and they had an ever-changing rotation of students who wanted to "learn from the best." The phrase made Josh uncomfortable, but it had come from an article written about the training facility.

She loved teasing him, saying he'd started the school just to get free cowhands. The "students" were often assigned basic ranch tasks, something both Josh and Harry told them was needed to learn the principles of balance, focus and hard work.

It seemed to be a winning formula. One of

their first trainees was doing especially well on the professional rodeo circuit this season and had been quoted several times giving credit to Josh and Harry for his improved performance.

Josh had also moved his horses down from McKeon's Choice in Canada. They were engaged in a friendly rivalry over their equine breeding program, but Josh admitted that his wife had him beaten. *For now,* he would clarify...then wink.

"Your jaw just cracked," Kelly murmured as he yawned a second time, even wider than before. "You should let me get up and change diapers part of the time."

"It's the least I can do when you're nursing them."

Josh was a stubbornly hands-on father. Grams and Kathleen complained that they didn't have enough time with the babies, but they probably didn't mind being able to sleep through the night. Hmm, *usually* they could sleep, that was. Both of the girls had extremely healthy lungs.

"Hey, guys, which girl is which?" Grant asked Casey and Marc as they waited in the carnival queue for tickets.

"That's Eileen, and that's Maggie," Casey said, pointing to each baby in turn.

Marc scrunched his nose; he still hadn't figured out how to tell his sisters apart. But at least with Josh's help, he was starting to be slightly less competitive with his brother.

"Oh, Kelly, they're beautiful," Betsy exclaimed, peering into the stroller.

"Thanks. How are your autumn travel plans going?"

"Everything is falling into place. We're leaving earlier than we originally thought," Betsy said. "Did you think you'd have twins again?"

Kelly smiled. "They run in the family, so I wasn't too surprised when we found out at the first ultrasound."

Josh put his free arm around her shoulders. "They had to scrape my jaw off the floor, but I thought it was great."

"What he means is—"

"Now, Kelly, that's private," he interrupted her. He didn't want anyone to know he'd passed out cold when Dr. Wycoff announced that twins were once more on the way. He'd compared it to the wildest bull ride of his life.

Kelly leaned into her husband. They still had heated discussions, but she couldn't imagine being happier. Who would have guessed that they'd find each other again?

She looked at her father.

Well, maybe Harry had guessed. He was, after all, responsible for inviting Josh to Kindred Ranch after all this time. She went over and kissed him. This was one wrong thing he'd gotten perfectly right.

* * * * *

Don't miss more great romances from author Julianna Morris available today at www.Harlequin.com!